FOOL'S GOLD

Also by Ted Wood

Live Bait
Murder on Ice
Dead in the Water

FOOL'S GOLD

Ted Wood

CHARLES SCRIBNER'S SONS • NEW YORK

Library of Congress Cataloging-in-Publication Data

Wood, Ted.
  Fool's gold

  I. Title.
PR9199.3.W57F66   1986   813'.54   85–27110
ISBN 0–684–18568–7

Published simultaneously in Canada
by Collier Macmillan Canada, Inc.
Copyright under the Berne Convention.

1 3 5 7 9 11 13 15 17 19   F/C   20 18 16 14 12 10 8 6 4 2

Printed in the United States of America.

For my son Ted,
who taught Reid Bennett how to fight

1

It looked like your standard domestic argument. A large him holding a smaller her at arm's length by the hair, while she swore and kicked and swung at him. I was four hundred miles from home, pulling my car into the parking lot of a motel. But I'm still a policeman, so I stopped with my headlights focussed on them and got out, hissing for Sam, my German shepherd, to follow.

There were about half a dozen men standing around them, mostly laughing, all dressed alike, rough heavy jackets and baseball caps. Miners, I figured, from the new gold mine twenty-five miles up the Trans-Canada Highway. And today was the thirtieth of the month. Payday. They were celebrating with a few drinks and some commercial female company that had driven into town for the occasion, probably in the recreational vehicle I could see at the end of the lot, which meant that this scuffle might not be a routine domestic. Anyway, I watched.

She was shouting, "You lousy sonofabitch. Gimme my money," and writhing like a snake as she kicked and flailed at him. He was laughing. He probably laughed at most attempts to hurt him, right before he tore the arms and legs off whoever tried it. He was six-foot-three and had the square-

1

as-a-door build of the lifelong manual worker. He looked and sounded mean.

"That was my goddamn money, bitch. You think I'd spend fifty bucks for a piece of ass?" he roared. Not domestic, I decided, the world's oldest professional argument.

I could see that the woman was thirtyish, slim, and blond. And she was spittingly, helplessly angry. When he let her go, I thought, he had better watch what she did with her feet. For the moment, though, he was in charge and he was enjoying himself. "You had a good time," he told her, and his circle all laughed. I guessed he was the camp bully. There's one on most sites and most men avoid trouble by Uncle Tomming him to death.

He grinned at the woman. "You shoulda heard yourself. You was nearly outta your mind. How long's it been since you had a real man?"

She flailed another useless hand at him and railed. "Real man? You limp-dick wimp." And that was when he hit her. Holding her aloft by her hair he slapped a cracking right hand across her face hard enough to make her body jump in the air, as if she had dropped to the end of a rope. Then he let go and she fell in a heap at his feet. He made a production of brushing his hands clean on his pant legs, looking down at her as if she was something he had just stepped in.

She pulled herself up on one elbow, shocked and stunned, hardly able to move. I went and squatted down next to her, making sure I had a clear view of the big guy. There was blood in her mouth.

The big man said, "You wan' her? Help yourself. On me." He laughed and one or two of the others laughed until I stood up and moved a step closer to him.

"Sounds like you ripped her off," I said evenly.

He stopped wiping his hands and looked at me, surprised, squinting through the beam of my headlights that lit up his big square face. "You her pimp?" he sneered.

"No. I thought you were. Only guys ever slap whores around are pimps and queers," I said. "Either way I could be right."

He was as dumb as he was big. He roared and charged me, head down like a bull. I sidestepped and kicked his right foot behind his left ankle as he passed. It sent him sprawling, face first, full length, scraping his hands flat out on the gravel. Behind me a man said in French, "Hey, he's fighting Carl, let's get him." I told Sam "Speak" and he sprang into action, stiff legged, moving out, barking at the menace as I went sideways so the light wasn't blinding me as the other guy got up, wiping his hands again. The woman was flapping away on hands and knees like an injured sea gull.

I watched the man, listening to Sam's working snarl behind me as he kept the others out of reach. Slowly the man reached behind him and I knew what was coming. He had a knife. "Bring that thing out and my dog'll have your balls," I warned him. "You wanna fight, forget the knife."

"I don't need no knife to cut shit like you," he said. He was calm now, with the first move made. He came toward me more slowly, arms half circled out to grab me if I tried to sidestep.

I didn't. Instead I dropped into a crouch and shot out a straight left that hit him square on the end of his nose, bursting it like a tomato. He howled and covered his face and I stepped in and sank a heavy right into his gut. He grunted but didn't fold and then grabbed me, both arms around me like a bear as he tried to sink his teeth into my face. I could hear his friends cheering above the metronomic barking of my dog and the sobbing breath of the woman who was standing up now, on the fringe of the tunnel of light, all of this in the moment before I head-smashed him on his damaged nose and scraped my boot down his shin and ground it into his instep. He was wearing work boots, but I hurt him enough that he yelled and let go. This time I made my fingers into a

3

chisel and dug them two knuckles deep into his solar plexus. He collapsed writhing, and I spun to face the crowd. "Who's next?" I shouted in French. "Who feels lucky?"

I wanted an encore about as badly as I wanted a case of herpes, but nothing discourages violence like the appearance of being crazy. I played it to the hilt, running toward them and shouting as they scattered in all directions, Sam snapping and barking at their heels.

I watched them go, then went back to my car and got in, feeling dirtied as I always do after fights, wishing it could have been avoided. I pulled along to a parking spot against the motel wall, got out, and whistled for Sam. He came to me while I got my bag from the trunk and I fussed him and set him to "keep" the area around my car—that way nobody was going to prove how big and tough they were by taking a knife to my tires. Then I opened the rear window and put him inside the car to sleep. He's an outdoor dog and the overnight chill wouldn't bother him any.

When I had Sam settled comfortably, I went around to the office. In the light from the little neon sign over the door I could see the woman bending over Carl as he sprawled on the gravel. I guessed she was getting her money back. I ignored her and went inside.

There was a woman behind the desk, working on something that she slipped out of sight under the counter as I came in. She was a dish, by my standards, handsome rather than pretty, but her face was unlined and her hair was set in a mass of curls that God hadn't given her. She was around five-two, one-twenty-five, built on a scale that my father, who was a Brit, used to call "bonny." She was in her thirties, probably a year or two younger than me.

"Hi," she said, and frowned. "What did you do to your head?" I reached up automatically and checked my forehead. It was wet with the other guy's blood.

There were tissues on the counter top. I took a couple and

wiped the blood off. "Sorry about that. I ran into some kind of tribal rite in the parking lot. That better?"

"Good," she said, frowning up again like a mother checking her boy's face for jam. "Yes, that's fine." She gestured to the door. "Another fight, was it? God! I hate paydays." I noticed a smear of color on her hand.

"You smudged your burnt umber," I told her, and she looked down at her hands and blushed, then looked up, surprised.

"You're not an artist?"

I didn't look like one. I was wearing the combat jacket I brought home from Nam and a heavy plaid shirt and jeans. I figured I looked like the rest of the guys she saw. But maybe that's how artists look these days, I've never met any. "No. But I owned a paint box when I was a kid," I told her, and she grinned. She had a nice grin, showing white, even teeth.

"Who was doing the brawling?" she asked, reaching for her box of check-in cards.

"An oversized rounder by the name of Carl. He was slapping a woman around and I objected."

"That bastard," she said passionately. "I hope you clobbered him." Then she gave a little laugh. "I guess you must have, you're here, unhurt, no marks. Good. I'm glad."

"It's nice to be needed," I said, just to keep the conversation perking along. I liked it a lot more than brawling in the parking lot.

She smiled again. "You're needed, believe me. He pulls this same stunt every payday. He generally picks on little guys. The police must have taken him in half a dozen times, nothing does any good."

There was no modest reply, so instead of shuffling my feet, I picked up the pen and started filling out one of her cards. Reid Bennett, Murphy's Harbour, Ontario. Company—I debated this one with myself. I'm still the police chief at the Harbour, but right now nobody needed to know. Finally I lied and wrote down "Prudential Assurance" and handed her the card.

She read it and laughed. "You're the damndest piece of the Rock I ever saw."

"It's a living." I tried to look sincere. The reason I was here was business, right enough, but not business I wanted known in the local pool hall. I figured insurance would cover me. Nobody would ask questions for fear of being sold a policy.

"How long are you staying?" She had blue eyes the color of Wedgwood china, and I noticed that her hands were free of hardware. Divorced, I guessed. No way a woman this attractive would have stayed single for thirty-odd years in what had been a logging town until somebody found gold just up the highway.

"I'm not sure, a couple or three days anyway. You got lots of space?"

"No," she said honestly, reaching for a key. "Since the gold strike at Chaudiere we've been crazy. Prospectors, chopper pilots, then the construction people setting up the new mine. These are boom times in Olympia. You're lucky we've got a room tonight, the Darvon people just phoned from the mine and cancelled their reservation." She waved the hand with the key in it. "They keep one all the time."

"My lucky night." I took the key. "Is the dining room still open?"

She nodded. "Be advised, have the lake trout, it's the only thing the chef can handle."

I raised the key in salute. "Thanks for the friendly advice and good luck with the artwork." I went off down the corridor between yellow-painted walls of concrete block, more cheerful than I had been since my ex-wife came to me for help. Maybe things would turn out well. Maybe I could go home in a week with the news that the police had been wrong, the body they had found in the bush with its head gnawed away by bears hadn't belonged to Jim Prudhomme, the husband of her old college roomie. I hoped so.

The room was down the end of the corridor and on the way I passed half a dozen open doors. Men, mostly in their shorts, were drinking and laughing and hoping that Miss America would wander by and fall in love with them and force her attentions upon them. It's crazy, but living in a bunkhouse will do that for a man.

The room was as I'd expected, walls of the same painted concrete block, two beds, a TV that drew its pictures from a dish receiver they had on the roof. Great. If Miss America didn't show, I could always watch "Gilligan's Island."

I freshened up and put on a sweater instead of my combat jacket and walked out across the lot to the two-story building all the rock music was pouring out of.

I looked around me as I went into the lot, but there was nobody there. Carl's friends must have taken him home to the mine site. Good. I was over quota for fights. I went to the car and spoke to Sam, who was curled in the backseat. "Good boy," I told him. "I'll bring you a burger on my way back."

The restaurant was built from the same block as the main building. Downstairs was the bar, filled to the walls with miners and construction men with a few, a very few women. Upstairs was dimmer and quieter—the dining room. I went up and checked. It was typical for this end of the world. The walls were covered with oil paintings one step above paint-by-number. I hoped the woman at the front desk hadn't been responsible, I'd been ready to admire her. There was a stuffed lake trout over the bar and a moose head on the wall by the door. Some wag had put a cigarette in its mouth.

Most of the tables were filled with men, dinner over, sitting with drinks in front of them. I judged them to be the upper echelon at the mine site—foremen, supervisors, the occasional engineer, people who didn't want to get into the buddy-buddy drinking of downstairs, even if they liked hard rock played at two thousand decibels. One table was empty so I took it.

After a minute or so the waiter came over. He was a big slow kid who looked as if somebody had told him a joke at lunchtime and he had just seen the punch line. "How're ya tonight, want something from the bar before you order?" There, hospitable as well.

I ordered a Classic and was looking at the menu when the door opened. I glanced up, wondering if it was friend Carl with his knife, looking for me. But instead it was a woman, the blonde from the parking lot, I guessed. She answered as much of the description as I'd picked up in the headlight's beam and one side of her face was swollen. She looked around and came straight for me. I wondered how the Prudential people would feel if they could see me now.

She had some seniority, but her figure was taut and good and she knew everything there is to know about makeup. Every guy in the room was watching her, and me. Her with admiration, me with envy. She was wearing a bright green velvet dress, high at the knee and low at the neckline. Someone must have told her it pays to advertise.

It was a nuisance. I just wanted to be invisible while I talked to people about Jim Prudhomme's death. If she was going to pull the My Hero stunt I'd be remembered for the rest of my stay. And I guessed she was capable of it. Hookers may not have hearts of gold, but they have tongues of brass. She would let the world know I was Sir Galahad.

When it was obvious I was the target I started to stand up, but she held out her hand, palm downward. "Don't," she commanded. "You already stood up for me when it counted." She wasn't joking. I had myself a fan. I pulled out the other chair for her. "Care to join me?"

She said, "I'd be delighted," as graciously as Nancy Reagan. I sat and looked at her, wondering what to say. I settled on, "Are you hurt?" She didn't seem to be. She was a touch puffy around the cheek where he'd cracked her, but she wasn't carrying her head in the whiplashed way I'd expected.

She shook her head. "No. Thanks to you. I think he was going to kill me."

"Probably not," I minimized. But she didn't agree.

"Guys never get rough, not normal guys anyway, unless they have trouble getting it on." So there was the reason Carl had hit her so hard. Now two of us knew his secret.

The waiter came back and set down my beer. He looked at the woman, then at me, then grinned as if someone had shown him dirty pictures. "Would you like something?" I asked the woman. She thought about it for a moment, then nodded.

"Yeah, please, a Coke, just to be sociable."

"You want rum with that?" the waiter asked. It was, after all, payday.

She shook her head. "Just plain old Coke." He grinned again and left.

I poured myself a little beer but didn't drink. She looked at me and then reached in her purse for cigarettes, Rothman's. She picked up the candle off the table and lit it. "I came looking to thank you for what you did," she said.

"It was for me, more than you. I don't like bullies." In this room it was hard to remember why I had tackled Carl. I had done exactly the same thing once before, in Saigon. It had been a much harder fight against a much better-trained man. Only that time I had ended up with the girl for the night. That wasn't on my agenda this time. I'm not nineteen anymore. I can go for hours at a time without the kind of first aid she dispensed from her Winnebago.

She drew a long pull off her cigarette, then took it in her left hand and stuck out her right. "I'd like to shake your hand," she said, and before I could move she added, "unless you're the kind of guy who doesn't like to touch women like me."

I shook her hand. It was cool and dry and the shake she gave me was firm and confident. I figured she could handle most trouble on her own. "Reid Bennett," I told her.

"Eleanor." She let go of my hand and sat looking at me while the kid brought the Coke and put it in front of her. I lifted the beer to her and sipped. She lifted her own glass. "Happy times."

I wondered what she would do next. If she felt dramatic she would go on talking about the fight—and I didn't need it.

"You're good with your hands," she said suddenly. I shrugged, but she dismissed the gesture with a wave. "No, don't screw around. You took out a guy who's taller than you, got a longer reach, weighs maybe forty pounds more than you do. I thought you were beautiful to watch."

"Thank you." I owed her no explanation, but sometimes guilt gnaws at me when I find myself using tricks that were taught me in the marines against people who don't want to kill me, just stomp me a little to be sociable. I told her, "The thing is, I was trained by experts. It was a while ago, but I haven't forgotten."

She took a long pull at her cigarette and then breathed the smoke out through her nostrils, something you don't see often since the surgeon general started telling fortunes on the back of cigarette packs. "I figure you for a veteran, only you're too young."

I said nothing and she did her smoke trick again and then put the cigarette down and snapped her fingers. "You're American, of course. Viet Nam."

"I was in Nam, but I'm not American." It's a story I've explained enough times now. About twenty thousand of us went south to the States looking for excitement at the time the same number of their guys were coming north looking for a safe haven. I'm still not sure why I went, but I'm glad I was there.

She stubbed out her cigarette and took a sip of her Coke. I

noticed that she had tiny green sparkles on her eyelids. She was loaded for bear on a night when the entire town was loaded for her. "You did me a favor," she said at last. "I owe you."

I said nothing and her face crinkled into a smile—a warm human grin, not a working grimace. "Bashful?" she asked innocently.

"Not exactly. I'm just trying to think of a polite way to say no, you don't owe me a thing."

"You figured I was going to invite you out into my magic trick truck?" she said, and grinned again.

"It occurred that you might. And it occurred that I would probably like it a lot, but not right now."

"You can take a rain check," she said, and then, "Look, I don't wanna embarrass you, anything. Like, I'm in your debt." She was anxious and vulnerable. She didn't believe in True Romances any more than I did, but I'd made the first spontaneous kind gesture she'd seen since some pump jockey offered to wash the windshield of her Winnebago. She was just redressing the natural balance, getting out of emotional hock. On impulse I decided to tell her why I was there. After all, she talked to a lot of men, maybe somebody had said something that might be useful to me.

"There is something I'd like you to do for me," I said, and she leaned forward.

"Name it." She was all attention and I studied her face. It looked intelligent.

"A friend of mine died up here around three weeks ago. He was a geologist by the name of Jim Prudhomme. He was attacked by a bear, I heard, somewhere north of Chaumiere. He was camped alone there on a lake and when the chopper came in for him they found him dead, torn up badly as well."

She nodded. "Yes. I heard about that last time I was in town. It was the biggest news since the gold strike."

I nodded and took a pull at my beer. "Yeah, it would have been. Well, anyway, I'm trying to find out whatever I can

11

about him." I improvised quickly. "We went to school together and I haven't seen him in a while. I wondered if anybody told you anything about the business, anything that wasn't in the papers."

She looked at me soberly. "I saw the papers, they had a picture of him from his company. He looked about twenty-five."

"That was a graduation photo," I explained. "He would've been thirty-eight now and he'd shaved off the beard."

She thought about it for a minute, staring blankly at the candle on the table, replaying some mental videotape of past clients. At last she shook her head. "Can't place him, you know how it is. But I'll keep trying and I'll ask around. You staying here?"

"Yes, room forty-seven." I raised my glass to her and she stood up. "Thanks. Take care of yourself," she said.

"I can, most times. But thanks again for what you did," she said seriously.

There wasn't anything to reply so I nodded and she raised one hand in farewell and turned away. Before she reached the door a table of men called her over and she sat down with them. She left with one of them before I'd even ordered my second beer.

2

The next morning I got up at seven and took Sam for a brisk run, maybe three miles, then fed him and left him in the car while I showered and went over to the dining room for breakfast. I had the place almost to myself. Most of the diners from the night before were back at the mine site, working their sixteen hours a day, trying to start bringing the gold out of the ground and into Darvon's pocket on schedule by the following summer. The salesmen were already off down the road with their smiles and shoeshines. Which left me, plus a succession of road-stained job-seekers, roughly dressed men who came in, about one every ten minutes, looking for work. By the look of them they had already been to apply at the gold mines and now they were anxious to win a stake to get them back to the city or farther west out to Alberta, where there was rumored to be work in the oil fields. The cook took time to give each of them a cup of coffee and a polite turndown. I guessed he'd been out of work himself once and remembered how it felt. It seemed he was getting stretched as the new people poured into town, following the gold strike.

The waitress was a girl of about seventeen who would have been attractive if she hadn't been addicted to chewing gum. But she brought me bacon and eggs over easy with home fries, and half an hour later I was down at the police station talking to the chief.

His name was Gallagher. He was an old-time copper, an inch taller than me at six-two, thickening slightly but still carrying an air of authority as unmistakable as a drawn gun. He had a grizzled moustache and dark brown eyes that looked as if they had already seen all the bad sights there are and would welcome something good. I wasn't it.

"You the guy who clobbered Carl Tettlinger?" was his first question.

"We never got around to exchanging names," I said, "but I did have a donnybrook with some big guy, name of Carl."

"I hear you decked him and scared the hell out of his buddies," he said, frowning.

"Kind of." I wasn't looking for glory, I wanted this man on my side.

He snorted out a sound that might have been a laugh. "Good," he said, and that was that. We were standing in the front office of his station, a frame building he shared with the local fire department. It looked a lot like my own police station at Murphy's Harbour: teletype, typewriter, a couple of guns. The only differences were a middle-aged woman clerk and a collection of police sleeve flashes from departments across Canada and the States. Gallagher watched while I looked things over, then asked, "You approve?" and we both grinned.

He threw up the flap on the counter and the little clerk glanced up anxiously as if he were giving away the secrets of the Masonic rite. He looked at her indulgently. "This gentleman is Mr. Reid Bennett. Anybody asks, he's with the—" He turned to me. "Which insurance company did you say?"

"Prudential," I told him, and he nodded.

"Yeah, the Prudential Assurance Company. You don't have to let anybody know that he's not—he's a police chief, like me."

I looked at him quickly. It wasn't a piece of news I had

14

intended laying on him or anybody else up here in Olympia. He waved me through toward his office, a comfortable little den down a short corridor. "Yeah, the name rang a bell when Alice at the motel spoke to my constable last night. Bennett, she said. Able to handle Carl without getting cut up at all. My guy told me today, so I checked with some old copies of the *Police News*. You're the chief at Murphy's Harbour, right?"

I nodded, but he wasn't really listening, didn't even turn, but went into his office, a homey little spot with carpet on the floor and bookshelves that looked as if he had knocked them together in his basement. There were revolver trophies around and the usual pictures of groups of policemen, obvious even in fishing clothes, holding up dead trout. There were only two chairs, one behind the desk, upholstered, the other in front, plain wood.

He pointed me to the plain one and sat behind his desk. "Yeah, I've read a few things about you. You were with the Americans in Viet Nam, then a spell in Toronto until you resigned, then Murphy's Harbour." He sat back in his chair and cocked his feet onto his desk. The top of it had black heel marks that indicated he did this a lot. "How come you quit Metro?" he asked softly.

It's a question I've been asked before, usually by policemen who see only the career path open in the Metro department, not the red tape and compartmentalizing. "I was off duty and found a bunch of bikers raping a kid from a milk store. They came at me and I took two of them out."

"Yeah?" He prodded me gently, craning up slightly to look over his boots. I noticed that the underside of the instep was polished. Ex-service for sure.

"So they arrested me for manslaughter. I got off but the media wouldn't let go, so I quit."

"It happens," he said softly. We sat and thought about that for a minute until the clerk came in with a pot of tea and two cups. "Tea?" he asked, smiling at the clerk and bringing his feet back down again so he could swing forward and do the pouring. When the clerk had gone out again he said, "Gladys is English. Been here for thirty years, bless her heart, good as gold. But damn if she's ever learned to make coffee. I gave up on it finally. When she brews up, I drink tea."

We drank tea and chatted about nothing for a minute or two, courteous as a couple of Arabs. Then, as he poured himself a second cup, he asked, "So what brings you to Olympia? Looking to find gold?"

I laughed, as he expected me to. "Hell no, wouldn't know what to do with it." I put down my teacup and leveled with him. "The widow of Jim Prudhomme, the geologist who was killed up here, she's a friend of my ex-wife and she's the one who asked me if I'd come up and talk to you, see what happened."

Gallagher pulled out a pack of cigarettes, lit up, placed the match very carefully in the clean ashtray, and said, "I don't know what she expects you to find out. The widow was up here herself when it happened, with her lawyer. Hell, he was the guy who identified the body."

I could see I was on thin ice. His professional pride was injured. What was another cop doing looking over his shoulder? "Well, you know how it is. My ex-wife, feeling helpful, suggests I come up and talk to you, see if the lawyer missed anything. I'm just going through the motions because I'm a month late with my alimony." The last part was a lie. All Amy had asked from me was distance. Big rough men who clobbered people were not what she had bargained for. She was happier with the computer salesmen she worked with.

But the lie worked, the chief was placated. He sat and smoked quietly and looked at me before asking: "You know the details, right?"

"Just in general terms. Prudhomme was out on a survey, working alone, didn't make his rendezvous with the chopper

16

so you set up a search party and they found the body, gnawed by a bear, unrecognizable."

"You got it." He nodded. "That's what made the papers get all excited. There hasn't been a case like it since Coffin was hanged for murdering those hunters. Before you were born, likely, happened in Quebec. By the time they found the bodies, bears had chewed the heads up. Heads and hands, the only portions exposed, I guess."

"How did you make a positive identification? From the clothing, what?" I pointed to the teapot and cocked my head, he nodded, and I poured us more tea. The case was on.

"Clothes and pocket contents," Gallagher said. "I was all set to get a check made on his dental records but she didn't want that. That friend of hers, the lawyer, he said he was sure it was Prudhomme right enough and that was enough for our coroner. After all, who the hell else could it have been?"

"How much of the head was left?" An ugly question, but I've seen enough injuries and wounds that I'm past worrying about the polite observances.

"Not a whole lot," Gallagher admitted. "The bone structure was mostly there but the skull was crushed and the lower jaw was gone." He swung around and opened the file cabinet closest to him, pulling out a long drawer and taking a folder from it. He shoved it toward me and I opened it. On top of the contents lay a couple of eight-by-ten photographs. "That's the whole case in a nutshell," Gallagher told me. "How about you take a look at it while I head down to the school for the safety lecture for the kids. I'm due at nine-thirty, be back in about an hour."

"Thank you. 'Preciate that." I stood up as he left me, reaching for his hat, which had two lines of gold braid on it. Pretty fancy. My own only has one, but then, he had six men working for him. I only had Sam. Scrambled egg doesn't impress him unless it's in his dish.

I sat down and took out the photograph. It was as the chief

had described it. Prudhomme's body was lying in a tangle as if it had been thrown down by some impatient giant. The face and most of the head were gone, so were the hands. Aside from that the body was intact, still dressed in a heavy canvas-type jacket with lots of pockets, what looked like jeans, and prospector's boots with thick, ridged soles for walking over rough terrain. The second shot showed a close-up of the head. It had been crushed and most of the contents of the cranium were missing. If a bear had done it, he must have been as strong as a grizzly, not one of our local blacks. And I couldn't help thinking that the injury couldn't have been better designed for disguising a body.

I read the police report next. Prudhomme had been reported lost by the chopper pilot, a man named Kinsella. When Prudhomme didn't show for the rendezvous the two had arranged, Gallagher had taken a couple of his own men and some volunteers and gone into the area to search. It took them two days, in canoes and the chopper, to locate the body on an island in one of the small lakes that dot the whole area. They were lucky to find him so soon but one of the searchers was an Indian, Jack Misquadis, which I happen to know is the Ojibway word for turtle. Misquadis was a trapper by profession and he had picked up signs on the second day on the portage leading to the lake where the island, and ultimately the body, had been found.

There were statements from Misquadis and Gallagher and the pilot all confirming the discovery in the dry language that police reports use to turn horror into paperwork. The only colorful statement among them was from Misquadis. He had written: "I have been trapping this place thirty years but I never saw anything like this before. This one must be a mean bear."

The other important document was the coroner's report. Prudhomme had been killed by a crushing blow to the head, the damage was compatible with a swipe from a bear's paw, and the teeth marks on the bone were compatible with the dental structure of a bear. That was it.

I read the rest of the papers. There was an itemized list of Prudhomme's personal effects: wallet, the usual ID and a couple of receipts, one of them from a place in Olympia called Keepsakes, two letters, gold watch, compass, tin of Erinmore tobacco, matches, pipe, all the etceteras you would have expected. In the ruined backpack there were cooking utensils, cup, plate, geologist's hammer, and a camp lantern. That was it.

The silent Gladys refused to make a photocopy of the file. Her face grew tense and she smiled like a Japanese diplomat, but there was no way I could make copies of anything without direct permission from Chief Gallagher. I didn't force it. I was sure Gallagher would let me take one later.

While I waited for him I went over everything twice more, looking for anything that jumped out and shouted murder. Nothing did. I was rereading the list of Prudhomme's belongings when Gallagher came back. I heard his rumble in the outer office and the tiny piping of the clerk explaining what a bad boy I had been. Then another rumble and Gallagher came down the corridor with her in front of him, like a frigate escorting a carrier. She stopped in front of me, bent slightly from the waist like a bird on a windowsill, and told me, "The chief says it's all right. So if you'll let me have the file, Mr. Bennett."

I thanked her and she swept everything away. Then Gallagher sat down behind his desk and reached for his cigarettes. "Find anything we missed?" he asked with enormous unconcern.

"You knew I wouldn't," I said cheerfully. "I appreciate the chance to look through it, though. And I do have a couple of questions."

He struck a match on the sole of his boot and lit up. "Shoot."

"Well, I was wondering if you'd mind if I talked to the pilot and the Indian," I began. "And secondly, I wondered if you came up with any kind of bag of rock samples at the scene."

He shook his head. "Nothing. I was a little surprised by that. He had that hammer they all carry, all the geologists, but no rock samples."

"Maybe he was just heading out from his camp. Hadn't had time to collect any," I suggested, but Gallagher shook his head again, looking huge and shaggy as a bison.

"No, he just didn't have a bag with him, period."

We thought about that one, but before I could go "Aha!" and stick my finger in the air Gallagher reminded me, "Don't forget that all the land around here is already licensed. Some of it belongs to Darvon, some to other mining outfits. Some of it belongs to moms and pops in towns like this. That's one mothering big lode out there. They say it's the biggest thing outside South Africa. And it's no secret to anybody."

"So don't go painting any picture of murder to conceal a big gold strike," I said, and we both laughed at the thought. "Pity, would have led us right to the guy who did it."

"I think he'd be called the culprit in that kind of story," Gallagher said, and then dropped the amiability. "Anything else you need?"

I shook my head. "No. Like I said, you've wrapped it all up. I just want to talk to those men, go home, and say I checked everything."

"Okay, then, I'll turn you loose." He stood up and shook hands formally. "I've got my summonses to get out for the month. Call me if you get stuck."

I shook hands with him—it was something like reaching into an oven—collected my photocopies, and left. As I went out I was going over the one fact that had come through so far. Joe Misquadis was a trapper, but nobody had asked him about bear tracks at the site of the killing. It looked as if he would be my next point of call.

3

I went back out to Main Street and looked up and down it. There wasn't a lot to see. At one end was Lake Superior, bigger than any other in the world, big enough to sink big freighters without trace. On the shore stood the pulp mill as it had for eighty years, with its pyramid of logs brought in by water and dumped, ready for turning into newsprint. At the other end of the street was St. Michael's Anglican Church. Across from me was the Loyal Order of Bison lodge hall, the Bank of Montreal branch, and one of the town's four taverns. Behind me was the police/fire station and the Hudson Bay store, a small, clapboard building stocked mainly with catalogs showing the swell chain saws and shotgun shells and Day-Glo lingerie available to mail-order shoppers.

Aside from that there wasn't much except a tiny shopping plaza back up toward the highway, with the basic stores—a grocery, a drugstore, hardware and work clothes, and the bus terminal. Somewhere there was a school and a couple more churches in different flavors and nothing else important, except for the streets of company houses—bungalows for workers, two-story for management. Out behind them, in what had been bush a month before, there were scars on the ground where new houses were being built for the workers who would flood in when the new mines went on stream.

21

I looked around and wondered if there was anybody in town who knew anything special about anything, let alone the death of Jim Prudhomme. But I was here so I started looking.

* First, I did the obvious thing. I called on Jack Misquadis. I figured if he'd been trapping thirty years he had seen other men mauled by bears. He might have something to add that hadn't gone into his statement.

The report had given me his address. I knew it was on the road to the town park, in a shack he had built himself. I wondered why he didn't live on the Reserve but figured he was a loner, halfway into the white world, making his money guiding fishermen and hunters, disappearing into the bush in fall to do his trapping. Today, on a bright Indian summer day with not a cloud in the sky and the temperature up in the mid-sixties, I expected to find him repairing his gear and getting ready for winter.

It took only a minute's drive to get out of town. I noted that there was a new campsite open. It had a couple of house trailers on it and one or two pickup trucks with cabin backs. There were tents there, as well, and a new sign that read: No camping in the same spot for more than one week. It was signed by the Olympia Health Department. I wondered if Gallagher bothered enforcing it. He was tough on the outside but he knew the unemployed men who had flocked to the mine site needed some place to live. I figured he left them alone as long as they stayed clean and quiet. I would have, and I thought we were cut from the same cloth.

I was right about Misquadis. He was outside his cabin with a stack of leg-hold traps beside him and a jar full of gunk that figured to be bear grease. He went on with his work, not speaking. Real Indian.

I got out of the car. "Hi, Jack Misquadis?" I asked politely, not trying to smile him into a better humor. He probably didn't have as many changes of humor as a white man. Most

Indians don't. If they're mad at you, you know it. Otherwise they act as if time was the cheapest commodity in the world.

He went on rubbing grease on his traps. "Who wants him?"

"Reid Bennett," I said, and waited. He was wearing blue denim pants and jacket over a thick check shirt. He had a pair of work boots on his feet; they were split in a couple of places and I could see that he didn't bother with socks.

He finished the trap he was working on and looked up. He had a good face, square and roughly handsome, like most Ojibways. His nose was unbroken and not mapped with boozer's veins. He was a steady citizen, I figured. He still said nothing so I plunged in. "I'm a friend of Jim Prudhomme's family."

"Yeah?" he said at last. He wiped his greasy hands on the dry grass and reached for makin's in his top pocket. I let him roll a cigarette, then pulled out the motel matches and struck one. He leaned into the flame, sucked down smoke, and said, "What's on your mind?"

"I'm just talking to the people who found him. Spoke to the police chief, he told me you found the body for them when Prudhomme didn't show."

More smoke. Then he said, "Yeah."

"I read what you put in the report they wrote, down at the station. You never mentioned any bear tracks there. Did you see any?"

I knew this was forcing the pace. I should have talked about the weather for a while, then his trapping and plans for the winter. Maybe, if I'd been cynical enough, I should have brought out a pint of rye. But I didn't want him thinking I knew anything about Indian protocol, and I don't believe in pouring drinks for people who may not need them. He stared at me for long enough to finish his cigarette. I waited politely and finally he said, "What makes you think there wasn't no tracks?"

"Figure a guy like you would've made a guess at the size

of the bear if there had been," I said. "Only reason you wouldn't is if there wasn't a track."

He dropped the shriveled little butt, stepped on it, and picked up another trap. "Didn't see none," he said.

He greased another trap without speaking. I stood and waited, sizing him up. He was just under six feet but couldn't have gone more than a hundred and forty. He looked as if he could walk the bush all winter with nothing more to eat than the meat he took from his traps, washed down maybe with the occasional pot of tea. He was one of the toughest men I'd ever seen. He could have been anything from thirty-five to sixty.

He looked up as he selected another trap. "You're the guy that beat on that big fella at the motel," he said. Fame!

"There was a scuffle, not really a proper fight. I figure he must've been drunk." I've been in the violence business long enough to know you underplay everything, wins as well as losses, you never know which side your audience is on.

Misquadis grinned. "Nephew of mine was up at the bev'rage room. Says you fixed him good."

I shrugged. "I don't like fights. I stopped him, that was all there was to it."

Misquadis looked at me out of ancient brown eyes. "He beat up on my brother's kid one time. Kid was drunk. He broke his jaw." I waited and his leathery face split open like a slashed football. "I been waiting for him to pick the wrong guy. An' you was it."

Good, I decided. I had made all the brownie points I needed. I grinned an Aw Shucks kind of grin and waited and at last he talked to me. "You was right. No sign of bear tracks, no bear shit, nothin'."

I waited and he spat and went on. " 'Nother thing, this was an island, not very big. I figure you could camp there safe. A bear's big as this one would've stayed on the mainland."

I put my question slowly. "You're saying there was no bear on that island?"

He sniffed. "We wasn' there long. I look aroun' a bit but not all over." I waited and he went on, "Only thing it looked like to me, it looked like the tracks was cleared up."

"Cleared up?" I felt the old familiar hunting jolt shoot through my arms and clear up to my brain.

He nodded. "I never seen nothin' like it before, not trappin' It look to me like somebody swep' the trail with a branch, something."

I whistled. "So there was a guy there, clearing up after the killing."

He shrugged. I paused to see if he was going to speak but when he didn't I asked him, "Why didn't you tell the chief about this?" I put the question gently. I didn't want to sound aggressive, that would shut him up completely.

He picked up another trap silently. I figured he was over quota on words. Probably he hadn't talked so long at one time in a month. It was my turn. I changed the subject.

"The way the head was chewed, and the hands. That wouldn't happen if the bear had killed him, only if he'd found him dead," I suggested carefully.

He nodded slowly. "A bear maul you, he rip you with his feet, front feet, back feet, he don't care."

I went slowly. "Did you tell any of this to the police chief?"

Misquadis spat carefully. "He never ask me."

"But he must've seen maulings before this, if he's been here all this time."

Misquadis looked up at me, still working the bear grease into the release of the trap. "He just been here a year. Before that he was down south someplace. He just hear me say bear and that was it. When it come time to write it down, he done it and read it to me."

I stood and thought about that for a while. Gallagher had looked like an old-time pro. But he might have fallen into the veteran's trap of looking for easy solutions to vexing problems. Maybe he had forced the pace. But that didn't mean he was the only guy who had made a mistake. There was the coroner to consider. He had said the facial damage was compatible with a bear's physique. This meant that Gallagher had gone to the end of his own experience and then allowed other people to fill in the appropriate blanks for him. Only they had left more than they had filled in.

"What about the doctor? What'd he say?"

Misquadis laughed. "Him? He was too busy lookin' at the teeth marks. 'Bear did that,' he said. 'First bear bite I've ever seen.'"

I had learned as much as I was going to learn here.

Misquadis wiped his hands again and dug once more for his makin's. "The chief tell you about the bounty?" he asked.

"Bounty, on the bear?" I was surprised. "Haven't heard about that at all."

He accepted a light and sucked in smoke. "Yeah. The chamber of commerce put a bounty on the bear, five hundred bucks. Been guys up there all week tryin' shoot 'im."

"And they came up empty?"

He grinned, grinning around the butt in the center of his mouth. "They're not Indian," he said.

"Yeah, but there must've been some Indians went out after that kind of money," I argued.

He looked at me without speaking, and for the first time I could see the pride that filled him. "They wouldn't go until I go," he said.

"And when do you plan to do that?"

"Tomorrow," he said softly, and then added the words I was hoping for. "You ever hunt bear?"

"Not yet," I said, and let it hang there while he finished his smoke. Then he asked me, "Got a gun?"

"Yeah, in the trunk." I don't hunt, but I was just back from an investigation in Toronto where a gun would have been useful so this time I had stuck the station rifle in its case and put it in the trunk. Call it a veteran's precaution, a reflex after a bad experience.

Misquadis nodded. "We take your car maybe." He waved

to one side of his shack where an aluminum canoe lay upside down. "I got some rope."

"Good, when?" I was falling back into the pattern of working with up-country people, white or Indian, no spare words at all.

"First t'ing," he said, and turned back to his traps as if I were not there. I nodded at his back, got into the car, turned it in the space on top of the bare rock in front of his cabin, and headed out toward town. I wasn't sure what I would find at the bear hunt but at least it would get me to the place where the body had been found, otherwise I was going to have to hire a helicopter and that would cost.

I was puzzled. If Misquadis hadn't seen a bear then there probably hadn't been a bear on the island. And if there wasn't, either Prudhomme had been killed somewhere else and moved or else somebody had killed him using bear's teeth and claws. And why would anybody do that? And if they did, why would they take so much trouble going over and over the exposed flesh until it was unidentifiable? It didn't make any sense. Unless maybe it was some grudge killing, some maniac hated the poor guy so badly that he had disfigured the body out of anger. And what had caused Misquadis to think the scene had been tidied up? None of this sounded right to me.

Still doing the same plodding things I would have done as a policeman, I drove back to the center of town where the tiny hospital stood. Like most of the other buildings it was made of white clapboard, square and ordinary. I guessed the builder had used the same plan he had used for the original school, it was the only way he knew how to build anything bigger than a house.

Inside it was like any other hospital, only scaled down. There was a comfortable-looking clerk on duty, tapping away on a manual typewriter, and a nurse behind the counter. The nurse was fiftyish and brisk. I went up and introduced myself and asked if Dr. Clarke was in. He wasn't, it seemed. There was a medical convention in Dallas, Texas, she explained helpfully. He would be back on Tuesday. I hung in, even then, explaining who I was and why I was there and pumping her very gently about Prudhomme.

Things must have been slack for her because she opened up like a flower, tutting over the poor shape the body had been in when the chopper lowered it into the hospital parking lot. "I thought I'd seen everything after twenty-three years in town," she said with a touch of pride. "I've had men in here with arms and legs gone from mill accidents. Bullet wounds we get by the score, every damn hunting season. I've taken fishhooks out of every portion of the male anatomy." I grinned at that one the way she expected me to, and she smiled and went on, "But this was something. The whole face had gone."

I said something sympathetic and she continued more briskly. "It's lucky for Chief Gallagher that Dr. Clarke was here at the time."

"Yes, I can see that," I agreed cautiously. "He's the only doctor within seventy-five miles, I guess."

"Oh, more than that," she said, giving her head a proud little lift that made her starched uniform rustle and let me realize that she was probably in love with her boss but would carry the secret to her grave. "Much more important than that. Dr. Clarke is possibly Canada's foremost authority on animal bites."

I looked properly respectful and she filled me in. "Yes, when he came up here first he was a young GP. There was no chance of getting out again to specialize anywhere, the town just couldn't spare him. So he decided to put the isolation to good use. He made a study of animal bites. We get all kinds of them here. Some of the trappers are incredibly careless."

She embroidered on this theme for about ten minutes, painting a picture of her employer as a Dr. Schweitzer of the north, toiling with microscope and textbook over the gnawed hides of an ungrateful population and taking his reward in the papers he read occasionally at conventions like the current one in Dallas.

Some world expert, I thought. The guy probably knew everything about a bear's dental structure but nothing about bears. He probably spent hours in his office, studying the way animal jaws closed around people, but had seen only a few real bites of any kind. Ah well, some medical fields are less crowded than others.

I thanked her and left and went to the greasy spoon in the plaza for a cup of coffee and a homemade donut. I scored the coffee five out of ten for quality, but the donut was great. The place was half full of men, nursing coffees and psyching themselves up for another round of calling at the mine sites, looking for jobs that had all been filled before news of the strike made the general pages of the papers in Toronto. I sat and looked over my notes. The only other witness to talk to was the chopper pilot, but he figured to be working through the day out of the chopper base about thirty miles away at a motel on the highway. No sense driving up there right now. Which left me what? I had an encore on the donut and read through the rest of the file. It seemed that Prudhomme had parked his gear at the motel while he was in the bush. I could ask about that when I got back.

I called the waitress back along the counter. She was a bright pretty girl around nineteen. In the city she would have been a secretary, at least. Here she would work in the restaurant until some young miner married her. The prospect didn't seem unpleasant to her, she was cheerful and happy to please. She knew all about Keepsakes.

"Yeah, sure. It's downtown, near St. Michael's on Mill Street. Just a house, eh, with the sign outside."

I thanked her and stood up. "What do they sell, souvenirs, that kind of stuff, Indian crafts?"

She laughed, a nice crinkling of her face. "Nothing fancy. What he is, Mr. Sallinon, he's an animal stuffer, you know, taxidermist."

I walked out, wondering what a taxidermist could have sold Jim Prudhomme for three hundred dollars. As far as I knew, the guy had never shot a buck or caught a fish in his life. Maybe he wanted a moose head for his rec room.

Arnie Sallinon was a white-blond Finn in his forties, soft and overweight, with skin so pale he looked like the Pillsbury Doughboy. He was standing in the converted parlor of his house, surrounded by a dead menagerie. Skunks and porcupines, a lynx and a couple of marten, seven or eight lake trout and pickerel, and a couple of moose heads filled the walls and the shelf space. He was something out of Charles Addams, even in his attitude. "What my customer buys is his business," he said firmly after I'd introduced myself. "I don't have to tell anybody."

"No, you don't." I agreed, sweet reason itself. "But the widow is a friend of my wife's"—ex-wife would cut no ice with a Scandinavian—"and Chief Gallagher was kind enough to help me and he gave me a list of all the evidence he had. It included the contents of Jim's pockets and that led me here. I'm just killing time until I can talk to the other witnesses and I thought I'd ask you what Jim bought."

He thought about it for a while, staring through me with those sky-blue eyes. "What the hell, it can't hurt anything," he said with a bleak grin. "Let me get the book."

He dug under the counter and pulled out a Charles Dickens–sized accounts book, opening it as if it were the family Bible. I had a feeling he was taking time for my benefit. He knew to the last tooth or nail what anybody had bought from him in the past twenty years. But I leaned on top of the glass counter full of immortal animals and waited. He ran back through the last four pages, item by item, then skipped forward almost up to date and said, "Oh, yeah, here it is." He turned the book so that I could look at the entry in his spidery handwriting in ink as blue as his eyes.

I read it aloud. "One mink, mounted."

I looked up and found him grinning the same thin-lipped grin. "Satisfied?" he asked.

"You charge three hundred for a stuffed mink?" His smugness was getting me down. He'd known from the start what Prudhomme had bought from him.

My question offended him. "Not stuffed," he said angrily. "That's all you laymen think it is, a sewed-up skin stuffed like a mattress. It was mounted, just as if it were alive. It even had a little mounted mouse in its mouth. Very lifelike."

"I'm sure it was," I said, "but three hundred bucks is a lot to pay." I walked over to the wall and pointed at the first thing that came to hand, a raccoon sitting up prettily, the way it might in the bush or on top of a garbage can in Toronto. "How much is this piece?"

He didn't answer for a moment and I turned to find him staring at me with the dislike plain in his face. "For you, three hundred dollars," he said mockingly.

I met his gaze and said, "Yeah, well, raccoons are a dime a dozen. Any kid with a twenty-two rifle could bring you in as many as you needed. But, a mink—that's different. Sounds like Jim got a deal."

Sallinon snapped the book shut, ending the discussion. "We negotiated a price," he said without looking up.

I didn't believe him, but dislike and disbelief are no reasons for pursuing an inquiry past its dead end so I did the obvious thing. "Well, thanks for your time," I said and left, clanking the cowbell he had hung down the back of the door.

I didn't dwell on Sallinon's lack of cooperation. Lots of small town people are resentful of strangers. They make their living from us and they smile at us from their eyes but their mouths remain set and their wishes are not for our well-being; they resent the fact that we have time and money to visit while they're stuck in their rut. I just stored my feelings away and went back over the suspicions Misquadis had brought into my mind.

Who could have swept up the campsite where Prudhomme was found? It wasn't him, obviously. Surveyors like him are usually tidy in the bush. They bury their garbage and clean up their campsites when they leave, but they don't sweep around with a big branch. And even if he had, if he was so compulsively house proud that he kept the site tidy all the time, the bear's arrival would have left tracks on top of his work. I knew that Gallagher had investigated and closed the case but it smelled suspicious to me. It smelled like murder disguised as a bear mauling.

I thought back to my few meetings with Prudhomme. We had never been close, I'd spent maybe three evenings in his company, back in my married days. My impression was of a quiet man with restless eyes, as if the sights of suburbia weren't enough to hold him. He would have preferred to be off in the wilderness, putting up with the flies and the discomfort for the sake of the peace and the chance of making a big strike that would earn him glory in his company and perhaps get him a vice-president's corner office in Montreal. And now he was dead. The bush he had loved so well had turned on him, as if he was just as ignorant of its ways as the rest of us who live in houses most of the time, instead of in tents away from the city. Except that his bear, if it had really been a bear, had cleaned up after itself.

Which left the question of why Misquadis had said nothing about that in his statement. Maybe he was right and Gallagher had been too forceful, putting down what he thought Misquadis had said and pushing it in front of him for a signature. Misquadis was an Indian and a bush Indian at that. As far as he was concerned the whole procedure was meaningless. A white man had been killed and other white men were filling up pieces of paper to make the body disappear. It didn't matter very much what was put on that piece of paper. If nobody had asked him about bear tracks, he wouldn't have volunteered the information. And when the bear horror story grew and the town put a bounty on the animal, he would have kept quiet out of good sense. He wouldn't need more than a day or two in the bush to come back with a bear carcass in his canoe. He'd have his winter's meat, a skin to sell to Sallinon, and a five-hundred-dollar bonus, big money for a trapper. Most of them make less than five grand a year—if he was lucky he might make ten. That was all.

I guess I should have gone hotfooting back to Chief Gallagher with my suspicions, but I didn't want to wear out my welcome too early. So I headed for friendly turf, back to the motel.

Sam was getting bored with the car so I let him out for a scamper before going into the front office. The same woman was on duty, working away at a painting below the level of the counter. She pushed it out of sight automatically, then recognized me and smiled. It was a nice smile and I was glad

I'd opted for talking to her rather than the chief. "Good morning, how's the insurance business?" she asked me.

I stuck out one hand and did the *comme-ci, comme-ça* gesture. "Tell me about the art business and I'll sing you the whole sad song," I promised.

Surprisingly, she responded. She drew out her unfinished watercolor and waved it at me, half embarrassed. I could see it was a landscape and it had a good feel to it; the washed sky reminded me of a thousand overcast mornings in the bush. "Hadn't you better keep painting?" I suggested. "I thought watercolors had to be finished in a rush."

"They should," she said, nodding firmly. "But an artist in a place like this is considered a bit of a freak so I can't work the way I'd like to."

I found myself hanging on her words. She was frankly pretty in daylight, wearing a soft blue wool sweater with big open stitches and a pair of designer jeans. She was getting to me.

"Consider your painting invisible while I'm around," I said, and she smiled and reached for her paints.

"Okay, you're on, as long as you don't give advice."

"Not a chance. I'm looking for some from you." That made her glance up as she dipped her brush in the water jar. "About what?"

"Well, I'm here to look into the death of Jim Prudhomme, the guy who was killed by the bear last month," I said carefully. It didn't clash with the insurance story I'd given her and I needed her help. She looked at me and nodded slowly, then looked down and went on painting while I continued. "I've been talking to some of the people involved—the Indian who found him and the police chief. Now I was going to ask you a favor."

"I'll help if I can," she said, mixing up green and black in her palette.

"Well, I understood that Prudhomme left most of his gear at the motel here when he went into the bush."

She worked at trees, not looking up, not missing a stroke

as she answered. "Yes, most of our guests do, geologists and pilots and so on. But his widow collected everything when she came up for the inquest."

"Yes, I imagined she would have. But I wondered if you saw the pile of stuff at any time." I waited and she thought for a moment, working more slowly.

At last she looked up again, almost frowning with concentration. "I'm trying to remember. Seems to me he had two suitcases—well, one case and one suit bag, you know, the folding type. And there were a couple of wrapped parcels."

"That was one of the things I was interested in. He's supposed to have bought a stuffed animal from Keepsakes in town. I wondered if it was among his belongings."

I waited and she slowly dipped her brush again and went back to creating trees. "If he had, it would have been bulky, wrapped up for protection, maybe in a box," she said. Another tree shook itself out of the brush and she dipped more paint and looked up. "There wasn't a box. One of the two parcels was fairly heavy, tied with thick cord. The other was small, maybe a pair of boots or something like that."

"Could the big one have been anything from a taxidermy shop?"

Now she set the brush down and looked at me. "As a matter of fact, it could. One corner of the paper was torn—I think somebody else's gear was stacked alongside it in the store-room and one of the geology instrument cases had caught the paper and opened up a tear. There was fur inside, black fur. Looked like a bearskin."

"I see." I didn't question how she knew it was a bearskin. Women in the north may not know fur coats very well, but they know pelts. Their fathers and husbands all shoot and they see the animals themselves sometimes, in the bush. She went on painting while I stood and wondered why Sallinon had lied about the item he'd sold Prudhomme. Just being ornery, I supposed.

But I've been a policeman for a long time. If Prudhomme

35

had bought a bearskin, no matter whether it came from Sallinon or not, the person who had killed him could have cut the head and claws off it and used them on him. Which meant this other person knew him well enough to be at the motel with him, maybe only socially, for a beer, but maybe they'd been seen together.

"Tell me, can you remember if Prudhomme was alone when he left to go on that last trip?"

"Yes." She nodded instantly. "I was in the office when he came in and asked me to store his gear. Then he drove off past the office window. He was alone then."

"Did he always work on his own?"

She put down her brush for a moment, flexing her arms at the elbows. "I've no idea what his pattern was. But when he was found they said he was alone on the island."

I looked at her, musing, and she looked down and picked up her paintbrush. "Are there many transients around? Guys he might have picked up on the highway?"

She glanced up. "This place is lousy with transients. Ever since the gold strike was made. Most days I turn away twenty or thirty men, unemployed guys from Toronto or the Soo or Thunder Bay, looking to wash dishes, wait tables, anything."

I nodded and said "I see" again. It jibed with what I'd seen in the coffee shop and her diner, earlier, and in the crowded campsite. I guessed too that Gallagher kept transients moving. Olympia wasn't big enough to support a bunch of welfare cases. The paper business had suffered during the recession in '82 and '83. Any charity the town could provide was spoken for at home.

She went back to her painting. "Did you have some work for somebody?"

"Not right now, but I might, you know how it is." Not exactly true, but on an investigation you often find yourself dealing in fractions of the truth. The whole thing is too rare for use outside a courtroom.

I stood and looked down at the curls on the top of her head, thinking more about her than about my investigation. As far as the world was concerned, that was a closed book. Anything I found was going to be an embarrassment.

She glanced up and caught my gaze. "You're looking thoughtful. Run out of questions?"

"Not quite." As I started to speak I felt the same awkwardness that always fills me at times like this. I'm thirty-five years old, divorced. I'm six-one and rangy and women have been good to me over the years but I don't have the assurance that some men seem to bring with them from their cradles. I don't feel irresistible. I usually start out with women from a one-down position, like always playing chess with the black men. "This is going to sound like a thousand salesmen you've heard while you've been in this place. I mean, I don't even know your name, but I'm unattached and harmless and I was wondering if you would see your way clear to having dinner with me."

She laughed out loud. "My," she said, "That's totally new, I promise you. It's mostly the salesmen who ask me out. Their idea of couth is saying anything other than, 'Hey kid, let's me and you boogie.'"

I laughed with her, feeling redder necked than usual, and she said, "Sure. I'd like to have dinner with somebody in Olympia who can recognize burnt umber. And just to set the record straight, my name is Alice Graham." She put her paintbrush down and reached over. We shook hands, grinning.

"How about this place while you're out?" I asked, wondering if we were going to eat in the dining room, with her having to leave the table every few minutes to attend the desk.

"I'll get Willie to mind the store," she said. "No problem."

"Great," I said, then realized I needed an exit line and added, "Who's Willie, anyway?"

She was painting again, using a pinkish-brown now for the face of a rock. She put it on in gobs, then smudged it expertly with the side of her left little finger. It took about a minute before she realized what I'd asked and told me, "Oh, Willie—

he's the waiter in the dining room. He's only there on paydays. The rest of the time the girl manages just fine on her own."

"I met him," I said. "He's a nice kid, but can you leave him in charge?"

She looked up again, putting her paintbrush down into the water jar and stretching her arms luxuriously. "No problem. We're full right up; all he has to do is say no politely." And then her grin widened and she added, "That's what I do, most of the time."

We set a time, kind of early by city standards, seven o'clock, but as she explained, the nearest place other than her own dining room was forty miles up the highway and she didn't want to eat with a patron in her own place.

It suited me. It meant an extra couple of hours in her company so I said sure and went back to my room and picked up the telephone. I got through to Carol Prudhomme's number in Montreal and she answered on the third ring. "Hello, Carol, Reid Bennett. I'm in Olympia."

Carol is a tall, dark, Latin type of woman. She was at Laval University with my ex but had done nothing with her education except marry herself a geologist and keep the home fires burning while he trekked all over faraway terrain trying to make them rich. As a result she is tense and has an underused quality that came across brittle on the phone. "Oh, Reid, this is so good of you, going to all this trouble. I mean, I don't know why Amy insisted. After all, nothing's going to bring Jim back." It sounded rehearsed. I imagined she had been living with the idea of me up here in the bush wasting my time when I could have been writing parking tickets in Murphy's Harbour, and she felt guilty.

"No problem. I just wish I could promise it would do any good." I had already decided to tell her nothing about my suspicions. It was bad enough being widowed—having to add murder by persons unknown as the reason would be too much to handle.

I kept my voice calm and reasonable. "I'm just calling to

bring you up to date. I'm sure everything is as you were told, but there are a couple more facts I'd like. First, the man Jim was working for. He's with the Darvon outfit, Amy told me that much, but she didn't have a name. I'd like to talk to him."

Her voice was suddenly breathy. I've heard the same kind of tone from suspects in interrogation rooms. She was very anxious about something. Maybe she was afraid I'd offend some vice-president of the Explorations Division and the company would take back her insurance money. "Is that necessary?"

"It may tell me something I don't know, something that's been overlooked up until now." When she didn't answer I went on, "Don't worry, Carol, I'll be the soul of tact. I understand how you feel."

There was another short silence on the line, and then she spoke in a tearful rush. "I'm sorry, Reid, there you are, working away for me and I'm being negative. I'm sorry. Anyway, the man you want isn't up there, he's here in Montreal. His name is Paul Roger." She pronounced the name the French way, accented on the second syllable.

"Thanks, Carol. I'm not sure I'm going to do anything about it but it's good to have the name. In the meantime, I'd like to say it out loud: I'm sorry to have this investigation to make. But while I'm here, I might as well do it right."

She said something pleasant, and I responded and then asked her the last question on my mental list. "By the way, what was in the parcel that was up here with Jim's stuff?"

The line sighed and whispered as she thought about that one. Then she said, "There was a pair of boots in one package and a skin of some kind in another."

I kept my voice nice and even. "Can you remember, was it a bearskin?"

"I don't know," she said, almost angrily. "When I got home I was so sick about everything that I took one look at it and gave it to Henri."

"Who is Henri?" Nice and polite, but still wondering.

"Henri Laval. He was a good friend of Jim's—his lawyer. He came with me to Olympia and took care of things for me. I saw that this was some kind of skin and I gave it to him."

"Did you notice if it had its head and feet on?"

She laughed, high and nervous. "Reid, you ask the craziest questions. No, I didn't notice. I'll ask Henri, next time I see him."

"If you would, please."

We exchanged a couple more politenesses and I hung up and sat back on the bed, thinking. There weren't many more rocks to turn over. It would be interesting to talk to the wonderful lawyer man and see if the head and claws were on the skin, or whether, as I was beginning to think, someone had hacked them off to use in disfiguring Prudhomme's corpse in the bush. This was all a leap in the dark on my part. It's a fact with homicide that most often the murderer is somebody who knows the victim. That meant somebody Prudhomme knew in Olympia, somebody who might have known Prudhomme had bought himself a bearskin that would come in handy in disguising the murder method. I knew it was all thin, but something was out of whack in this case and my guess was as good as the next clairvoyant's.

Aside from that I had nothing to go on, nowhere to look. Roger, the geologist in Montreal, wouldn't know much. He might just be able to explain why Prudhomme wasn't carrying rock samples, but that wouldn't move me much further ahead.

I was still sitting there thinking when the phone rang. I picked it up, expecting to hear Alice's voice with some message about the evening. Instead a woman said, "Hi, Mr. Bennett?" It took me a moment to recognize her—Eleanor, the prostitute from the night before.

"Hi, nice to hear from you. What's on your mind?"

"You," she said, with professional charm. Then she went

on, excited. "You know you asked me about that guy who was missing—Prudhomme, wasn't it?"

My own excitement matched hers. "Yes, what about him?"

Like most people who don't get a chance to talk much, she milked her moment. "Well, I was trying to remember, all last night, and then today, just when I woke up, I remembered. He was a trick of mine, just once."

"Are you sure?" I didn't want to throw cold water on her help but there was no doubt she had a lot of customers and probably didn't pay much attention to what most of them looked like.

"Yes, I'm sure. I remember that he was really up, you know, the way a guy gets when he's been through a lot, been in the bush for a while or that. And anyway, I got a photograph of him."

I sat staring at the wall, my mouth open. "A photograph? That's incredible. How did that happen?" I thought it might have been in a bar. Maybe she had an arrangement with the girl who circles with the Polaroid, some fee-splitting arrangement. But she was even smarter than that. "It's kind of a habit of mine, in the van. I take a shot of everybody as they come in. They don't know, but, like, it could be useful." Her voice hesitated. "Like I wouldn't want this getting around, eh? I mean, people might get the wrong idea, only a friend of mine put me up to it."

I said nothing. There was only one reason a prostitute would take pictures: for blackmail. It lowered her in my estimation, but what the hell, she had to live, and by the sound of it she had a pimp to support.

When I didn't answer at once she broke into the silence. "Yeah, I know what you're thinkin'. Like I said, I don't want it getting around. I wouldn't tell people normally, but I owe you."

"I appreciate the help, Eleanor. Thank you," I said. Then I framed the important question. Prudhomme's body had been identified on September fifteenth, two weeks and two days previously. "Do you have any idea when it was taken?"

"Yeah," she said, and gave a little girlish giggle. "That's what makes it a gas. This was the last time I was in the Soo, which would have been the eighteenth of the month, a fun-filled Saturday night."

5

I've been a copper too long to accept good news just because it's welcome. I asked the obvious question. Was she sure he had been Jim Prudhomme? She was honest with her answer. No, she didn't remember meeting him before, but this guy was a ringer for the man in the photograph in the Thunder Bay newspaper, allowing for the beard and the fact that he had aged twelve years. That was when I asked the sixty-four-dollar question. How did he sound?

"French," she said without hesitation and then added the clincher. "An' he had like a slush sound in his voice, y'know, an impediment, I guess."

I remembered, as if he was talking in my ear. Jim was born Jacques; Jim was only a nickname. And he had that hissy sound that you hear sometimes and wonder if the person is wearing dentures. There was no doubt about it. She had found Prudhomme for me three days after the body on the island had been identified as his.

"Normal enough trick, wanted half and half," she went on cheerily. "No way I'd have thought anything about him but he was like the picture in the paper, and you asked me."

"Where's the photograph now?" First things first. Let's get our hands on some evidence. I knew a prostitute's testimony

43

wouldn't last two minutes in court. Some slick lawyer would crucify her and smile his way back to his seat, leaving any case in ruins. A photograph would give me the credibility I needed to reopen a formal investigation.

"I've got it right here with me," she said, and my pulse started to jump. "Don't tell me where you are," I almost shouted. "Just fix a rendezvous, somewhere we can meet and you can give me the picture."

"Why the hell wouldn't I tell you?" she asked, and laughed. Then she must have thought about it because in the few seconds I remained silent she said, "Hey, you don't think somebody's listening in?"

"No idea." I tried to sound cheerful. "But I was in a small war once and they taught me one thing."

"What was that?" She genuinely wanted to know.

"Tell them nothing," I said. "That's the whole of it. Tell nobody anything."

She laughed again. "Well, that's heavier than I normally worry about, but okay, I can give you the photo tomorrow."

"Why not tonight?" I was full of the old familiar hunting lust, the thrill of an investigation. It makes you feel like a caveman on the trail of your dinner. No other thrill matches it, except for its big brother, of course—patrol in enemy-held territory.

"Honeylamb, tonight is the men's social," she said patiently, and told me the name of the do-gooding organization whose membership was gathering that night to tell jokes, smoke cigars, drink eight-year-old rye, and watch Eleanor in the embraces of one of their younger members. "Two and a half yards easy money," she explained.

"What time will you be through?"

"Not till maybe three. Some of these old goats may get ideas and that means a little extra action for me. I could make five hundred."

I never dwell on lost causes. "Where and when tomorrow?"

She thought about that one. I could imagine her, twisting her blond hair around one finger as she worked out what to do.

"Well I'm in, well, like, around Thunder Bay. So how about I wait for you at the Terry Fox memorial at five o'clock. Know where it is?"

I did. Terry Fox was the gutsy kid who lost a leg to cancer and then set out to run across Canada anyway, trying to raise money to fight the disease. The secondaries returned in his lung before he reached Thunder Bay and there's a handsome statue there with the name of every goddamn cabinet minister who could swing the connection any way at all after Terry died. It's a few miles east of the city. "Yeah, I know where it is. If you're certain that's the best time to get together."

"Unless you've got five big ones to buy me off tonight," she said teasingly. I said nothing and she went on quickly, "Just kidding. Believe me, if I wasn't promised for months now, I'd leave the old farts to jack off on their own."

"Tomorrow is fine, Eleanor," I said. "Thanks for worrying about it. It's great."

"Five o'clock then. The cocktail hour. Maybe we could have a drink," she said.

"I'd like that a lot," I said. "See you at the monument at five tomorrow."

She hung up and I got up at once and drove down to Jack Misquadis. He had finished his work and was sitting in the doorway of his cabin, staring out at what little view there was, perhaps fifty yards to the stunted evergreens.

I told him I had to meet a guy the next day. I could be ready for a bear hunt the day after, would that be suitable?

He heard me out and nodded. Sure, the day after would be good. First t'ing. I nodded thanks and left. His attitude is one of a lot of things I admire about Indians. You don't have to make a big thing of arrangements when you're dealing with them. The old cliché about white time and Indian time is very true. They're not concerned with big hands and little hands on a clock, their time runs from events. They don't say, "See you at eight o'clock"; they say, "See you after supper." Now, if I chose to put some other event before bearhunting, that was fine. We would hunt bears later.

With the arrangements made I felt better. I would have liked to have the photograph of Prudhomme in my hands, but that would come. And then I would have enough evidence to open the inquest up again. This time we wouldn't take the word of a man who recognized the clothes Prudhomme's body had been dressed in. We would disinter the body and check the dental record for the upper jaw. I had a feeling that we would come up with some information to startle all the Prudhomme mourners.

It was hard to set thoughts of the case aside, but I had no choice. Tomorrow I could roll up outside the police station with the photograph and stir things up. Until then, I had nothing to do but prepare for my first honest-to-God date in I didn't know how long.

What I did first was to drive out of town with Sam and find a logging trail. There I pulled off the highway and stripped down to jeans and T-shirt and put myself through a solid workout. It's a habit I've been in since the service. As a copper, your major piece of equipment is your physique. You never know when you're going to need the most it can give you in strength, agility, or response time. It pays to get off the seat of the patrol car every day or so and make sure everything is still in working order.

It was. Soaked with sweat, I kibitzed with Sam for a while, then worked him through his paces once or twice and finally drove back to the motel.

I had a long, luxurious shower and changed into the best clothes I had with me, a good pair of corduroy pants, what my dad used to describe as the Bennett tartan, Viyella shirt, and a tweed jacket. Not exactly evening dress but plenty formal for this far north.

46

Alice was in the front office talking to Willy, who had widened up his grin a notch when he found she was going out to dinner. He looked at me, ignoring Alice, who was giving him instructions, and asked, "Had any more fights?"

Alice looked at me over his shoulder and threw her hands up in mock despair. Then she finished her briefing and I walked her out to the car. Sam was in the backseat and I let him out first.

"This could be a problem—I don't have anywhere else to leave him, except the room. Do you mind sitting in front of him for forty minutes?" I asked.

She looked at me over the top of the car, her face a pale smudge against the surrounding darkness. "It won't take forty minutes," she said firmly. "Leave him in the car."

I opened the door for her, then let Sam in the back again. If she thought the interior smelled a little doggy she didn't mention it; she had gone quiet on me. I wondered if I had offended her. Her next words put me straight.

"No sense driving all the way to Esterhaven for dinner," she said. "I can cook rings around the guy at the restaurant there."

"You're sure?" I tried to sound casual but I felt like a high school kid on his first date. "If I'd known I would have picked up some wine or something."

"You couldn't buy anything but domestic sparkling rosé around here. I bring mine in from Toronto when I order for the motel."

Even with Sam in the car I could smell her perfume, light and subtle, and I noticed that she had changed when I picked her up. I guessed she had a pad at the motel as well as some place of her own. "Head back toward town," she directed quietly. I turned left from the entrance, away from the Trans-Canada, down the four-klick side road to the middle of Olympia. After a minute or so we started to come to houses. She indicated one of them, a small place, in darkness, set up on top of a sandy slope. "In here," she said.

I pulled up beside the door and she got out matter-of-factly and unlocked the side door. I followed her in and she turned on the light. The place had been gutted by somebody who knew what he was doing. The standard sparse little rooms had gone. In their place was a single room, decorated like the loft of a girl I met in New York once on liberty from the Marines. There was a wood stove in the center, low, comfortable furniture, and a pine bar at one end with the kitchen behind it. The walls were cream-colored plaster, hung with pictures, most of them watercolors. There was an open staircase against one wall, leading up to a balcony that filled half the upper area, leaving a tall ceiling space over the rest of the room. A big, tropical-type fan hung there to keep the heat from the stove down where it would do most good, I guessed. You don't have to worry about cooling, not north of Superior.

"This place is beautiful, a real studio," I said. She grinned and wagged her head deprecatingly.

"I had some of the local women in here last year, working on a fund drive for the hospital. They asked me which magazine I'd seen the design in."

I stood at the door, still looking around, and she took her topcoat off and hung it on a pine coatrack on the wall. "How about you get the stove going while I pour a drink?"

I was looking at her, admiring the sheen of her hair and the aptness of the green color in her silk blouse. "Sure," I said. "That's something I'm good at."

There was a box of pine kindling close to the stove with a pile of birch bark on top. I laid some thin sticks on a piece of the bark and lit a match. Within moments the big Fisher was warming up and the crackle filled the room with comfort.

She had gone to the other side of the bar. As I waited to put a log on the sticks when they were ready, she brought out a couple of glasses. "What's your tipple?" She sounded a little tough, as if she were not sure she had done the right thing and was scared I would come after her like a rutting moose.

"Rye and water, if you have it, please."

"Coming up." She busied herself with the bottles, still not looking up. I went over to the wall and started looking at the pictures. Most of them were landscapes—hers, I judged, all with the same sad light I had seen in the current painting she was doing. But there were two small oils; one of them looked as if it might be a genuine Tom Thompson, the first guy to paint the Canadian bush in an impressionistic way. And there was a very fine watercolor of a man sitting in a canoe, laughing out at me. He was about thirty, big, judging by the scale of the paddle in his hands, fair haired and blue eyed, with a strong chin. He had the confidence you see in prewar pictures of buddies who died in combat. I guessed instinctively who he was, and with a small chill of presentiment, what had happened.

She came over to join me, carrying two glasses, rye and water for me, what looked like Dubonnet for her. She gave me mine, not meeting my eyes, looking sadly at the picture.

"Thank you," I said, and then, "Was he your husband?"

Now she looked up, like a startled bird. "Why did you ask 'Was he?' "

I sipped my drink and shrugged. "It's got a 'Paradise Lost' feel to it. I've been to the homes of buddies of mine who were killed in Nam and their folks have pictures like this on the wall, photographs usually, but with this kind of sadness to them."

She looked at me, clear eyed. "You're sure you're not psychic or anything like that?" Her mood suddenly changed and she waved one hand almost impatiently. "No, that sounds silly, but you certainly go right to the heart of things."

"I'm sorry if I opened up any old wounds." I sipped my drink again, taking one last look at the man in the picture and then turning away to check the watercolors close to it. "All your work?"

"Don't tell me they're good," she said almost angrily. "They're competent, able even, but they don't have the real touch."

49

"I don't know that I would recognize it in a landscape, even a brilliant one." I turned back to her and saw a frightening brightness in the corners of her eyes. She put her drink down and went to the counter for a tissue. She blew her nose and then turned back, smiling again.

"Sorry about the dramatics," she said with a wide smile. "Some nights it hits me that he's never going to come in through that door with a string of pickerel and three days' growth of beard."

"When did it happen?" I knew what—from the picture I guessed he had been an outdoorsman, one of those guys who out-Indians the Indians, paddling alone into lakes where only bears and trappers ever penetrate. That kind of guy usually tempts Providence one step too far at some point.

"August seventeenth, last year. He was alone, like always. He was heading upriver in his canoe, then carried it over the portage to some place he loved. I never found out what happened. His canoe was there, on the river below the rapids. The guy who found it figured he was trying to shoot the white water on his way home. His body never surfaced."

She looked so frail in that moment that I wanted to put my arm round her, would have done it if I'd known her longer. Instead I said "I'm sorry," and turned away to look at a watercolor.

She came up beside me, pointing out a rock in the foreground. "That's where we sat, the night he asked me to marry him. It was the same lake he was heading for when he . . ." She let the sentence dangle for a heartbeat and then finished it bravely, ". . . when he died."

"And it's the same lake you've been painting ever since?"

She nodded, then laughed awkwardly. "Can't paint the damn place out of my mind. I'd never done landscapes before, I always was a portrait painter, in watercolors yet, it made me halfway unique and I was good. I was very good, but since Ivan died, I haven't seen any faces I wanted to paint."

I left her looking at the painting and went back to the stove to check on the logs. This wasn't going to be the evening I had expected—a few drinks, a little steak, a gradual warming up that might have led anywhere while I was in Olympia, maybe longer. This was like the time I visited the widow of a man in my platoon, a plain girl with glasses who knew she had lost the only husband she would ever have and spent the evening in tears. I felt clumsy and inadequate.

Then she came over and sat on the couch next to the stove. "You do good work," she said brightly. "That's going just fine. Now if you'll pick out some music I'll think about tearing some lettuce up and scraping the frost off some fish fingers."

I laughed with her and the bad moment was over. She had a good record collection, light on rock, which is fine with me, but heavy on classics and, surprisingly, country. I picked out Willie Nelson's "Stardust" and sat across from her, enjoying the warmth of the stove.

She spoke first. "Sorry to seem such a Harlequin Romance character," she said. "It's just that you remind me of . . . of the way things used to be. He was big, like you, only blond, but he had the same blue eyes."

I took the reins of the conversation and steered it away gently. "That's what you get from an English father and a Quebecois mother. Black hair and blue eyes. You should see my sister, she makes the combination work."

From that we moved to safer ground. I even told her about my divorce, and the reason for it, the aftermath of the encounter I'd mentioned to Gallagher.

She picked up her drink, still almost untouched, and went back to the counter, where she made salad and put steaks under the grill. We were talking easily now. She was as bright as she had been the night before when I walked into the office at the motel. It seemed that Ivan was a forgiving ghost. Now she had paid her dues, the chill was off the evening, the way it had gone from the room under the influence of the big Fisher stove.

She brought out a bottle of California red wine. The name meant nothing to me, but it was better than most of the French wine you can buy in Ontario. We ate and drank wine and listened to Willie and talked. She had a cheesecake, made by a German woman in town, she confessed, and after that coffee and Hennessy and a seat, side by side, in front of the stove.

And then, in the warmth of the fire and the friendship we had built up over the few hours, we kissed. Her mouth was soft and when she pulled away she looked into my eyes and smiled. "You've done that before, haven't you?" she said.

"I did warn you I'm an ex-husband, a secondhand man," I told her. She reached up again and this time when we broke she said, "Come with me."

I followed her up the open staircase, like a companionway on a ship, and found that the whole second floor was a bedroom. She turned at the top of the stairs, one step higher so that we were eye to eye. "You like?" she asked playfully.

"I believe I could grow to love it," I said, and picked her up and carried her over to the bed.

It must have been three when I left. She was half asleep and I kissed her on the nose and got dressed. "Love 'em and leave 'em, eh, Bennett?" she said drowsily.

"I'd love to stay but I live in a small town myself. I know the neighbors are going to be watching by daylight." I stroked her hair. "It's up to you."

She sat up then, the sheet slipping down so her firm breasts were uncovered. I kissed them both. "Maybe you're right," she said. "Will you be in town tomorrow?"

"I'm here for a while and my dance card is completely open."

"Good," she said, and settled down again. "Lock the door as you go. And put me down for the next boogaloo."

The northern lights were flickering across the sky as I went out, and the air was colder. I stood and looked at her house for a minute, then got into the car and drove back to the motel.

Sam was restless and I let him out for a while before going in through the side door into the corridor of the motel.

The whole place was in darkness except for the emergency exit light behind me. I was surprised. Most places, even this far north, would keep the hall lights on. But I found my room and tried the key, scraping it slightly as I searched for the lock. It swung open and I stepped inside and stopped, still in the short corridor that led to the room itself. My hair was prickling on my neck. Something was wrong, I could feel it. The light didn't go on when I hit the switch and I could smell cigarette smoke in the air. I crouched instinctively, left arm up over my head, staring out through the darkness toward the translucency of the gauze curtains, lit from outside by the sky. And as I watched a form sprang into my vision, reaching up to swing a club as hard as a Blue Jays batter trying for a homer.

I had an advantage. Whoever it was had put himself between me and the window. I straightened, arm still raised, stepped forward under the club, and brought my knee crashing up into his testicles. At the same time I uppercut a solid right hand, bringing it up into his descending face like a hammer.

He collapsed like a falling wall, the club clattering uselessly behind me. I stepped back and felt for it with my foot, listening for other sounds than the anguished gasping of the man at my feet. I could hear none, but I crouched carefully and retrieved the club. It was a piece of rough lumber, still with the bark on it, about four feet long. It felt like a small fence post. I held it by the middle, like a Parris Island pugil stick, ready to block or swing in any direction, up, down, across. Still nobody moved. Whoever had set me up had sabotaged the lights. They had probably left one plugged in, most likely the one that switched on from the bed. That way they could have sat back and put the lights on to prod my body with one toe and laugh when they had me on the floor, moaning.

There was no alternative. I swung the stick, trying to be silent, cutting the air in front of me in every direction as I inched for the bed. When I felt it against my shin I edged along and found the bedside switch.

As I clicked it on, the other man sprang for me, leaping across the bed, swinging his club sideways at my head. Maybe if we'd been somewhere high enough for him to come overhand he would have decked me, but the ceiling was too low. I parried his swing with my stick and then windmilled him with both ends, twice each in the head, scattering his teeth across the floor. He gave a half scream of pain and collapsed, bleeding from his mouth and his nose.

I ran back to the bathroom and threw up, dry bile and undigested fear and horror at my own ferocity. Once I'd spent hours in boot camp working with a padded pugil stick, wondering why the hell they wanted me good with the thing, learning it only so the DI wouldn't be able to pound me anymore. But it was a boxing glove compared with the bare knuckles of the post I had used tonight. Even the day my training and practice had paid and I squared myself with the DI, knocking him on his butt, he had been on his feet shouting orders, first bounce. Now I had used a raw club without pads and smashed a man. The fact he had been trying to kill me didn't stop me from being sick. But I beat it, soon. And though I felt filthy, I kept the club in one hand in case either of them got up and tried again.

I was wasting my worry. Neither one of them moved and I came back into the room and turned the first one face up. It was Carl from the night before, moaning soundlessly, both hands clutching his groin. I left him and checked number two. He was conscious but shocked beyond speech.

He looked at me blankly and I let go of him and picked up the phone, dialed the operator, and asked for the police. Surprisingly, I got right through to Chief Gallagher, patrolling in the scout car. In the instant he responded "police chief," I realized he must have a shunt through the radio at his station and thought about getting one installed in Murphy's Harbour.

"This is Reid Bennett at the motel. Two guys jumped me with clubs in my room, number thirty-four."

"Two of them, eh?" His interest was clinical. "Both still there, are they?"

"Yeah, I think they could use an ambulance."

"If it'll wait until I've been there, hold onto them for five minutes, I'm down at the mill."

I hung up and looked around. They had broken into my case and taken out the bottle of Black Velvet I had brought with me. Both the motel glasses were on the table, used, so I took a slug straight from the bottle. It calmed me and I sat and waited until Gallagher arrived. The men moaned in pain, but I've seen guys with worse injuries waiting hours for the choppers to come in.

Gallagher came in without knocking and checked both of them. "Shit," he said respectfully. "Remind me not to get you mad. What'd you hit them with?"

I showed him the post I'd taken off the first man. He whistled, surprised but not shocked. It looked as if I'd been right in my instincts about him. He was the typical copper. His presence in the room was like the return of daylight after a bad night. The blood on the carpet seemed less vivid, the two men less grotesque in their pain. I held out the whisky bottle without speaking and he took it and pulled himself a good taste. "Thanks. What happened?"

I told him while he reached for the phone and called the hospital. He asked them to send somebody to the motel, pick up a couple of fighters. Then he asked, "Where were you, until now?"

"I was out visiting."

He grinned, a bleak, copper's grin. "Thought that was your car at the Graham place," he said, and asked, "What happened?"

I spelled it out for him and he nodded. "I believe you, but in the morning the magistrate is going to find it difficult to credit that they ambushed you."

56

I shrugged. I knew firsthand that he was right, but there was nothing to say about it. It sure as hell looked like excessive use of force, even to me, and I'd been there.

"You gonna charge them?" he asked, flopping down on the edge of the bed, making it look casual but dodging the bloodstains. He took off his hat and tossed it aside. "Might be an idea, ya know," he urged. "Otherwise some shyster is going to suggest they charge you with assault."

I didn't answer him directly. Instead I picked up one of the clubs, four-foot hunks of cedar, cut with a hatchet, judging from the marks. "They both had these," I said, tossing it to him.

He caught it casually and reached down to prod the second man. "Either one of you two scumbags wanna charge Mr. Bennett with assault?" he asked. The man groaned.

Gallagher tossed the club back at me. "Give him a good night's sleep and some dental work, he'll be chirpy as hell again, certain to think of some reason for pressing charges. You should charge them."

"Okay, break and enter and aggravated assault. Should get them out of your bailiwick for a month or two."

He stood up, suddenly angry. "I hope they get ten years," he said savagely. "That bastard there"—he pointed at Carl with one toe—"he's beat up more guys. But none of them will press charges. It's not like the city, you know. Up here, working on mine construction, you have to love thy goddamn neighbor or the bastard's likely to drop a pick down the shaft on your head. Only they're afraid to do it to him. He deals in terror, constantly. Nobody ever charges him. He thinks he's King Kong."

He walked over and tapped Carl on the shin, lightly, but the man looked up out of pained, dull eyes. "How're you feeling now, big shot?" he asked. "Finally picked the wrong guy, didn't you?"

Outside I could hear a siren wailing toward us. Gallagher turned toward the window and sighed. "He really needs that, to clear the traffic away at three-thirty A.M. in Olympia, doesn't he?"

"It's his only chance," I said. "It's to let his wife know he's working."

I went to the outer door and directed the ambulance men in. They had a stretcher with them, but they looked at Carl in dismay. "He's a heavy sonofabitch, ain't he, Chief?" one of them said to Gallagher.

Gallagher nodded. "Hope you been eating your Wheaties," he said casually. "The other one is walking wounded." He reached down and tapped the man on the shoulder. "On your feet, sunshine, these nice men are taking you to the hospital."

The injured man stood up slowly, pulling himself up on the bed, then putting both hands back over his mouth. I felt my sickness rising again but hung on. If they'd surprised me as they intended, I'd have the injuries of both of them, plus others.

The ambulance men grunted Carl onto the stretcher and staggered out with him. We followed. I left the light on.

We went to the hospital first. From there Gallagher called one of his men, waking him up and asking him to come down and guard the pair of them. He arrived ten minutes later, with the drained look of someone woken from a sound sleep.

He looked at me wide-eyed when Gallagher filled him in and we left as a nurse brought him coffee. Gallagher drove me down to the station and let us in.

"You know the routine," he explained casually. "I need a formal complaint and I can lay the charges. No doubt in my mind it was like you said."

"Does this mean court in the morning?"

He nodded and grinned. "Which means you'll be lucky to get five hours' sleep. Welcome to police work, in case you forgot."

I sat there while he typed up the occurrence and took my

statement. Then I asked him the question I had thought of back at the hospital. "You think there's any more to this than revenge for last night?"

"More? Like what?" His eyebrows pulled themselves together and he leaned over the typewriter, taking his weight on the arms of his chair.

"Well, I've been asking a lot of questions about Jim Prudhomme today. You don't think that has anything to do with the town thug taking a crack at me?"

He left himself relax, leaning back slowly and opening the drawer of his desk. He took out Juicy Fruit gum and pulled himself a stick, not offering it to me, and pushed it back in the drawer.

"What makes you think the Prudhomme thing isn't closed?"

I looked at him, at the obvious squareness of a lifelong copper, a hard-nose who never took anything for granted. I've known a lot of policemen and a lot of tough guys earning a hard dollar in tough places. All of them have the same iron quality to them—not in the face, in their core. I knew I could trust him. "Because I'm starting to get a whiff of something funny about this business. It wouldn't surprise me at all if Prudhomme was alive and well and the body in his grave was the body of some drifter."

"You were talking to Misquadis?"

"Him and some other people." I let it sit at that and he chomped his gum a time or two and then sat forward again.

"And he told you there wasn't any bear on that island?"

"He said he didn't see any tracks," I said carefully.

Gallagher snorted. "Neither did I."

We sat there, our eyes locked. When I spoke I was careful again. "But you said Prudhomme was killed by a bear."

Suddenly Gallagher stood up. He looked down at me as if I were a petty thief and this was our first meeting, while the loot I'd picked up lay on the table between us. "No I didn't," he said angrily. "I never made any such damn suggestion.

59

That was the coroner. I told him there was no bear spoor, no tracks. You know what he did?" He paced away from his desk and turned suddenly, "You know what he told me?"

"I guess he told you he was the doctor and you were the copper," I hazarded.

Gallagher laughed. At least, the ugly sounds that poured out of him might have been called that. To me they were the gurglings of a man in misery. "Ten out of ten," he said. He turned to the wastepaper basket and threw his gum into it, looking down as if he would like to kick the basket into ruins. "That could've been his exact words. And because I'm fifty-seven years old with nowhere else to go before retirement, I let him say it. And I went along with his finding. And I tore up my first report, which called for an investigation at the site of the killing and a proper search by Misquadis and a proper investigation by the forensic people at Queen's Park in Toronto. I let him tell me how to do my job, because without him and the rest of council there isn't any goddamn job to do and I'm still too young to be dying of old age in some single room in Toronto."

He sat down again, bonelessly, collapsing into his chair. I waited for him to continue but he didn't. He sat and looked down at his desk until I spoke. "It's the same in Murphy's Harbour, the same in every small town. They hire you and they think they own you."

He looked up at me. His face was bleak. "You've still got time," he said. "You can quit, find some other kind of work. But I'm stuck. I'm a copper with maybe eight good years left. After that I'd be lucky to get a job in security, letting people in and out of some oil company office in Toronto."

There was nothing to say, so instead I waited for a while, then filled him in about Eleanor and her photo. He whistled softly. "Well, there's one smart little hooker," he said. "Always struck me she was better than the job she does. She's got brains and she's got spirit but she still keeps on peddling her ass like it was fish. It makes you mad." Not a word about the evidence.

I waited a moment or two, then told him about the bearskin Prudhomme had bought, and about the fact that Sallinon had said it was something else.

"I was starting to figure that somebody killed Prudhomme and tried to dress it up as a bear mauling," I said. "But when the guy owned the murder weapon already and when he's found alive and well enough to get laid some days later, I wonder just whose body that was up there on the island."

Gallagher sat up. "If this Eleanor is right—and we'll know better when we get that photo—then you've got to think that Prudhomme killed some other guy and dressed him up in his own clothes."

"Why?" I wondered out loud.

Gallagher stood up and paced around his desk. "Hell, I don't know. Why does anybody kill anybody? Maybe he was in over his head with a loan shark? Maybe he was sick of his wife and wanted to drop out of sight. We don't need a motive, we've got a goddamn body."

"Yeah. But that raises another question, for me anyway. If he bought that bearskin from Sallinon, why did Sallinon lie about it? Did Prudhomme ask him to, I wonder?"

"Beats the hell outa me." Gallagher said. At last he began to grin. It started around his mouth, cold and hard, a flexing of the muscles. Then it spread until it lit up his whole ugly face. "Go to it, Reid. Let's bring this case back to life and show these arrogant bastards that they know nothing It won't make any difference to them, they're in too solid in a town this size. But it'll show them there's more to life than taking the plane to Chicago or Los Angeles and standing up there talking bullshit about animal bites."

I wondered why he had such a personal anger against the good doctor. Was he perhaps interested in the big nurse? It was a thought, but I let it slide. "Okay. I'm heading to Thunder Bay tomorrow. As soon as I've got the picture we'll turn this investigation on its ear."

He didn't say anything. Instead he reached across the table and shook hands with me. "Come on," he said. "I'll drive you back to the motel."

7

I was up at eight after four hours' broken sleep.
First I let Sam out of the car, fed him, and gave him a brisk
run, then I went for breakfast. The same girl was on duty
and I ate the same breakfast, looking through the same window at the same grand view. After that I went down to the
little courthouse, ready to tell the magistrate what had
happened.

First I had to sit through half a dozen hearings of vagrancy.
In each case Gallagher gave the same evidence. He had found
the men panhandling in town. He had driven them all to the
city limits and give them five dollars and told them to head
back down the highway, there weren't any jobs vacant in
Olympia and there was no room for beggars. All of them had
come back into town and taken up panhandling again. He
had arrested them, given them a night's shelter in the cells
and a solid breakfast, and brought them to court. In each
case the magistrate cautioned the men, told them they would
get thirty days next time, and advised them to leave town
for keeps. They had all agreed to do so. Two of them had
stopped on their way out of court to shake hands with Gallagher and thank him. He brushed it off, but it increased my
respect for the man. He was a good copper and a kind man.

I didn't get a chance to talk about the attack. The town

lawyer was there on behalf of the two men, Tettlinger and Gervais. He asked for a one-month remand, telling the magistrate that his clients had suffered a severe beating, frowning at me as if he expected me to go red. I didn't. My initial horror was over. These two were bad news. They deserved a jail term. I would do what I must to see they got one. In the meantime, thanks to the Bail Reform Act, they were freed on their own recognizance and told to return a month later for the hearing.

There was only one florist in town, but he had yellow roses. I bought seven of them, then went to the grocery and picked up an empty carton to hide them in. It had previously held somebody's toilet tissue, but I didn't figure that was too outlandish to carry into a motel.

Alice Graham was at the desk, looking as perky as ever. She had some miner type with her, checking out, so I set the box down carefully and waited. She glanced at me over his head as he bent to sign the credit card form, and winked. "A little early for deliveries," she said.

"They told me this was an emergency," I said, and waited until he had gone.

Suddenly, without his presence, she was a little shy. I didn't let it cool me but lifted the box up onto the counter. "Never judge a carton by its cover," I told her.

She looked at me, her eyes wide, face still neutral, and opened the lid. She peeked in and closed it down immediately, bowing her head. Then she opened it again. "This is good-bye, isn't it?" she said quietly.

"How about *au revoir*?" I asked. "I have to drive to Thunder Bay this afternoon and I won't be back until midnight."

She pulled the roses out of the box and sniffed them. "You know where I live," she said. And then the phone rang and she was all business again.

I waved and left. It was noon and Thunder Bay was four hours of driving away, at least. Sam was glad to be moving. He sat up next to me for the first fifty miles until we reached the restaurant where I'd expected to eat the night before. I pulled off and had fish and chips, having to specify no gravy on the fries. By then it was one o'clock and I settled back for the rest of the journey.

The weather was perfect. The sky was brilliant and all the hardwoods were changing color. Right in that section, the Trans-Canada highway has to be one of the most beautiful roads in the world. There are little mountains peeking out of the endless trees, sheer cliffs, and the occasional view to the shores of Lake Superior. I knew that in one month there would be snow up to the hubcaps, but on an afternoon like this I could envy the lonely people who live there. Each of the scenic lookouts had cars at them, mostly carrying American license plates. Moms and pops were snapping their Instamatics at their Oldsmobiles with the view in the background. I stopped at a lookout about an hour from Thunder Bay to let Sam stretch and to get my mind away from Alice Graham and back to the case. I've known my share of women, but this one was a rare delight in a town like Olympia. She was intelligent and spirited and almost beautiful. I found it hard to get her out of my thoughts.

But I concentrated, and when I got back in the car I had worked out what I would do. It was simple. I would pick Eleanor up and drive her into town for a quiet drink, perhaps dinner. I'd take her through the story enough times to be sure she'd got the date right. Then I would thank her and take the photograph back to Olympia and let Gallagher see it for himself. From there on, he could take over the investigation and I would do any legwork he suggested. And in the evenings, I would spend what time I could with Alice.

As I came up the slight slope from the east, I could see a Winnebago at the foot of the Terry Fox monument. There were a couple of other cars parked there. One, I noticed, had Michigan plates; the other was Ontario. People were standing around the monument, reading the words at the base, taking photographs.

I pulled in next to the Winnebago against the low wall that surrounds the scenic lookout. Eleanor wasn't in the driver's seat, but that didn't surprise me. Her vehicle was a home. She was probably relaxing in the back, maybe making herself a cup of coffee on the propane stove. It occurred to me that she might be carrying through on the reward sequence she had sketched for me the night I fought Carl Tettlinger. Maybe she was back there in a housecoat, waiting to show her gratitude in the most obvious way she could think of.

I grinned at the thought. I'm no prude, but I didn't need the gesture. I'd rather be her friend than just another john. I tapped on the door and waited. Nothing happened. I tried it, but it was locked, I went around to the other side where the main entrance door was located. I knocked again but there was still no answer. A pulse in my throat started to kick. This wasn't right. You don't have to beat the door down to be heard in a motor home. If she was inside she was in no shape to answer. And I wondered why. I turned the handle and found the door was open.

That was unusual. It's not smart to leave a recreational vehicle open. Kids could swarm through it and rip off everything that wasn't screwed down. It could happen, even here in the true north, strong and law-abiding.

I stuck my head in and called "Eleanor." My voice echoed. Slowly I climbed the first step and called again. Still no answer. The interior was tidy. The double bed was made, covered with a silk bedspread as close to scarlet as I've ever seen. It had been ruffled, as if someone had lain on it and got up hurriedly, but there was no sign of her. I glanced around. The only inside door led to the head. It was shut. I tapped politely and called again, "Eleanor." All I got was silence. Working now on a policeman's instinct, I opened it.

Her body fell out with a slithering rush and sprawled at my feet. She had been shot, at close range, through both eyes.

8

The next six hours were a replay of a dozen homicides I've dealt with in my time. I got the couple in the next car to call the police. They came, a couple of uniformed patrolmen. I showed them my Murphy's Harbour ID and filled them in. They called the detectives. The detectives called their homicide guy, just one for the peaceable folks of Thunder Bay. He came. So did the CID people with their fingerprint gear and their cameras. And then the ambulance, picking its way through the crowd that had swarmed there: sightseers, reporters, cameramen, gum-chewers. By nine o'clock I was in the police station, drinking bad coffee and making a statement.

They started off suspicious but slowly thawed out. One of the detectives called Olympia and spoke to Gallagher, who told them I was kosher. Then they went over all the contents of the Winnebago, pulling out everything—from the milk in the little fridge to the working girl's wardrobe of garter-belts and fancy lingerie they found in the drawers under the bed. There was the usual amount of sniggering over all of that stuff, especially from the uniformed coppers who were still young enough to think that everybody's sexuality except their own was a scream.

They uncovered her camera, hidden behind what looked like a smoked-glass pelmet over the window facing the main entry door. It had no film in it. There were no photographs of any kind in the camper.

The detective, a big Nordic blonde by the name of Pedersen, sipped his coffee with distaste and asked me, "Who all would've killed her?"

"No idea. I only met her two nights ago, like I told you. I was coming here to see her about some customer she'd had that looked like a man I'm after."

He sipped again and looked at me as if I smelled bad. "So it's likely your fault she's dead," he said in a growl. "That shooting through the eyes, that's somebody's way of saying she'd seen too much."

"That's the feeling I got. But I don't know who could've done it. It could've been some trick she was blackmailing. She didn't strike me as the type, what I saw of her, but I don't know any more about her than you do."

"Less, probably," he said, crumpling his coffee cup. "I was in high school with her." He stood very straight and scrubbed his tired face with the heels of his hands. "Bright as a goddamn dollar. Some asshole tourist knocked her up and her family kicked her out. She couldn't get a job that paid enough to support the kid so she took to hooking. And now this." He looked at me for any sign of smugness. I didn't show any. Women like Eleanor don't make me feel superior. They make me feel fortunate to have been born male. We don't get landed with her kind of trouble. The bad ones among us cause it, the rest of us mostly blunder through our lives without having to touch the sides.

Pedersen must have sensed sympathy in my silence. "She was fifteen when it happened. Grade ten. Her folks ran a campground, lived out there all summer. She stayed there, picking up paper, working the kitchen, all the chores a kid would do to help around the place. That was my last year.

Grade thirteen. She was in ten, so I guess that makes her thirty." He corrected himself, "Made her thirty, when she was still alive."

I said nothing. There isn't anything to add to that kind of story. A lot of social workers would have you believe all the women on the street get started that same way. It's not true. Some of them are lazy, some of them hate men and take out their resentment by accommodating them, enjoying the power they hold over them for the time it takes. Others are just unlucky, like Eleanor. My mother, rest her soul, would have said a Hail Mary for her. I don't say prayers much, since Nam, but I felt for Eleanor.

After an hour or two they secured the scene. Her camper had already been towed into the police car pound and they had sent four uniformed men scrambling down the escarpment in front of the lookout, one of them with a metal detector, searching for the murder weapon. It hadn't shown up by midnight, although they must have turned up fifty bucks' worth of beer cans, so they called two of the guys off and left the others to guard the scene against souvenir hunters until daybreak. Me they let go, with a warning to stand by to be recalled for the inquest.

I drove back down the dark highway, boring through the blackness with my lights on high beam, going thirty miles at a stretch without seeing a house or another car. In one spot a truck had hit a moose and a pickup full of Indians had appeared from nowhere to butcher the carcass. They looked up at me over the big bloodstain in the road, eyes gleaming red in my headlights as I barrelled through.

I made Olympia at five A.M. and drove down to Alice Graham's house. It was in darkness, but the door opened almost as soon as I turned off the engine. I paused to let Sam out, leaving him in the predawn chill as I slipped in past Alice, who was shuddering in the cold, wearing a nylon nightdress that Eleanor might have been proud of. I picked her up under the elbows and kissed her on the forehead. "Sorry I'm late. I ran into trouble."

"It was on the radio," she said softly. "They said a local woman had been murdered in her Winnebago at the monument and police were questioning a man." She tilted her face to kiss me quickly on the chin. "I put two and two together."

She closed the door and stood a foot away from me in the darkness. "You want to talk about it?"

"Nothing to say. She had some information for me. I went to pick it up and she'd been killed and the evidence was gone. It looks as if somebody learned about it and beat me to it."

Now she reached out and turned on a low reading lamp. Her house looked dim and comfortable, like a stage set for a romance, only I didn't feel romantic. I felt dirty and hungry and disappointed. "And that's all it meant to you?" she asked soberly. That somebody beat you to it?"

"No, it meant the end of a remarkable women. It makes me sad and it makes me angry and I'd like to catch the sonofabitch who did it and break his arms and legs," I said, suddenly angry. "I'm not a machine, Alice. I like people, I want them to stay healthy. I liked what I'd seen of that woman and now she's dead."

She shivered quickly, then reached out and hooked a coat off the peg by the door. It was a red mackinaw jacket, barely long enough to cover her hips. Frothy white nylon spilled out underneath, transparent against the low light. "I'm sorry. You just seemed so matter-of-fact about it. Would you like some coffee, a drink, what?"

My empty stomach rolled and I reached out and stroked her cheek. She caught my hand and held it against her face, then quickly let it go as if her mother might come in and see her playing with the boys. "Have you had anything to eat?"

"Not since one o'clock yesterday, and I want to be in Chief Gallagher's office as soon as he gets there."

"Then you need bacon and eggs," she said. "I'll put some on." She went over behind the counter and opened the fridge. I had half expected her to go for a housecoat, but she didn't, she moved around in her crazy half-sexy, half-practical outfit as if I wasn't there. For the first time in three mostly lonely years I felt like a married man.

I sat stupidly, wearily, watching as she laid strips of bacon in the pan. I noticed the roses I'd given her in a crystal bowl on the bar. Part of me wanted to go over and hug her, not for the sex but for the closeness to somebody who cared about people, me and poor dead Eleanor. But I was too aware of my own presence, the stale lived-in feel of my tired body. I had no right looking for proximity, even to a girl in a mackinaw jacket and a nylon nightdress.

So instead I went over to the stereo system against the wall and dug through her records. She had a copy of the "Four Seasons" and I put on side one, the "Spring" section.

Alice looked up from the stove. "Nice," she said. "I didn't know you liked Vivaldi."

"Grew up with classics. My father was a brass band man in the Old Country. He taught us what music was, saved me from being a rock fan."

She smiled, a quick beam that looked as if she meant it, then turned the bacon and reached for eggs. The coffeepot bubbled, filling the room with fragrance. I swallowed hungrily, waiting for breakfast and for something to go wrong. I figured it had to. Women don't often get out of bed to cook me a breakfast. It's hello, good-bye, generally. This time was a lot more fun.

She lifted the bacon out onto a paper towel and cracked eggs, three of them, into the pan. "Over easy, right?" she asked, and I must have grinned because she grinned back. "You men are so goddamn predictable."

I waited while she finished cooking and set the plate on the bar top and ordered me to start.

She diplomatically did nothing but make toast for a few minutes until I'd finished. "More coffee?"

I shook my head. "No, thank you. The charitable thing for me to do would be disappear and let you get an hour's sleep."

"You think that would be charitable?" She laughed.

I looked at her, surprised, I guess. She had been so buttons-and-bows domestic for the time it took to cook breakfast that I had thought we were going to settle for polite handshakes at the door. Instead she slipped out of the jacket and tossed it on the couch. "You've still got a couple of hours before you start working again, Mr. Detective."

I was standing up as she said it and her words stopped me like a punch in the head. "Who told you I was a detective?"

"Nobody had to. That story about being in the insurance business is hokey. We have a Prudential man in town and he's never heard of you. And all this work and worry over this geologist. I want you to know that the drinkers in the cocktail lounge have you pegged for a detective."

I straightened the rest of the way up and she turned away toward the staircase. "And what do you think I am?"

She laughed again. "If I told you out loud, my mother would wash my mouth out with soap. Come on, it's getting early."

She paused on the stairway and I came up below her and put my arms around her, my skin tingling at the feel of her warmth through the nylon. She shuddered and pressed herself close to me. "Come on," she said urgently, and led me up the stairs.

It was nine before I got to the police chief's office. The little clerk beamed nervously and ushered me in. "Chief Gallagher said he wanted to see you right away."

By now I was shaved and showered and wearing a clean shirt, but Gallagher looked at me and grinned. "Hard night?"

"A long drive," I said carefully.

He laughed again. "Don't break my heart. I called your room at seven, you weren't in yet."

"I'm here now." His locker-room jocularity was breaking one of the few rules of gentlemanly conduct my father ever drummed into me. You don't kick a man when he's down and you don't talk about women.

Gallagher hadn't gone to the same school. He held onto the topic for a sentence longer while he poured coffee. Only now his face was grim. "Don't get the idea she's some kind of roundheels. You're the first guy she's taken to since her husband drowned. That's a whole lot of grieving for a woman as ripe as her."

I said nothing and he passed me coffee and we sat each side of his desk. "So, I talk too much. It's difficult not to, living so far from people worth talking to. Sorry if I stepped on your toes."

"No offense taken," I told him. "You want to hear about Eleanor?"

"I think I got the most of it already from Pedersen at Thunder Bay," he said, sipping his coffee. "She was shot at close range with a small-bore weapon, likely a twenty-two pistol. The fact that it was through her eyes looks like a very specialized killing. I figured whoever hit her did it that way because of something she'd seen."

"That's the way I read it," I said. "I was looking forward to getting that picture and opening up this case again. I don't believe Prudhomme's dead, but I don't know if we've got enough evidence to go for a disinterment order."

Gallagher looked at me over the rim of his cup, both elbows perched on the same arms of his chair, head hunched down on his thick neck. And he grinned. "And what would you do with the remains when they dig him up?"

"Check the dental record. That's the safest bet. Even if he only had his top jaw left intact. He was a typical middle-class guy, he must have gone to one particular dentist. We could get the records and make sure it was his jaw, and that means his body."

Gallagher set down his cup and stood up, still grinning. "Good thinking," he said amiably. He went over and leaned on the top of his file cabinet. "Only I don't think we should go to all that trouble, moving all that dirt an' all."

"You're stringing me along," I said, trying to stay as happy as he was.

"Well no, but I can do you a favor," he said. "Turn your back a minute."

Something in his forcefulness triggered my alarm mechanisms. I don't turn my back on trouble of any kind, especially physical trouble. I looked at him unblinkingly, and he laughed. "No sweat. I just have to open the office safe. You can wait outside the office if you want."

I turned away and heard the click of the wheel on his little safe. Then he spoke. "Okay, take a look at this." I turned back. He was holding out another file folder to me. "I didn't submit this one with the rest of the material in that folder I made up for the files," he said, and passed it over.

I opened it and found two pieces of paper in it. The first one had a dozen or so lines of typing on it. "Look at the next one," he told me. I did, and whistled in surprise. It was a clean sheet of paper with a crescent-shaped series of indentations on it. "Right," he said happily. "That's what one jaw looks like biting down on a piece of paper held by a dumb, handicapped chief of police."

"You mean you took an impression of his jaw?" I looked up, astonished. "Why didn't you say so before?"

"For the same reason I told you last night," he said, and all his amusement had gone. He was stoney eyed. "Because nobody in this town wanted to know. But I took it and I kept it. And the first sheet lists all the peculiarities I could make out. Gaps, fillings, what looked like old chips out of the front teeth, everything."

"Then we've got it." I glanced down the written sheet. It may not have been what a dentist would write, but there was no doubt it was as complete as a layman could make it, complete enough to check with a professional record.

He nodded. "Yeah. I guess you could say we've got it. Only what do we do with it now?"

9

We talked it over for an hour while some out-
raged citizen with a parking ticket waited in the front office
for the chief to go out and explain why he couldn't park
against fire hydrants, even if he was a thirty-third degree Free-
mason passing through this one-horse town. It all came down
to one thing. We had to get the imprint checked against
Prudhomme's dental record.

"We can do it one of two ways," Gallagher said over his
fourth cup of coffee. "Either I can call the Montreal police
and ask them to do it, or you can head down there. One way
it takes three weeks, if we're lucky. The other way you have
the answer tomorrow."

"Then what?" I was prepared to go, for the sake of the
investigation, but I had a reason for staying in town now
that hadn't existed when I arrived in Olympia.

Gallagher put it all on the line. "Then I can put out a
warrant for Prudhomme, suspicion of murder. Because if that
wasn't him dead in his clothes, someone killed the guy who
was wearing them, and the logical suspect is Prudhomme.
And I can see that fat prick Sallinon and ask why he lied
about the thing Prudhomme bought off him. And I can show
the yo-yos on council that I'm a policeman, not a night
watchman."

"Why not head down there yourself?" It was the obvious question, but he had the obvious small town answer.

"Because everybody knows everything about everybody else in this town. If I go, the news will be all around by noon and anyone with anything to hide will have it well hidden by the time I come back with the evidence," he said wearily. "And if that doesn't warn you to get the hell out of the place you run before you're too old, I don't know what will."

And so I went. First I drove to the motel, where I found Alice painting, as usual, only this time she wouldn't show me what it was. I respected that and asked her a favor. "It's about Sam. I can't take him on the airplane with me without a lot of hoopla. And another thing, Carl Tettlinger and Pierre Gervais were released this morning. They're a bad pair and they might come looking for me and find you instead."

She laughed, although her eyes were serious. "And your dog will take care of me?"

"Against a troop of cossacks," I promised. "Let me show you what he can do." She left the phone untended and we went out into the lot. I did that on purpose, hoping that the help was watching from the dining room or the bar, taking notes on how good Sam is. It would be something to talk about that evening, something that would get back to the cowardly bastards who had tried to jump me in my room.

I put him through the simple stuff first, the "speak" and "keep" commands that did all my crowd-control work for me back in Murphy's Harbour. Then I got my leather sleeves out of the trunk, along with the dummy knife. Sam watched me out of his dark, intelligent eyes and I took a minute to stroke and fuss him. Then I straightened up and spoke crisply, going through the handing-over routine I had worked out for him, passing his control to Alice. "I want you to act as if I'm trying to attack you. When you think it's gone far enough, tell him to fight." I whispered the last word so Sam couldn't hear and miscue.

"You're the boss," she said nervously.

77

I shook my head. "Not any more. You are. Wait and see," I promised. I held the knife the way a kid from the South Bronx taught me on a slow weekend in the marines when we couldn't afford to go to town, and started walking toward her, doing my best to look mean. It doesn't take that much. I'm six-one, one-eighty, dark. The best day I ever saw I seemed like a menace to most people. As I drew nearer, Sam stiffened, but did nothing until Alice spoke.

He jumped for me, grabbing my right wrist, the hand that held the knife. I wrestled it into my other hand, struggling against the crunching pressure on my right wrist, kicking out at him. He didn't hesitate. He grabbed the other wrist. I relaxed, dropping the knife, but he hung on, tugging me off balance until Alice remembered what I had told her and called "Easy."

"Good. Now stroke him, pat his back. Tell him good boy," I said. As she did it I reached down for the knife and again she said "Fight" in her high, nervous voice. And again he had me.

"There. See what I mean?" I didn't break the protocol I'd established by reaching out to pat Sam. I let Alice do that. As far as he was concerned, she was his boss until I got back and we put the same procedure into reverse.

We went back into the office and Sam curled on the rug in front of the counter. I thanked Alice and said good-bye. She looked at me with an intensity I have only encountered once before, in Nam, from a bar girl, a fragile Chinese beauty of seventeen who was killed in a bomb blast in Saigon. I kissed her, quickly, as if we were in a crowded railroad station, and went out to my car.

They have a small airport at Olympia now, since the work started on the gold mine. I parked there and took a local hop to the Soo—Sault Ste. Marie—where I got a Nordair flight to Montreal.

It was after five when I finally reached Dorval Airport and I took the bus downtown along the elevated expressway that was built in time for Expo '67, when half the world came to Montreal. It takes you past the industrial section of the city and then along the backs of streets of those typically Quebecois apartments with outside stairways to the second floors. In the gathering dusk there were lights and warmth coming from the windows, and I could imagine the smells of good home cooking and the clatter of French as tired men opened beers while wives cooked in all those kitchens.

I took a room at the Queen Elizabeth. It's fancier than I needed, but Gallagher had given me a couple of hundred bucks expense money and I intended to head down to Chez Pauzé for a lobster once I'd seen Carol Prudhomme. I checked in and called her. She was in, just as tense-sounding as she had been when I called from Olympia.

"Hi, Carol, Reid Bennett. I'm in town, can I come over?" There was a five-second pause before she answered. I'm enough of a policeman that I measured the pause and decided she was not alone. It seemed as if she was all through mourning. I sensed a man in the house with her.

She said to come right over so I took a cab, directing the driver in French, which was my mother's native language. My French is good enough that the driver took me for a local and spent the trip beefing about the black Haitians who had cornered the cab-driving market. Racism isn't a peculiarity of WASPs, despite what you read in the newspapers.

Carol answered the door as soon as I knocked. She was wearing a black dress that looked too chic to be widow's weeds, and her makeup was perfect. I figured she was going out for dinner. I've never been close to her, despite her friendship with my ex, but close enough that we exchanged French-style kisses on the cheek. I got a whiff of her perfume and guessed my estimate was dead right. She was loaded for bear. "Come in, please," she said, smiling like a geisha girl, all formality, no warmth. I followed her into the living room, furnished in the kind of spare elegance you see in the magazines that dentists keep on their waiting room tables. The most conspicuous item in it was a man—tall, dark, with that elegant, hollow-cheeked look that French movie stars cultivate. He was holding what looked like a Dubonnet on the rocks. Lover-boy, I figured.

I don't expect people to leap to their feet when I come into a room, but most guys would make some kind of gesture of recognition. He didn't. He drew on his cigarette and looked bored.

Carol introduced him. His name was Henri Laval. He stood up to shake hands but kept his cigarette dead center in his mouth. He also tried to crush my hand, but I didn't do anything about it.

"*M'sieu*," he said. He looked like a suit advertisement.

"Reid Bennett. Glad to know you." I didn't think Carol knew I spoke French and kept the news to myself; it could prove useful.

It did, almost at once. "This is the policeman you told me about. His feet are big enough," he said to her in rapid French, smiling at me divinely at the same time.

I smiled back. "And you must be a lawyer, your head's plenty big enough," I said, in English.

He was cool enough to laugh, while Carol gasped in embarrassment. "I apologize," he said. "It is an old expression, and you are very much a policeman."

I beamed back. There's nothing like being one up to bring out your good nature. "I assume you're Carol's lawyer."

He blew smoke through his nostrils and stubbed his cigarette as if he had suddenly realized the cancer stories were for real. "And friend," he said ambiguously.

Carol fussed about getting me a drink and I took rye and water and we sat and looked at one another until Henri was finally curious enough to ask, "What brings you to Montreal? This sad business of poor Jim?"

"Yes." I sipped my drink and let him think about that for a minute. He said nothing so I pushed on. "I understand that you identified Jim when he was found."

He shrugged, an expression that painted a picture of his selfless devotion to helping the poor widow. What else could a friend have done?

I glanced at Carol. She was very carefully pushed into the back of her armchair, about as relaxed as a heart patient waiting to hear the prognosis. "I'm sorry, Carol, I have to ask some questions that may disturb you. Do you mind?"

She fluttered a look at Henri, then back at me, and shook her head silently. I nodded my acknowledgment and bored in with the first one. "How certain were you that the remains were his?" I asked Henri.

"Really," he said angrily. "This is very distressing for Carol."

"That's why I apologized in advance," I reminded him politely. "Sudden death is always distressing. I'm asking for a very good reason."

Now it was his turn to look at her. He was the perfect gentleman in that glance, anxious to spare her suffering, impatient with this big-footed policeman, certain of the truth. I waited, and at last he turned back to me.

"I was absolutely certain," he said.

"Did you check anything other than the clothes he wore?"

He frowned at that one. "I do not understand."

"Well, I wondered if Jim had any identifying marks, scars, tattoos, anything that made you certain."

Carol spoke now, her voice high and reedy like a soprano sax. "Jim didn't have any marks like that." She was very eager to give me the news.

I nodded thanks and smiled. "Of course, you would know, Carol, but I wondered whether there was anything else than his clothes used to identify him. Understand that I'm just being careful."

Henri took out cigarettes—Gauloises, of course—and lit one, making an angry little pantomime of it. "M'sieu," he said coldly, "if you had seen poor Jim's remains for yourself, you would have realized that the only way to identify him was by the clothes. He had been mauled by a bear." He broke off and spoke soothingly to Carol, "Forgive me, Carol, this is painful." Then to me again, "You have never seen anything so terrible."

I had, plenty of times, in Nam and since, but this wasn't the time for tall stories so I continued. "You will appreciate, as a legal authority, that anybody could have been wearing those clothes."

He was suddenly all lawyer. He stood up and walked up and down as if I was a jury he had to convince. "And this 'anybody,' he made Jim disappear and then dressed in Jim's clothes and was eaten by a bear?"

"I have a witness who can swear that Jim was seen alive after you had identified the body," I said.

Carol slopped white wine down her cocktail dress and gasped in horror. Henri turned to stare at me in fury. "Produce this witness," he said. He suddenly gave up on English and spoke rapidly in French. "My God. This poor woman is just being reconciled to the fact that her husband of ten years is dead and now this imbecile comes here with these stories."

I waited until he stopped, then went on, in English. "No, I don't believe it, either, but that's why I came to see you. I wondered how thorough your identification had been."

"Thorough enough," he said. He sat down and crossed his legs, like a girl who has lost an argument. "I do not wish to pursue this unpleasant conversation any further."

"Did you, for instance, take an imprint of his teeth and compare it with his dental records?"

He threw up his hands. "My God, what are you saying? Do you suspect me of complicity in some crime?"

"Just a question," I said amiably. "If the incident had happened in my own area I would have taken a dental imprint and compared it with Jim's records. It's routine practice. I wondered if you'd done it, that's all."

He sucked on his cigarette as if it were an air hose. "There wasn't enough left to get an impression," he said.

82

"The top jaw was intact. I saw the photograph." I was polite, reasonable, but he stayed mad.

"If you have ever seen a friend as badly hurt as poor Jim had been, you wouldn't put anybody through such suggestions," he said snottily. This time I handed it back to him.

"I appreciate how you feel. It happened to me many times in a war I fought in. Please excuse the unpleasantness. I am only doing it because there may be a chance that Jim is alive."

Carol got up and fled the room. We both stood up automatically and Henri followed her a few paces before turning back to me, shaking his head in disbelief at my behavior. For myself, I was beginning to wonder whether Carol was upset by the thought that Jim might sweep her into his arms again at some point or whether she was wishing he would stay dead.

Henri spoke first. He put out his cigarette and this time dropped a lot of playacting as well. "What do you intend to do?" he asked quietly.

"Well, I'd like to make a comparison between Jim's teeth, at least the teeth on the body, and Jim's records," I said, just as quietly.

He looked at me unblinkingly. "And to do that you would" —he searched for the word—"disinter the body?"

"If necessary. It's grisly, I know, but there is a witness who saw Jim days after that body was found."

He uncrossed his legs and sat looking down at his knees for a moment, straightening his creases with tiny little tugs. When he looked up there was a hint of his original arrogance in his eyes. "I'm afraid it's too late," he explained. "The remains have been cremated."

I sat and smiled back, saying nothing, wanting to find out what he would do next. He savored his triumph for about thirty seconds and then decided I wasn't impressed enough. "So you see, *M'sieu*, it is too late. Carol does not have to go through the distasteful experience."

I pulled out the envelope which I had folded, carefully, so that the imprint of the bite wasn't creased. "She won't have to anyway. I have an impression of that jaw, right here. All I want from you is the name of Jim's dentist."

I guess he'd seen all the right movies. He knew exactly how to take the statement. "What a relief for everybody concerned," he said. "No need for all that digging. If you will excuse me, I will ask Carol for the information."

He left and I put the envelope back in my pocket and sat and finished my rye and water. He was gone so long I was wondering if I'd be welcome to pour myself a second shot. Then they came back together.

Carol had been crying. I stood up and spoke first. "I'm sorry about all this, but once the dentist has checked the imprint we'll know for certain and you can put all this behind you for keeps."

She looked at me levelly. "It was already behind me," she said. "I had no idea that Amy would ask you to do all this crazy digging on my behalf. It's a mistake and tomorrow you'll know that and I will ask you to go home and forget all about this."

"That's my plan exactly," I lied.

"Please understand that I'm grateful for your efforts, but they are misplaced." She was in such tight control of herself that she was speaking English as if it were her second language. I nodded and waited and she gave me the name and address of the family dentist. It was a place in a shabby end of Montreal and she felt obliged to apologize for that. "Jim was always very loyal to old friends and people who had known him before he started to make good money."

"Yes, he was a very nice guy, and I'm sorry for your loss," I assured her.

She stayed on her feet, Henri at her elbow, so I took the hint. "And I've taken up too much of your time already. Thank you for the help. I'll call you when the dentist says what we all expect him to say." Tactful, Bennett, put yourself on the side of the angels whenever possible.

Henri showed me out, all amiability. "Do you know Montreal?"

"A little, enough to know where the best lobster in town can be had."

"Ah, and where is that? I must see how well you know our city," he laughed. If I'd been more couth we would have looked like a scene from Noel Coward.

"Well, I lean to Chez Pauzé," I admitted, and he sucked in his cheeks and nodded acknowledgment of my cleverness.

"An excellent choice," he said. "Enjoy your dinner." He stood at the door and watched until I reached the sidewalk.

I walked to the corner, flagged a cab, and went for the lobster, which was excellent, with a couple of Bras d'or ales. I was feeling on top of the world when I came out onto the sidewalk again and turned along Ste. Catherine Street toward the hotel. But I wasn't drunk. I was aware of my surroundings, as I always am, ever since I first walked point on patrol in the Marines. And so, within a few seconds I had seen the two black men in the doorway opposite and I wondered why they were watching me so carefully, not moving along or talking or smoking, like the few other pedestrians.

Montreal is a safe town, not as safe as Toronto—few places are—but nothing like New York. I stood for a moment on the curb, looking as if I was debating taking a taxi, then wandered away toward the hotel, stopping a time or two to look at traffic. It gave me a chance to see that they had split up. One of them had gone back to the corner behind me and was crossing the street, the other was walking rapidly toward the next corner.

They were very professional. The one in front crossed and was waiting as I reached the corner. He had a dollar bill in his left hand and he spoke to me politely in English. "Par'n me, sir, have you got change for a dollar?"

It's an old trick. The sucker puts his hand, his good hand, in his pocket, and the other guy clobbers him a good lick.

But I'd met men who had been rolled this way so I stepped back against the wall and told him, "Sorry, no. But I have a gun. Would you like to see that instead?"

He raised both hands and grinned. "That's cool, man, that's real cool with me."

And then his buddy bounded up beside me and tried to hit me in the head from the side—throwing all his strength into it.

I stepped forward at the last moment, slamming the first one in the gut so he doubled over as the other guy passed behind me. Then I whirled to face the second one as he recovered and came back, pulling a knife. I grabbed his knife hand and tugged, sticking my left leg in his way so he fell face first on the sidewalk. The first one was already up but slow on his feet, and I sunk my fist in his kidney and he went down again. Then I kicked the knifer on the inside of his knee as he tried to stand and he buckled into a heap on the sidewalk, moaning. I picked up the knife, a big switchblade, and dropped it into the grating at the curb. Then I pulled the owner to his feet and ran him into the wall, head first. He groaned some more, but I had his arm behind him and he couldn't escape.

"Who sent you after me?" I hissed. Behind me the first one scrambled to his feet and staggered away down the sidewalk, trying to run. I let him go. The one I was holding moaned and I cranked up the pressure on his wrist. "I can break your arm real easy," I promised. A middle-aged couple was coming along the sidewalk, looking into store windows. They saw us and the husband grabbed the wife and headed across the street at a dead run. The man I was holding moaned again. "I'm sorry. We pick d' wrong guy, tha's all. I'm sorry, man. I don' have no job. I gotta eat."

It could have been true, but I could still hear Henri's voice asking me where I was going to have dinner. I'd been set up and I wanted proof so I could put the oily bastard away.

"Who told you to mug me?" I pressed up on his wrist and he half screamed. "I dunno. I was play pool wid Georges. He get a phone call. We come here, we wait. He see you. He say, 'That's the guy.' I come for you. Okay?"

He was terrified. By the smell I judged his bladder had failed him. But I'd picked the wrong man. I did what had to be done, frisking him over for more weapons. He had another knife, hung down his back Scandinavian fashion, where he could reach over his shoulder and pull and throw in one gesture. I took it out and dropped it on the sidewalk, then marched him to the curb and waited for a scout car to come by. It took five minutes, and then another fifteen of explanation before they took us to the station and booked him for assault with a deadly weapon. The detectives questioned him casually, more interested in the damage to his face than in the evidence I was looking for.

In the end he was out on bail before I left the station. The detective apologized. "You know how it is. You're a flic," he apologized. "The goddamn law says he is innocent until you can prove him guilty."

"I only wanted the name of the guy who set me up," I explained. "I've seen this happen enough times, it doesn't get me hot anymore."

He shrugged. "In the old days, he would have told me. Now . . ." He shrugged again, the resigned gesture of a man doing a hopeless job. "Maybe, if you come to court six, eight times, maybe next year sometime he'll go to jail for a couple of months. You should have broken his neck."

"It was close," I said. "Thanks anyway. Can you drop me at the hotel?"

"If you prefer. I was going to dinner. Perhaps you would join me for a nightcap."

And so, in very civilized fashion, I had a brandy with him at the kind of tiny family restaurant the tourists never find. I heard about his own troubles, his lousy marriage and the son who played hooky from school and the daughter who smoked grass. And I sympathized and relaxed, and wondered how Henri had rounded up his help so quickly.

He dropped me at the hotel around two o'clock. I was up again at seven, running down Ste. Catherine against the incoming traffic, sweating out my anger and waiting for the dentist to get to his office.

At nine I got there. It was an east end location, over a drugstore. At least, it had been the night before. This morning there were firemen rolling up their hoses and complaining to one another that nobody around had brought them out any coffee. The drugstore and the offices above it were gone. The captain explained it for me. "Very strange, *M'sieu*. We have stores that need the insurance, they burn all the time. But this man has a good business. He does not need a fire. I find it very hard to explain, this one."

I didn't. But it put an end to any chance of matching Gallagher's imprint with records. The only thing remaining on the dentist's floor was his chair with the little sink attached, leaning crazily down through a hole into the drugstore ceiling. His files, of course, were gone.

10

I stood there, crunching broken glass under my feet and cursing quietly. I was back to square one. Except for the fact that all my misfortune had started from the moment I spoke to Henri, I had nothing. But I didn't have to be Sherlock Holmes to know he was in this up to his Gucci bootstraps.

I didn't want to let Carol know my suspicions in advance, so it took me an hour of going through the yellow pages to locate him. He was a full partner in a middle-sized firm of lawyers who had a general kind of practice. His secretary told me that he was away from the office, so I made an appointment in the name of Georges Claudet and said I would come around later and talk to someone about my problem, which was too personal to discuss on the phone. She probably thought I was another divorce statistic waiting to happen and didn't quibble. She would "fit me in" with a lawyer.

The first thing I did was to take a cab to Carol's house, dropping it at the corner and walking in quickly and quietly so she wouldn't see me from the window. That was just in case Henri had spent the night there, carried away on waves of hot Latin passion.

I was wrong. The only one home was a Haitian housekeeper who told me in French with a pinched African accent that madame was out and would not be back until late. She was small and nervous and looked at me as if she was certain I had come to rape and pillage, so I thanked her politely and left without pushing my way in to see if she was telling the truth about madame.

I was out of luck at Laval's office as well. He was out. His secretary turned out to be a fortyish spinster who obviously wanted to use her job as a dating service. All the signs were there. The clothes just a fraction too tight, the neckline just a fraction lower than necessary, and her makeup could have been applied by Mary Kay herself. I smiled at her like a grunt just out of all those womanless weeks at boot camp and moved in. "I assume you are his confidential secretary?"

"Of course," she said, matching my smile tooth for tooth. "I prepare all his correspondence, there are no secrets."

I looked impressed and stood thinking about it for a moment while she went on beaming. I don't like role-playing around women, but I needed information and she was the key. I checked my watch. It was eleven-forty. "I wanted to talk to M'sieu Laval—a friend recommended him to me— but I must leave the city this evening. Perhaps as it is so close to noon, you would do me the honor of having lunch with me and we could talk." I was shoveling on the charm the way French chefs shovel on the garlic, but she was buying.

"It is not regular," she said sternly, but immediately unbent when I looked anxious. "But as M'sieu Laval will be away for a few days, I could do that."

She took me to one of those ordinary-looking Montreal restaurants that serve magnificent food at prices that keep them filled up with locals. Everybody knew her and she chattered with the patron about the special of the day and we ordered it, sole Veronique and, at her recommendation, a carafe of the house white wine. It cost me a small fistful of Gallagher's dollars but it was worth it.

She ate with great enjoyment while I told her a little fairy story about coming home and finding my wife missing overnight. It took about five minutes, and then I sighed and acted philosophical and started pumping her gently about Henri, who had gone, she told me, to an important client in New York.

She was ready to talk. I ordered another half liter of wine and we sat there until two o'clock while she explained what a wheel her boss was and how important his clients were. A couple of them were local biggies, but she went on to say that he was also a very important criminal lawyer who had defended men on heavy charges, one of them accused—wrongly of course—of murder. And then she played her ace. He also had a number of clients who were involved in the gold business. She used the word "gold" with the kind of respect King Midas would have appreciated.

"Gold?" I looked properly awed and she elaborated.

"One of them was the man who discovered the deposit at Chaudiere. He found gold where hundreds of others had missed it, not a hundred meters from the highway at Chaudiere. And then, only last month, he was working in the bush alone and he was killed by a bear."

I took her through that one fairly quickly and got her onto the subject of his other clients in gold. She was unfolding like a rose by now, under the warming influence of the wine and my attention. I was beginning to despise myself for taking advantage. She was still attractive—not beautiful, but handsome and charged with that implicit sexuality that Frenchwomen all seem to radiate so effortlessly. She was smiling more easily, putting on less of a show, relaxing and getting ready to handle the proposition she expected me to put to her once the bill was paid and we left.

But I kept on working and she told me that Henri had many important clients, businessmen from New York and Buffalo as well as from Montreal. That made me think. Calling them "businessmen" rather than executives was pretty open-ended. And both New York and Buffalo are notorious Mafia towns, as is Montreal itself. Maybe Henri was connected. I was chewing this over when she told me the most interesting piece of news yet. It seemed that her boss handled the business affairs of the vice-president of the company that was opening the mine at Chaudiere. He was a geologist.

She was telling me this when the patron came alongside with the suggestions for coffee and dessert. We ordered coffee only and suddenly the spell was broken. It was as if the thought of coffee, the lubricating fluid of the business day, made her realize she was still employed by a law firm, and she became all business again.

I've seen the same thing happen in a lot of interrogations. When there are two of you working it's easy to break through. One of you changes the subject for a while and the other comes back to it later. But I was alone with her and there was no way back. So I did the sensible thing, probing her on other subjects. She kept up her momentum, but everything now was unclassified. She had been at the law firm for longer than she cared to remember, since before M. Laval joined them. He was a good boss, a thoughtful man. Why, only last month he had given her a beautiful present, something a client had given him.

I said something obvious about how gracious that had been, and asked what the present was.

She spread her arms wide. "The skin of a bear, bigger than this. I have it on the floor of my living room."

"In front of the fireplace," I suggested, and got a slap on the wrist. I grinned and shrugged. "Well, I was imagining the bear smiling at you with his big teeth."

"Oh no." She shook her head and laughed. "No, I could not look at such a thing. Fortunately this bear has no head, no claws. He is a soft bear."

This fit exactly with my notion of somebody taking the bear's head and claws and using them to gussy up a murder, but I said nothing and tried not to look excited and we laughed and the patron offered more coffee and I glanced at my watch and exclaimed at how late it was.

I paid and led her back to the office and took her hand at the door and thanked her for her patience in listening to a familiar story.

"Sad stories are never familiar," she said, with charm. "I am sorry for what has happened, but I thank you for a superb lunch. When will you be back?"

"In one week. I have to go to Vancouver. Will *M'sieu* Laval be here by then?"

She gave a little "don't know" pout. "I am not sure, but perhaps you will come into the office and check."

"I would never again miss the opportunity," I assured her, and squeezed her hand and gave a small bow and left, feeling like a louse, but an informed louse. I headed for the nearest pay phone and called Olympia.

Chief Gallagher was at his desk, eating a hamburger, he informed me cheerfully, and wondering what was happening down among the bright lights. I filled him in and he wondered out loud what Laval was doing in New York so soon after I figured he had set me up and had the dentist's office burned down. He had the same policeman's suspicions as me. When I mentioned that his clients were "businessmen" in Buffalo and New York, he made the same jump any Ontario copper would make. "I wonder if he's running with the Mob?"

"I wondered the same thing," I agreed. "If he was, he'd certainly know how to find people to give me the kind of trouble I've had this past twelve hours."

"Right now I'm going to check with Prudhomme's boss," I told him. "After that, I'll take the evening plane to the Soo and back to Olympia."

"Okay. I'll meet the plane," he said, and hung up.

Twenty minutes later I was in M. Roger's office. He was a big, soft man, heavier than he would have been if he had been out in the field as much as his underlings. He was chain-smoking American cigarettes and fiddling with files and worrying and answering telephones as if there were nobody else in the company.

I didn't take much of his time. I flashed my police chief identification from Murphy's Harbour and told him I would appreciate learning what Prudhomme had been doing when the disappeared.

"Why would a policeman from another jurisdiction want to know about Jim?" he wondered, leaning back in his chair and lighting up a fresh Camel.

"My ex-wife is a friend of the widow," I explained. "I had some vacation time left and she asked me to take a nose around and make sure that the local police had been thorough." I shrugged. "I'm convinced that they were. I've met the chief and he seems a good man, but you know what it is when women get into the act."

We exchanged knowing, male-chauvinist smiles over that one and then he took the precaution of having all his calls held for ten minutes and gave me the facts. Prudhomme's work had been just about finished up there. He'd been a first-class field man, looking for new deposits. He had been one of several company geologists who had made the Chaudiere discovery. It was big, maybe the biggest ever outside South Africa. He even drew me a rough sketch of the probable outline of the find, a big circle with Olympia close to the southern rim. It might possibly have been caused by volcanic action millions of years ago. Prudhomme had analyzed the signs more cleverly than all the other clever men who had been looking in that region for close to a century. "Jim only drilled three test holes," Roger said proudly. "Two of them didn't turn out as he hoped, but the third one hit a real find. It assays at a quarter-ounce a ton, and there's eighty million tons at least—maybe more. In fact, I think there will be once we get down to it. We didn't get all of it, of course; there's two other companies involved right now, but we sure staked a big one. It could be worth six, seven billion, maybe."

"Could you tell me one thing? Is all the land up there claimed by now, all the good gold prospects?"

94

He coughed on his cigarette smoke. "It was claimed within a month of our initial discovery. Every sonofabitch and his brother was up there staking claims. It's tied up so tight it'll take years to work out who owns what."

"And is there likely to be another reef, if that's the word, as rich as the one you're working?"

He shrugged. "Could be, the whole area has much the same geology. There could be ten more finds this size up there, any one of them worth a couple of billion bucks."

"And Jim, as an employee of Darvon—could he have claimed land in his own right?"

Another cough. "No. Absolutely not. He was locked into us by his contract. Anything he did, geologically speaking, was our property." His phone rang, then stopped, then buzzed. He picked it up and said "Yes?" snappishly, then, "Oh, okay, if I have to," and pressed the button and began to speak.

I got up, making a small motion of thanks. He replied in kind but kept on talking and I left the office, certain that I had the news that was pulling this whole case together.

I had a quiet flight to the Soo, getting there in time to transfer directly to the flight to Olympia. Gallagher was waiting for me in the scout car and I filled him in as we drove. He wound down the window and spat into the darkness. "You making the same of this that I am?" he wondered aloud.

"Like Prudhomme staked a bunch of claims of his own in a company name maybe, then rigged his own death so his widow could get the insurance. She goes her way, he goes his, coming back sometime in the future, carrying the ID of the man he killed, sells out his claims to Darvon or some other mining company, and lives happily ever after," I said. I'd spent the whole of the flight putting the pieces together.

"That's how it looks," Gallagher nodded. "From what you say, this lawyer is thick with Prudhomme's widow, or wife, whatever. She's taken care of, marries her fancy man, and everything's peachy."

"Except for the poor schnook you found on that island," I

said, "it all fits like a glove. The only thing is, we can't prove that Prudhomme wasn't the corpse. If we can do that, we can open the case and bring in some national help looking for him."

Gallagher cleared his throat in an angry growl. "Or maybe if we can find out who the guy was who was killed up there. That would help."

I had a thought, one of those odd threads of intuition that bail you out sometimes in cases like this one. "I wonder if Prudhomme ever had his teeth fixed anywhere else? Like, for instance, is there a dentist in town?"

"I already checked that one out," Gallagher said, turning off the highway down the now-familiar road to the motel. "We do have a Painless Pete of our own, but Prudhomme never went to him."

"Pity," I said, and we both snorted.

He swung into the driveway of the motel and stopped. The lot was full of cars. "Looks like you may not have a room here tonight," he said. Then he chuckled. "If you need one."

I got out of the car and reached in for my bag, saying nothing. He was starting to bug me, breaking the rules again by sniggering about Alice. "Thanks for the ride," I said, and suddenly he reached out and held my sleeve anxiously.

"Listen. No offense. Like I said, she's been on her own for a year and you're an unusual kind of guy. The only thing is, I don't want anybody, including you, screwing her around."

There was real passion in his voice and I suddenly understood. I was careful when I spoke. "That's not my way."

He let go of my sleeve and sat back in his seat. "No, I guess it isn't," he said quietly. "I just don't want to see that woman hurt. They don't come like her very often." I shut the car door gently and he waved and left. I watched him go, then turned to walk into the motel. Alice was at the desk, registering a guest who turned and looked at me and then away without interest.

I could tell by his clothes that he was American. There's

something about the casual assurance in the way an American dresses that you never find in Toronto or even Montreal. Good clothes, a little softer and looser than a Canadian would wear. I wondered idly what he was doing up here. A salesman, I guessed, tougher looking than most of them and with noticeably bad skin, but they don't deduct marks for acne when you're selling drill bits.

Alice was behind the counter and I winked at her without speaking. I didn't want my greeting tangled up with the other guy's business. Sam was beside her, on his feet with his tail wagging, staying close to Alice but anxious to remind me that he had recognized me.

I waited until she had given the other man his key and directions down the hall, then I reached over the counter and pulled her close. Her kiss was soft and we lingered over it, craning awkwardly over the counter until Sam gave a tiny, miffed bark.

Alice pulled back and laughed. "Looks like we both missed you," she said.

"That's doubly nice. Just tell him, 'Good boy, go to Reid,' " I instructed, and she did and Sam jumped on the counter and down my side and wagged his fool tail off. I crouched to fuss him, rubbing his big head and telling him he was good and letting him know that the feeling was entirely mutual. Most of the time he's the only living creature around to let me know he cares if I'm alive or dead and I wanted him to know I appreciated it. Then I told him "Easy" and straightened up.

"If you're looking for your old room, you're out of luck," Alice said. "Mr. Wallace from Buffalo, New York, has just taken it, you saw him."

"So I sleep in the car," I said, and she laughed.

"Not if you play your cards right," she promised. "It's good to have you back."

"I hated to leave in the first place. Did anybody miss me, besides you two sentimental slobs?"

97

She shook her head, but she had stopped laughing. "Nobody. But I was glad of the company last night. There was someone outside the house around two A.M." She pointed at Sam. "I'd told him 'Keep,' like you showed me, and he barked for about ten minutes, then stopped." Her face was serious. "I've never had prowlers before, even now when the town is full of guys from out of town, looking for work."

"That could have been those two rounders who tackled me. I'm glad you had Sam with you," I said, and when he heard his name, Sam gave a happy little bark. "Listen, if you're on duty, hand off the ball somewhere while I give Sam a walk, then we'll head on home."

God! it felt good to use that word. I still didn't think of my place at Murphy's Harbour that way. I'm square enough that I need a woman around to make it complete. Over the eighteen months I'd been there I'd had a couple of volunteers, but nobody I wanted to assign the duty on a regular roster.

"We're slack at the bar tonight, I'll close up and leave a card for people to speak to the barman over there if they have problems," she said. "You do the thing with Sam while I lock up."

That's what we did. I put my bag back in my car and then took off my town jacket and ran halfway to the highway and back, with Sam springing beside me like a kid let out of school. A couple of cars came by, slowing to see what was going on, but Sam ignored them, happy to be back with me again.

I was sweating by the time we got back and found Alice waiting in the doorway of the office. "I've got a lake trout thawed out at the house," she said. "Put Rin-Tin-Tin in the car and let's go."

I hugged her, feeling more like a kid than I had since I left Sudbury to enlist in the Marines. In the back of my mind was the sick certainty that this couldn't last. But I've grown with that feeling since Nam. This was like a quiet time on patrol, no snipers, no booby traps, nobody trying to infiltrate. I was happy to enjoy it and let the next day take care of itself.

I drove to her house and she invited both of us in. "The hell with sleeping in the car, he's family," Alice said.

The house was cool, but I lit the stove and then showered while she put the fish in the oven and opened one of the bottles of Pouilly Fuisse I'd picked up in Montreal. And then, as we sat down to eat, she gave me the news.

"I heard something funny today," she said, "Wanna hear it?"

"I'd rather hear there were seconds on the trout, but fire away."

She helped me to another slice. "Well, that Indian friend of yours, Jack Misquadis. One of his nephews was in the bar, early on. He'd had a few beers and it got to the point where I didn't want to see him snockered, so I asked him to leave."

"And Sam gave you the required minimum use of force," I said.

"No," she frowned. "He went okay, that wasn't it. But instead of trying to break the place up he said something that stuck in my head."

"What was that?" I didn't really care about barroom chat, but her animation made her even better to look at so I listened.

"Well. He went, but he said, 'My uncle Jack could buy this place up, no trouble.' I didn't know any of the people in the band were rich, did you?"

"He sure doesn't live rich." I remembered his shack, crude and comfortable but worth maybe five hundred bucks total. He had that and his traps and his old twenty-dollar World War II rifle and his canoe, that was it.

"Well, I didn't argue. You don't when somebody says something like that. It's kind of like, my dad can whip your dad," she explained. "But then he said something else."

I stopped eating and looked at her. Her oval face was lit

from above by the Tiffany lamp and she looked beautiful. I didn't much care what any drunk had said, I just wanted to watch her repeating it. "What was that?" I prompted.

"Well, he said, 'Jack's the real owner of all them claims.'" She frowned slightly. "Does that make any sense to you?"

I put down my knife and fork and looked at her seriously. "It makes more sense than anything else I've heard since I came up here."

11

We had no prowlers. If it had been Tettlinger who'd been hanging around the previous night he must have recognized my car and stayed away. But I wasn't sure he would keep on staying away. Guys like him don't let go of a grudge. And now he had even more reason to dislike me—the threat of a jail term. He might decide that the best way to stay free would be to stand off and blast me from a distance with a deer rifle. Before the sound died away he could be gone, melted into the bush that reached back behind Alice's house until he found a nameless lake to throw the gun into. I'm not paranoid, but there was something particularly ugly about that guy that worried me.

That's why I insisted Alice keep Sam with her while I went down to the police station and talked to Gallagher.

He was in his office, preparing his duty roster for the coming month. He waved me to a seat. "Try some of the lousy coffee. This won't take but a minute," he invited. So I did, and found he was right. Bad coffee seemed to be an art form with his secretary. But she, or somebody, had brought in a box of donuts and one of them took the taste away and within a couple of minutes Gallagher was ready.

I told him what Alice had repeated. He listened, looking at me narrow eyed as if he'd found me shoplifting the donut.

"I never knew an Indian yet ever staked land," he said. "Did you?"

I shrugged. "There's nothing minable in Murphy's Harbour, but no, I'd have to agree with you."

"Which means what?" he wondered out loud. We stared down one another's eyes blankly for a minute and then I put forward my idea.

"I wonder if maybe he's acting for somebody else. Somebody who doesn't want the world to know he's staking claims."

"Could be," Gallagher growled. "But if his nephew says that he owns the claims, they must be in his name. That means they're his property, that's no good to anybody else."

"But what if he's acting for a company? The ABC Mining Corporation. He's a vice-president, they tell him. He gets to register the claims but they belong to the company. He's just one of the crowd, a guy doing the clerical work. That way, when Darvon or somebody wants to use the claims, all the management gets a share, including him."

"And including the rounder who set him up," Gallagher completed for me. "Yeah, that would work. Let's go see him."

We took the scout car and drove to Misquadis's shack, but he was gone. The shack was unlocked—it didn't even have a lock, for that matter. A lot of cabins don't, up that far north. A place is there to be used if somebody doesn't have a roof and the weather turns vicious. People go in, stay warm, use what they have to, and then leave the place as they found it, paying for the stay by topping up the wood pile before they go.

His old car and canoe were missing, so we guessed what was happening, but Gallagher opened the door anyway and we went in. His rifle was gone, so were the blankets from the bed. "Gone hunting," Gallagher said. "The fool council put a bounty on that bear that's supposed to have killed Prud-homme. I'll bet a million bucks to a cup of Gladys's lousy coffee he's up there on that island shooting one."

We went out and stood in the pale fall sunshine and

thought about our next move. "I guess the best thing would be to check the claim files and look for any unknown names," I suggested.

Gallagher snorted. "Have you got any idea how many crackpots got into the act? Hell, when they found that ore deposit, you couldn't find anybody in town for a month. Everybody was out registering claims. Old Yoong at the laundry was out there, even. Must be seventy, but he trekked out and looked for gold. No, I'd rather go find Misquadis and talk to him. He's a straight guy, if there's anything he can do to help, he'll do it when I explain."

I objected. "He likely left yesterday. I'm not sure where this place is that he's going to. But it's a couple of days' paddling and portaging and then we could draw a blank. Can you afford a helicopter to head in and check the location where the body was found?"

"Me?" Gallagher laughed a big, square-mouthed, mirthless laugh. "Helicopter nothing. It's all I can do to squeeze enough out of the council to run the scout cars."

"In that case, let's go at it a different way. If this is what we think, and Prudhomme set it up, he'd have made sure the claims were all in the richest area he could find. How can we find out where that is?"

Gallagher straightened up and tapped his hat more firmly on to his head. "Let's go ask the expert," he said. "Get in the car." He took the wheel and poured on the gas, up the highway to the site of the new mines.

There were three of them, all within a mile of one another, the shiny new headframes visible above the trees at roadside. We passed the first two and drove to the third one, the Darvon mine. Gallagher nodded at the headframe as we turned into their roadway. "Look at that. A fortune in gold lying not a hundred yards off the Trans-Canada Highway. And the poor slobs down in Olympia have lived and died on what they make at the pulp mill for damn near a century. No justice, is there?"

He stopped at the barrier and a prettyish girl in a hard hat let us in, directing us to the office up the road. It lay on the other side of the construction site where earthmovers as big as a house were removing broken rock. Gallagher switched off the radio. "They ask you to do that. Damned if I see how it could set off their dynamite, but mining is dangerous enough without extra risk."

The flagman on the road let us through between loads, and we drove to the work office. It was a cluster of sixty-foot-long house trailers set up on waist-high stands and interconnected by a central passageway. There were pickup trucks with the insignias of a dozen construction and building trades companies parked alongside. Opposite stood a similar complex, without any parked vehicles.

"Those are the miners' quarters," Gallagher explained as we got out. "Not like the shacks the old miners used to live in. They've got showers, TV, everything except women."

Inside the office was the kind of clattering busyness that can't be faked. Draftsmen were working, women were typing, men in big construction boots and hard hats were clumping in and out with plans in their hands. Gallagher nodded to a few of them and they nodded and grinned and called him "Chief."

"That's what gets to you about being the kingpin in a place like Olympia," he confided over his shoulder. "The town's going to double in size. All of these people will be in my patch before they're finished. And I'm tryin' to get to know them all before they settle." He expanded on it as we walked on. "A year ago I could police this town like being dad in a family. When the bonspiel is on at the Legion, I'd park up there, and when a drunk came out I'd take his keys and tell him, 'Take a cab, Eddie, pick up the car tomorrow.' They liked that and they respected the law. Now I'm going to have to treat 'em all like strangers. It's the only way to be fair and it's the end of the hominess of this town." He sucked his teeth and sighed, not looking at me.

There was a small private office at the end of one of the trailers. Outside it sat the prettiest girl in the whole place, tapping something out on a word processor. She looked up and beamed when Gallagher approached. "What's up, Chief, Mac forget to pay his parking tickets?"

Gallagher warmed to her smile and I realized how much he thought of women and wondered why he was up here alone. Maybe he had a story like mine to tell. In any case, his looking like a bear didn't seem to be stopping him from winning real affection from women. "No. He's been a good boy. I just wanted him to meet a friend of mine. Is he busy?"

"Always," she said, with another grin. "I'll tell him you're here." She got up and tripped into the inner office, moving nicely. She kept the door tactfully half shut around her as she talked to the man inside, then turned and pushed it wide open. "Come on in, please."

"Thanks, Sue." Gallagher smiled his big honey-bear smile and we went on by. The man inside was as big as he was, wearing green work pants with a good shirt and tie. He stood up and stuck out his hand. "Hey, Chief, nice to see you. Who's this?"

Gallagher introduced me and we shook hands. I learned that his name was Walter McKenzie and he was the construction manager for the mine. He had a good handshake, powerful but not crushing.

"Siddown." He waved us to a couple of old wooden chairs. We sat and he asked, "What brings you out here? You majoring in crises?" We all laughed and his phone rang, then stopped.

Gallagher said, "Reid here has been asking around about the last days of that guy, what's his name?" He turned to me and I supplied Prudhomme for him. "Yeah, you remember, the guy who was killed by the bear."

McKenzie looked at me with new interest. "Checking up on the chief?"

I shook my head. "No, just an insurance hassle. But I'm trying to look into all the things I can while I'm here, and part of it is trying to get an idea of where he was working, generally, before he died."

McKenzie waved over his shoulder toward the window. "The whole shooting match," he said cheerfully. I noticed the faint buzz of the Highlands in his speech. He was another expatriate Scot, I think maybe they're the most widely scattered race in the world.

We all grinned at his joke and I acted humble and added some detail. "No, in particular I wondered if he had been following up something logical, something connected with the ore body. The chief said he didn't think so, that he was outside the area, but we thought you could spare me a minute to tell me where that runs."

McKenzie looked at me under eyebrows that seemed to bristle more every minute. "Y're in a curious kind of insurance work, Mr. Bennett," he said.

Gallagher took his cue. "Don't worry, Mac. I checked him out good, he's legit."

McKenzie took out an old pipe from his desk, looked at it grimly, and put it away. "Giving it up again," he said, then looked at us. "If you're happy, Chief. Sure. I can tell you." He stood up and walked to the wall where there was an oil company map of the area pinned to a board. "The survey maps aren't small enough scale to show the extent of the whole area that interests us," he said. "This is the biggest deposit I've seen in all my years in mining." He indicated a semicircle with a radius of about thirty miles. "This whole area is worth looking at closely. You won't necessarily find another deposit like this one, but you might."

"So Prudhomme was just looking around in a general sort of way," I suggested.

McKenzie's phone rang, then stopped. He tapped the map with his finger. "No. He was found here, on an island in this lake. The thing is, he'd already looked there, it was in his preliminary report. Hell, we'd already drilled a test hole there and come up empty. He had no reason to be there."

"And what about the other deposits you think are around? Are they all the same quality, or what?" I asked.

He gave me another frown. "Now this isn't my area, you understand, but so far we've only identified one deposit for sure, right here on the highway, where all three companies are opening their mines. Like I say, the geology is promising for the whole region, but so far this is the only strike we've made for certain. And that's fine by me, it means we can build right on the highway. It's so damn convenient, you can't believe it. It saves millions in construction costs alone, not having to build a road in."

I had to ask him: "Excuse my ignorance, but what kind of a find are we talking about? For a layman, you understand."

McKenzie didn't even look around. He had the figures on the top of his mind and he rolled them off at me. "We're estimating nineteen million ounces of gold. And just so you'll get the idea, that's six times the amount that came out of the whole Yukon strike in the last century." Now he turned and grinned. "In case you're counting on your fingers, that comes to something close to six billion dollars' worth if gold stays at three hundred dollars an ounce." I whistled with respect. Six billion is enough to cause all kinds of disappearances.

Gallagher took over, asking the next question so naturally that McKenzie would never have known it was loaded. "And I suppose you cagey bastards have sewn up all the hot spots where there might be gold," he said.

McKenzie laughed and took his finger off the map. "I wish," he said fervently. "By the time we'd made our first claims there was a rush on. For all I know there's three more deposits as rich as this one. There's a fortune waiting for the people who find them and put up the capital."

Gallagher moved back toward his chair and I followed suit. "And I guess that'll be Darvon once you've made your money back from all this." He thumbed casually toward the outside.

"We won't wait that long," McKenzie told him. "We'll be moving out there as soon as this one is in production. We've got the lawyers out already trying to buy up promising claims. Plus we're still prospecting everywhere. For all I know somebody's already found what we want. And if he has, why, you could say he's sitting on a goddamn gold mine."

The phone rang and McKenzie looked at it anxiously. "I'm always expecting trouble," he explained. "Anything from complaints about the food to breakage on the drill they're using to sink the shaft. Whatever happens, I'm in the hot seat."

Gallagher stood up. "We'll leave you to it. Thanks for the time, and if you want a game o' chess some night, call me."

"I'd like to have the time," McKenzie said. He reached out to shake hands. "If there's anything else I can tell you."

I shook his hand and said, "No, I don't think so, you've been very kind." And then I dropped my next question, as casually as I could. "Oh, there is one thing. How did Prudhomme get in and out? Did he go by chopper?"

"Nothing but the best for Darvon guys," McKenzie said. "Yes, he flew in everywhere. Always used the same outfit, the guy who reported him missing."

Gallagher said, "Sure. I didn't give Reid all the details yet, I'll fill him in."

We left, Gallagher stopping to say good-bye to Sue warmly, like a departing uncle, and then we walked back through the corridor and out to the car.

"I thought it was in the report, about the chopper," he said as he unlocked the cruiser.

"It was, but I wondered if he ever got in and out on his own," I said. "Now we know he didn't. So maybe I'll go and talk to the chopper pilot while you put somebody on the claim search, try and find out if Misquadis is a registered owner."

Gallagher started the car. "And which of my minions would

108

you suggest I use?" he asked. "I don't want the whole damn world to know what we're up to here."

"In that case the choice is limited," I said. "And I'm going to talk to the chopper pilot."

He checked over his shoulder and drove off, slow and careful, past a gaggle of miners who were getting out of a yellow bus, looking round-shouldered tired, the way a man looks after eight hours on the muckstick, raking broken rock. "I guess that's the way it is," he said. "You high-powered investigators have all the fun while we coppers do the work."

"That's life in the fast lane," I told him. "Can you take me to the chopper pad? Unless you'd rather take me back to get my own car."

"No sweat." He tapped his hat more firmly on his head. "No sweat, but say, if he starts offering free rides, ask him to show you where the body was found. Then, if Misquadis is doing business with the bears up there, drop in and ask him about the claims."

"Will do," I said. "Let's find the pad. Who knows, it could lead us to another six billion bucks."

12

I had thought the mining companies would have choppers of their own, but that wouldn't have given them the same tax breaks. Instead of owning birds, Gallagher explained, they were just plain folks, hiring as they needed them. Which meant that they did business with Olympia Lift Corporation, a helicopter company up at the big motel a further five miles east.

When we arrived there was only one chopper at home, on a flat gravelled area in front of the main motel building. Beside the landing pad there was an office, an army-type Quonset hut with the name of the company painted badly on a sheet of plywood.

"This is it," Gallagher told me. "I have to get back. If you find anybody to talk to, wave from the window and I'll take off. When you're through, give me a call and I'll come back. You can get a beer at the motel while you wait."

I nodded and got out, taking a quick check of the chopper as I walked to the hut. It looked like the standard Hughes 500, the civilian version of the Hughes OH-6 Cayuse that I'd seen in Nam. They were small and quick and had been used only for scout work. I'd never flown in one.

I went into the building and was time-whacked right back

into the service. Most of my flying had been done in the field, scrambling in and out of choppers in LZs in the boonies. But once, on my way out of Saigon, I had been in a flight office, carrying a message from the captain to the flight crew. This place was the same. There was the same smell of jet fuel, the same temporary, kicked-around look to the interior. The only difference was a counter at the front, about eight feet from the door. I walked up to it and called, "Anybody home?"

Somebody in a room at the back called "Yo" in a way that told me he'd learned his social skills in the same finishing school I had, or else he'd seen the same movies.

I waited and a man walked out. He was my age, fair, rangy, negligent-looking in his manner, but with the underlying toughness that comes from military training, from being sure of what you can do. He was wearing brown pants and a leather windbreaker with the company crest over his left nipple, where his wings would have been if he had still been in the service. He looked tanned and relaxed. "Yessir," he said in a voice that was friendly but not overenthusiastic. A vet, for sure.

I matched his grin. "Hi, you're the pilot."

"The very best," he said. "Looking for transportation?"

"Not right this minute." I held out my hand. "My name's Reid Bennett. I'm in insurance, looking into the death of Jim Prudhomme."

He shook hands. "Paul Kinsella. I'm the guy who was there when they found him. And I also flew him around in the fall of last year when they made the discovery. What can I do for you?"

I held up one hand for a moment and went to the door and waved Gallagher away. He nodded and drove off and I came back in. "Well, I'm not sure. I wondered if you could remember where all he went, what he did—just background stuff for my report."

He looked at me levelly. "You talk like a cop, not an insurance adjuster. This guy do something bad?"

"No, I just got roped in because of the crazy way he died. We never paid off on a bear mauling before and head office wanted to double-check everything."

He still wasn't buying, so I fed him another crumb. "And you're partly right. I used to be a cop, but the hours were lousy and I was never home, so I switched to this job. Smart, eh?"

Kinsella laughed at that and flipped up the flap on the counter. "I've got some coffee out back, wanna cup?"

"That would be great, thank you." I followed him into the little room. It was like a lot of other male domains. There were magazines everywhere, most of them a year or so old, a coffee maker with half a dozen dirty cups around it, ashtrays filled with butts, a deck of cards and a cribbage board.

He found a clean cup and poured me some of his coffee and then topped up a mug that stood by the most comfortable chair in the place. "What would you like to know?"

Like most of the other moves in an investigation, there was no quick answer to that one. I had to dig first and then look at what I'd turned up. "I'm not sure," I confessed. "Did you know him well, can you remember anything about him?"

He took the good chair and cocked one foot on the edge of the table. "Not a hell of a lot," he said, and sipped his coffee. "He was a geologist, sounded French. I'd say he was kind of an anxious guy, always double-checking everything. If we were leaving at seven, he'd be here at six. Always questioned everything you did. Stayed in Olympia, although he could have stayed here a lot more conveniently."

That all sounded like Jim Prudhomme. I nodded and sipped. The coffee was excellent. "Did you drop him on his work locations a lot?"

"Maybe half the time he flew with us. Frank, the other pilot, he used to take him when he was here. He's got the Bell, it's bigger. My usual machine is the one outside."

"The Hughes 500."

He looked up at me sharply. "You know the difference?"

"I was in the Marines. I've seen the Hughes used, but I've never been in one."

He took his foot down from the table and sat forward. "You were there?" He didn't have to say where.

"Two fun-filled years," I said, and he whistled. "Gung-ho sonofabitch, weren't you? Two full years there. Combat?"

"Most of the time. I was in Saigon for a month once and in the hospital for another couple. Aside from that, it was the boonies all the way."

He reached forward and shook my hand again. "Nice to know you," he said sincerely. "The only guys I've met who know anything about the war were in college in the World, organizing sit-ins to protest it."

"I wasn't. Which outfit were you with?"

He told me and we played old soldiers for a few more minutes, then got back to Prudhomme. Now, for a fellow sufferer, he took the trouble to remember properly. Most of Prudhomme's work had been carried out west of the main find. But they had drilled a test hole on the island where his body had been found. Kinsella had been involved with transportation, lifting supplies in, lifting core samples out as the drilling progressed.

"Any chance you'd be heading out that way again, soon?" I asked innocently.

He straightened up and grinned an old sweat's grin. "You wouldn't be joshing now, would you? Like you wouldn't just be trying to hitch a free ride in my mo-sheen?"

I laughed at his hillbilly imitation. "Not really. But I'd like to look, if it didn't cost me an arm and a leg. Head office is death on expenses."

He looked at me and shook his head grudgingly. "You know what it's like with aircraft of any kind. Once it's airborne, the meter's running. I have to add the time to the log and somebody has to pay for it."

"How much would it cost to take me out to where Prud-homme's body was found? Like I say, I don't have deep pockets, but if it's just a half hour I could swing it."

He didn't answer at once. Instead he picked up his coffee cup and drained it. "Well, I have to admit I was having a little trouble with the radio earlier. I've switched the board in the set and it works okay on the ground. But maybe, for an ex-grunt, I could carry out an air test."

He went over to a tall cupboard at the back of the room and took out a bundle tucked into a big canvas bag. "Sleeping bags," he explained. "We've still got Indian summer, but the forecast is for colder and I wouldn't want you to freeze your ass off if we're forced down."

I picked up the bag and nodded and waited while he phoned somewhere to report he was going up to air-test the radio. Whoever was at the other end squawked a little but Kinsella stayed cheerful and a minute later was locking the front door of the office and we were walking out toward the chopper.

The Hughes is mostly glass in the body. It's a bit like a kid's soap bubble with the bubble pipe still attached. Kinsella opened the door carefully and we got in. He shut it again, just as carefully, something that marked him for a pro. It's part of the same plastic bubble, but worth about as much as a new car. You slam it at your own risk.

There was a headset on each seat. He put his on and pointed to mine. I put it on and he ran through his quick rosary of preflight checks and started up. The familiar whine and then the crack of the start and the steady whup-whup-whup of the blades put me into the same time warp I'd experienced in the hut. I had been in choppers a lot, always for the money—heading in on a landing somewhere, or out with a prayer in my heart and a hot situation behind me.

Kinsella looked at me and grinned. His voice was thin, filtered through the headset. "Takes you back, huh?"

114

"Right back," I told him, pressing the microphone button on the headset lead.

He reached down for the throttle on his left side and spoke again. "Hang in. It's easy this time, Charley's not out there waiting."

He wound up the rpm, lifted the stick, and we were away, slowly and gently. Whatever kind of cowboy he had been in Nam, he was a civilian now and his motion wouldn't have worried an old lady. When we were thirty feet up he shoved the control stick over and we swung left and away, still climbing, until the motel and the road were nursery toys on a green floor beneath us.

"I'm heading three hundred twenty degrees," he told me. "It's maybe twenty minutes from here."

"Wake me when it's over," I kidded, and he laughed and swung us sideways, onto his true bearing.

I stared down at the terrain, dark green with pines and spruce and occasional lakes. Somebody once said that Ontario is like American beer, nine-tenths water. This end of the province isn't typical—there is less water surface than land, but there are still plenty of lakes. We crossed a sizable river. In the past, before there were roads and trucks big enough to make it worthwhile, that was the main route for the pulp logs they processed in Olympia. Now it traced a band of smaller trees, second growth after the first generation had been sent down to the mill. And then we were in country so repetitious it was almost featureless: lakes, none of them big, the occasional high, bare outcropping, and never-ending trees.

Kinsella pointed down. "See that bare-ass rock there." I nodded without switching on my mike. "Yeah. That's the landmark for the lake where Prudhomme died. It's about three hundred fifty degrees from it, maybe three miles more, with three islands, two small ones together and a big one." I nodded again and watched carefully as he tilted the stick and moved to the new heading.

"There it is." I pointed and he nodded.

"Same place as before," he said, and we both grinned. "Hang onto your false teeth, we'll go down and take a look." This time he did show off his combat skills, dropping us like a stone, then tilting again to take us over the biggest island.

It was about a quarter mile long, half as wide, about thirty acres altogether, most of it rock. "Looks a bit small to have its own resident bear," I said.

"That was my feeling, but he'd sure as hell been chewed up and the doctor said it was bear teeth did it." Kinsella was enjoying himself, swinging the chopper along the shoreline all around the island. Down low the speed was obvious again. It was like driving a race car. For me, it was a memory of a lot of approaches to LZs I had known. I could almost sense the presence of the other guys, the smell of sweat and gun oil, the murmur of cursing and the occasional prayer. I found my fists were clenched tightly and worked at slackening them.

Kinsella grinned. "Now you remember," he said, and I nodded. He laughed, off microphone, and turned the far corner of the island, hanging almost sideways under the blades, like a weight slung at the end of a cord. My breath caught in my chest but we swung back vertical again and I relaxed, feeling a tingle of the old familiar exhilaration. And then I saw something floating ahead of us in the water. I switched on my mike but Kinsella had beaten me to it. He pulled us up and slowed the forward progress so we hung in the air, fifty feet from the object, thirty feet above.

"It's an aluminum canoe, like the one Jack Misquadis owns," I told him.

"Yeah?" Kinsella worked the controls, bringing us down ten feet above the canoe and a little to one side where we could see it clearly. "You mean the Indian who found the body?"

"That's the one. He was coming in today to shoot the bear. They put a bounty on it." I was staring down at the canoe, seeing that it was empty, sunk to within a couple of inches of being completely submerged, held up only by the Styrofoam buoyancy floats under the metal at the bow and stern.

"Well, I hope he was wearing a life jacket, because he's nowhere that I can see," Kinsella said.

He edged a little closer to the canoe, bringing it under my side. "Anything in it?"

I checked carefully. "Not a thing. That means he's either tipped it and everything fell out, or it drifted away after he'd made camp."

Kinsella sucked in his lower lip. "He didn't strike me as a drinker," he said, "and I can't think of any other way an Indian would get careless about tying up."

We looked at one another and I asked, "Can you bring me down on it? I'll tie the bowline to the skid and we can take it to the island."

He rolled his head thoughtfully. "I guess you've been in and out of enough choppers. Just be goddamn careful, all right?"

"I promise," I said fervently. He edged the machine closer and I unsnapped my seat belt and slid the door back. The downstream from the fans filled the cabin, taking my breath away. I fought hard to grab air, then eased out, keeping my head low, and stood down on the skid. The downdraft was boiling the surface of the water, flattening the slight swell that covered the lake, pressing the canoe deeper into the water. The noise was filling my head, it was hard to breathe. I was eighteen again, jumping into the unknown.

I forced in another big gulp of air and reached down for the edge of the canoe, keeping my left hand tightly around the upright support of the skid. The water was cold as it swirled around my hand and wrist but I didn't let go. I pulled the canoe along under me until I could reach the bow. The line running from the front eye was thin white nylon, strong enough to pull a powerboat. I found it, six inches under the surface, and pulled. It should have come easily, rolling up into my hands, its weight neutralized by its buoyancy. Instead it was hard to move, snagged on something under the water. I hung on tighter to the upright and reefed on the rope as hard as I could.

Slowly, as if I were pulling in a log, the rope came up to me, six feet, twelve, fifteen. And then, through the black murk of the water I could see the end, snarled around something that was trailing reluctantly. I pulled harder and a moment later I found out what it had been caught on. It was a man's ankle and he was very dead.

I wrapped one leg around the upright and used my free hand to gesture to Kinsella. His eyebrows went up and he mouthed the words "Hang on." I took a tight grip of the man's cuff, sliding my hand up inside the trouser leg against the deathly chill of the swelling flesh beneath it. Then I hung on tight to the upright and fought for breath as Kinsella inched the chopper toward the island. There was a long flat rock on the shoreline, slipping gently down into the water. With my arms trembling from the stress I held on until we reached it, then hopped down, keeping low, let go of the stay, and let Kinsella lift farther up the rock clear of the water and cut the motor.

He was out beside me before the blades had time to stop turning. He grabbed the leg I was holding and we eased the body up the rock, turning it over so the face wouldn't grind itself against the surface. When I saw who it was I whistled with surprise.

"Holy Hanna. That's not Misquadis," Kinsella said. "That's Jim Prudhomme."

I nodded grimly. "You're right. And this is his second time at bat."

13

I didn't waste time searching the body or carrying out any kind of investigation. Kinsella and I folded it into the rear seats and then beached the canoe, drained it, and tied it to a tree. Kinsella had explained that he couldn't take it out with him. It would mess up the balance of a chopper; it would have to be flown out underneath a float plane. When I'd finished lashing the canoe securely, Kinsella got back into the chopper and started up. I got in after him, closing the door and buckling in. He lifted off vertically and swung back on a southeasterly course that brought us within sight of the plume of smoke from the mill within five minutes.

Kinsella radioed the Olympia Airport that we were planning to land at the parking lot behind the hospital and described what we were carrying. The girl on duty was pro. She didn't break stride as she confirmed that she would notify the police and the hospital. I wondered if there would be a security leak. We didn't need a lot of onlookers when we arrived, but there were bound to be ham radio operators in the area tuned to the airport frequency. And once she made her first phone call the chances for leakage would be increased time after time.

Kinsella came in high over the town and I could see at once that word had gotten around. There was a ring of cars at the parking lot and a crowd of upturned faces as we pulled in over their heads and began the slow, sweet descent.

Gallagher was alongside the machine before the blades had stopped turning. I opened the door and he leaned in to look at the dead man's face. "Sonofabitch," he said. "We were right."

He stood back as I got down and a couple of orderlies from the hospital ran over with a gurney. We loaded the body on and covered the face with a sheet, then Gallagher went with it into the hospital while I talked to the constable Gallagher had brought with him.

The crowd was shoving in close and I spoke to the constable and he ordered them back, away from the machine. He was young and inexperienced, a gum-chewer, covering his lack of knowledge with a thick layer of machismo. But he knew how to handle the crowd so I left him to it and went into the hospital and looked for the chief.

He and Kinsella and the body were in an examining room. The nurse I'd met was in there as well and she frowned when I entered, but Gallagher held up one finger. "It's okay, Millie, this is the guy who found the body. Reid Bennett. He's a p'liceman himself."

She frowned harder. "Indeed," she sniffed. "Mr. Bennett told me he was an insurance man."

Gallagher nodded, not looking up. "I know, Millie, he was working under cover. Now he don't have to anymore."

She smiled when he spoke to her and I wondered quickly if I hadn't been mistaken about who she was crazy about. Maybe it wasn't her boss after all, maybe it was the chief. They were close to the same age and had the same appealing toughness about them. Gallagher could do a lot worse, I thought.

She left and Kinsella sat down on a tall stool and lit a Rothman's. Gallagher asked me, "Okay, now what happened, exactly?"

I told him and he asked a good question. "How come the rope was tied around his ankle?"

120

"Most likely for security, in case he fell out. I've seen guys do that before. It's dumb if you're in fast water, you could snag and drown, but in a lake it means the canoe won't drift away before you can pull it back under you."

He nodded. "Makes sense, I guess. Anyway, he'd have been missing if he hadn't done it, so it's a good thing he did." He paused and thought for a moment. "Right, then, so far, so good. There's a doctor on call in town. He's been phoned and he'll come in and take charge of the medical end of things. Let's you and me examine the body first." He turned to Kinsella. "D'you mind, it's police business now; I'd like to keep it in the family."

Kinsella slipped down off his stool. "No sweat, I'll go put the make on Gloria." He left and we turned to examine the body.

We set to it, starting by checking for injuries. There were none on the head or hands and no marks on the front of the clothing. But there was a neat hole in the back of the parka on the body, just left of center, under the shoulder blade.

"Bullet wound," Gallagher said. "Looks like a fairly big caliber."

"There's no exit wound. That means we can dig out the slug and do some ballistic testing," I said. "And I'd say you're right about the size. This wasn't the gun that killed Eleanor."

"Could be anybody's gun," Gallagher said angrily. "Every goddamn wall in this town's got a gun hanging on it. Everybody puts a moose in the freezer in the fall. Unless we pick up somebody carrying, it won't be worth spit finding that slug."

He rolled the body on its back again and we started searching, taking notes of everything we found. In the pants pockets there was a clasp knife with a shield on the handle and the initials JP. "No bastard told us this was missing when we identified that other poor slob," Gallagher said. "Looks crookeder an' crookeder all the time."

I said nothing and felt for the dead man's wallet. This was more valuable to us. It contained all the identification of a man called Andrew Wagoner. There was his social insurance card, a driver's license with an address in Toronto's West End, a Canadian Tire credit card, and a couple of photographs of a woman in her forties.

"Had any queries about a missing person called Wagoner?" I asked, and Gallagher shook his head.

"Doesn't mean a thing," he said. "This whole area's been stiff with transients since the gold mine opened up. It all adds up this way to me: Prudhomme met him at the motel, having a beer maybe. He talks him into coming into the bush, to make a few bucks helping set up camp or some yarn like that. Then he clobbers him, changes clothes with him and takes his identity. Then, when he'd got the other guy in his gear, he marks him up with the bear teeth and claws."

"It sure looks that way. It also gives us a motive for the killing on the island. Prudhomme needed a new identity."

Gallagher nodded. "Up till now I wasn't certain who'd done what to who. Anybody could have killed that guy on the island. Now it seems stone cold certain that Prudhomme set it up himself."

I sucked my teeth and said, "I didn't think Prudhomme was tough enough to club that guy down with a bear paw and smash his head the way it was smashed."

"Well, somebody did," Gallagher said. "And when you find Prudhomme carrying some stranger's ID and you have an unidentified body, it's hard not to think he did it all himself."

He turned back to the body, opened the parka, and ran his fingers over the thick wool shirt beneath it. "Something in here," he said. He unbuttoned the breast pocket and brought out a few folded slips of paper, soft and almost transparent from the water. He laid them on the steel table and opened them as carefully as a scholar working on the Dead Sea Scrolls.

122

I looked over his shoulder as he examined the first one. It was a hotel receipt from Sault Ste. Marie, where Eleanor had reported tricking with Prudhomme. The date was for three days, at the time she had said. "Looks as if Eleanor was right," I ventured.

"Yeah." Gallagher had taken out his notebook and was writing down the name of the motel, the dates, and the phone number. "Gives us a place to start our investigation," he said cheerfully.

He checked the other papers. One was a list of phone numbers. There were no names on it but Gallagher copied them into his book carefully, checking them all twice. I glanced at them but the exchange numbers were strange to me, except for one. "That's a Montreal exchange," I said.

"There's no area code with it," Gallagher argued gruffly. "Could be anywhere."

"Yeah, but one of the anywheres is Montreal. Let me check my own notes a minute." I reached in my pocket and found the paper on which I had written the phone number of the law office where Laval worked. It had the same exchange as the one on the list but a different last four numbers. "Yes, here it is, in the area where his lawyer works, that guy Laval I told you about."

"Small world," Gallagher said. "You make any connections down there that would be useful?"

"Yeah. I got friendly with one of the detectives. I figured he'd check it out for me, as a favor."

Gallagher looked up and grinned, then wiped his hands on his pant legs and took out a stick of gum, carefully not touching it as he folded it in between his front teeth, holding it by the foil cover. "Maybe you can collect on that favor when we get back to the station."

I nodded and he unfolded the last piece of paper. It was covered in figures, all in Prudhomme's neat handwriting. Gallagher shook it aloft in his fist. "Well, well. Lookit that.

He did us a favor after all. That's his list of claims, all by number. Now we can take this down to the office and find out. who all staked them and when."

We looked at one another and nodded like mandarins, not saying any more. Then Gallagher said, "This is going to take a while. Whyn't you see if you can scare up a cup of coffee?"

Kinsella was leaning on the reception desk, talking to a nurse who was rosy and delicious as a McIntosh apple, a blonde, smiling like sunrise as Kinsella chatted.

I could see that she wasn't wearing any rings and I guessed she and Kinsella had a thing going so I left them to it after she'd promised to bring some coffee in, and I headed back into the examination room.

Gallagher looked up. "Where's the other guy?"

"Playing nice with one of the nurses," I said. "Looks like they've met before."

"That'll be Gloria," Gallagher said. "Most guys would rather see her with no clothes on than you in your best suit." He paused and added, "That includes me."

We both laughed, ignoring the gray-faced corpse on the table. Then Gallagher slapped his hands together. "So okay, let's look at what we've got." He ticked off on his fingers. "First, we can follow up on the Wagoner ID and see if he's missing from home. If he is we can use that dental chart to get an identification on the body."

"Right. Then what about that Montreal phone number? Can I check that, see if it's Laval's number at home?" The excitement of the case was getting to me. It's always good when the breaks start happening and the pace of the investigation picks up. I figured I could call my Montreal cop and get the information right away.

Gallagher grunted and ticked a second finger. "Okay, do that. Then, three, maybe he can find Laval, and ask him how come he identified the body of the wrong guy. Nice and friendly."

I held up one finger. "It still leaves us the question of who

124

killed Prudhomme. It's odds on he's still up there in the bush. I guess we have to get back up there and look for him."

Gallagher grunted again. Like a lot of senior police officers, he hated acknowledging that anybody else's idea was worthwhile. "That brings us to the main question. Who could've shot Prudhomme, anyway?" He stopped talking and stared at me as if the answer might be written on my face.

"The obvious choice is Misquadis," I said. "That looks like his canoe and the bullet hole is big enough to have come from that old army .303 of his."

We thought about that one some more. Gallagher reached up and took off his cap as if air to the scalp might speed up his thinking processes. He ran his hand over his hair and put the hat on again, not touching the shiny peak. A longtime uniform man, I thought automatically.

"Did he strike you as a murderer?" he asked at last.

I shook my head. "No. He looked straight arrow to me. He makes a thin living by my standards, but he has all he needs."

"And he's not a drinker," Gallagher added. "He's never been in any dutch since I got here, anyway. So he didn't get wingy and just blaze away."

"That wasn't a blazing-away shot," I said. "That was a killing shot. It looks to me like the work of a real hunter. Or a hit man."

Gallagher frowned. "What makes you say a hit man? I told you, every guy in town is a hunter, even the goddamn undertaker heads out at fall and comes back with his winter's meat." He stood silently for a long moment, thumbs hooked into his gun belt, chewing his gum in silence.

"Not many men have shot at other men," I said. "That was a heart shot, from the back—it's the way a hit man would take a guy out. And if we're right in thinking that Prudhomme is involved with a few jillion dollars' worth of gold, there could be some heavy people who wanted him dead now his part of the work is done."

Gallagher scowled, thinking. "It's worth a thought," he

125

allowed at last. "But first, I think we oughtta cross off all the obvious possibilities. That means finding Misquadis and seeing if he's got his canoe with him, and test-firing his gun for comparison with the round we take out of Prudhomme's chest."

"How're we gonna do that?" I wondered. I could see what he had in mind for me, but my own ambitions were for working in town and spending the night at Alice's house.

"I think we should take a party back into the bush. We'll use Kinsella's chopper, lift in you and one of my guys and maybe that dog of yours, and see if we can come up with him."

"Not much sense going back in tonight, there's only a few hours of daylight left," I said, and Gallagher grinned.

"Yeah, well, I wouldn't want anybody to miss any rest. We'll go in tomorrow first thing. That way we can hear what the quack says about Prudhomme. Could be that the bullet wound didn't kill him." He snorted at that one. "Yeah, I know that's bull roar, but we have to listen to the doctor."

"He might be able to tell us how long Prudhomme's been dead," I suggested.

"Don't hold your breath," Gallagher said. He turned and pointed accusingly at the gray corpse on the table. "The only way you can ever assess the time of death is if you know for a fact when he ate his last meal. And we don't know boo-all about this guy except he got laid two weeks ago."

"Well, anyway, let's fingerprint the canoe, see if we come up with anything. And after that, we can check those claim numbers and see who registered them," I said. "That will give us some kind of a motive, at least."

We left it like that. My chore was to call Montreal and find out whose number was on Prudhomme's list. After that I was nominally free until the next morning, when I would head into the bush with one of Gallagher's men, looking for anybody who was in the area where we'd found Prudhomme. In between there was all the opportunity I needed to hang

126

around Gallagher while he investigated. I wasn't keen to, but I knew I would, even though I'd done what I'd set out to do, however awkwardly. I'd proved that Prudhomme was dead. So I arranged to meet Gallagher at his station later. He nodded without speaking, and I left.

Kinsella was out front still, with his nurse, chuckling and talking quietly with her, leaning over the counter as if it were a neighborhood bar. I told him we would be flying to the lake the next morning and to keep us the necessary booking on his machine. He responded with a negligent wave, the kind of hand signal any serviceman would give another when he was making good time with a girl. I didn't wait for anything more formal, but walked out into the pale afternoon sunshine to find a cab back to the motel.

Alice was in the office, talking on the telephone. When she saw me she winked and held up one hand to let me know she wouldn't be long. Then she wrapped up the conversation, hung up, and stood to lean over the counter close to me for a kiss. I squeezed her shoulder and said, "Hi."

"Hi yourself," she said. "We missed you, didn't we, Sam?" She turned to look down at Sam, who was wagging his tail and looking at me like a kid waiting to be let out of class.

"Turn him over to me," I asked, and she did. Sam whisked himself up on top of the counter and down beside me, wagging his tail off. I patted him and fussed him for a minute, then settled him down and straightened up. "I guess you heard what happened."

She nodded. "It was all over the town as soon as you reached the hospital. I just hung up from the second person to call me. What's it all about, anyway?"

"I'm still not sure, but the thing is, I'm going again tomorrow morning to look for whoever's out there. In the meantime I have a call to make and then I have to go down the station again for a while. After that I'm all yours to work your wicked way with."

She grinned, but not so widely as I would have liked.

"What's up?" I asked. "You look like I just disappointed you."

"No. I'm glad you're here overnight. I'm just not crazy about your going up there tomorrow. There's some nut out there with a gun. He could shoot you before you even saw him."

"Not with Sam along," I promised. "Come on now. I've been shot at before, they always miss."

She bit the tip of her left thumb, not looking at me. "Men," she said at last. "You're a bunch of damn kids. You're off to play cowboys and Indians while I sit here waiting."

"I've told you, don't worry. The whole thing's probably an accident. Somebody's gun went off by mistake. They hit Prudhomme and we found him. Meanwhile they're only concerned with getting a fire going and waiting until we show up to rescue them."

She wasn't convinced, so I changed the subject, and just because I'm a longtime policeman, I asked her about the guests registered. I wondered if any of them might be out of the ordinary run, maybe far enough out of it that they had brought a rifle up here to take out Jim Prudhomme for keeps.

She wasn't eager to play but she did go through the list. A couple of guys were here for the first time, including the one from Buffalo I had seen the night before. But there was nothing concrete, so I went down to my room and called Montreal. I reached the station, only to find that the man I wanted was off duty. That figured, but I pushed my luck and asked for his phone number. Maybe it was because I spoke French, but the policewoman at the desk took my number and offered to call the man and have him call me. I poured myself a smash of my Black Velvet and lay back, wondering how I was going to break the news to Carol Prudhomme.

Normally you don't phone news of a death. You call the local police and have them send someone around. It's painful for them as they stand there twisting their cap in their hands, but it prevents the person at the other end from thinking she's being fooled by somebody with a Halloween sense of humor. The difference this time was that Carol already considered herself a widow. I thought about that as I sipped on my rye. On the night I'd seen her playing cozy with Henri Laval I'd wondered whether Prudhomme might have disappeared because of her affair. Maybe they'd set it up between them so she could have his company life insurance and he could get a fresh start. She had acted jumpy enough to ring a little guilty to me. And if she was, she was going to be startled to find herself widowed for real.

I compromised by phoning my ex-wife. After all, it was her fault I was up here in the first place. She was closer to Carol than I had ever been or would ever be. I reached her in her office. She sounded brisk and businesslike, probably taking me for a client. "Amy Bennett."

"Hi, Amy, it's Reid, how are you?"

Give her marks for couth. She still didn't treat me badly. She hated the work I do but she wasn't bitchy to me. She was as polite to me as to a stranger. What more can you ask?

"What's going on? Are you still in Olympia?"

I filled her in, not painting any pictures, just playing out the facts like a man dealing the cards for solitaire. She listened, as she always listens, and asked the practical question. "What can I do?"

"I'd like you to call her and break the news. I figure she thinks I'm a bit of a heavy. The news is bad enough without coming from somebody you don't like."

She agreed, and we talked a minute or two more and I gave her my phone number in case there was anything Carol wanted me to do, and she hung up.

Almost at once the phone rang again. This time it was my drinking-buddy copper from Montreal. He was at home, cooking the dinner for his kids while his wife had her hair done, he explained, but what could he do to help? I gave him the telephone number to check and he did it while I waited, just by digging into the phone book. "*Oui*, 'enri Laval, like you say. In the book like 'e got nothing to 'ide," he told me. There wasn't anything else so I thanked him and hung up and sat there for a while, finishing my drink and thinking about going on patrol again the next day, out in the boonies looking for a man with a gun. It would be like Viet Nam, all over again.

14

I called the station and found out that Gallagher was down there. Because it was daylight and Alice didn't need the support, I took Sam with me. He's too well trained to show much emotion, but he was glad enough to be with me again that he sat up straight in the front seat instead of snoozing as he usually does when I drive with him in the car. I reached over and fussed him with one hand as I drove. He's a good buddy and he was going to save me a lot of wasted motion in the morning when he went with me into the bush.

He came with me into the police station, pacing quietly, his standard six inches behind my left heel. I guess Gallagher's clerk was a little house-proud about station cleanliness. She tutted when he came in but didn't say anything. I just waved at her. "The boss in?"

"Out back, in his office," she said briskly and went on typing as if Sam were a mirage and she didn't want to admit to seeing it.

I lifted the counter flap and walked down the short corridor. Gallagher was hanging up the phone. "Hi. D'you get anything from Montreal?"

"Yeah, that's Laval's home number on Prudhomme's list. Any luck tracing the others?"

Gallagher got up and came over to pat Sam, who stood for it patiently. "I gotta get myself a dog," he said. "Not as fancy as this guy. Just something that'll be glad to see me when I get home. Even if it's just because I feed it."

"Should I get out my violin?" I ribbed, and he scowled and straightened up.

"Smart-ass. You youngsters are all the goddamn same." He sat down again and picked up his notebook. "I checked the other numbers, came up with some surprises," he told me, referring to his list. "The first belongs to a woman in Thunder Bay who has the same last name as everybody's favorite animal stuffer. Sallinon."

I whistled. "Now there's the kind of coincidence that makes coppers get suspicious."

"Right." Gallagher nodded grimly. "As soon as I've cleaned up a few things here, I'm heading up to see him. In the meantime, I'd like to track down Laval and have someone we trust have a word with him. You think you could talk to your contact again?"

"I can ask him. He's a bit of a loser, but I made friends with him the other night; he'd do it. What's on your mind?"

"I'd like to ask Laval why Prudhomme had his phone number in his possession," Gallagher said. "I mean, he wasn't alive anymore, not officially. He was supposed to be this Wagoner guy, but he still had Laval's number. They were still in contact. That means to me that Laval knew he was alive. I want to lean on the sonofabitch a little. He might just open up for us."

"I doubt it. He's a lawyer, he knows all the reasons there are for not saying anything. He's also slick as a whistle, he isn't likely to bend because some detective comes knocking on his door."

"Well, let's try it anyway." Gallagher rubbed his face thoughtfully. "Looks to me like he's in this up to his armpits, it wouldn't hurt to stir him up and see what comes of it."

"All right, I'll call my man. What else is there?"

Gallagher sucked his teeth. "Not a lot until the claim office opens on Monday and I can get a man in there to start looking up those numbers. That may give us a lead to the company that's registered them and we can chase up the members and see what their tie-in with Prudhomme could be."

"Well, if it was somebody from town who shot Prudhomme in the back, he'd have needed a flight into the area. We could check on that."

"I'm ahead of you there," Gallagher said. He fumbled in his in-basket and pulled out a sheet of paper. "I've talked to all the chopper companies in the area. None of them flew anybody into the bush yesterday. Or"—he waved one hand brusquely—"make that none of them flew any strangers anywhere near where you found the body."

"From what I saw of the terrain, he'd have needed a chopper to get in there that quick," I said. "It's a good thirty miles away and the river's got some rapids on it, so he couldn't have taken a powerboat in. He'd have needed a canoe, and then needed to portage about three miles through the bush. That's a solid day's traveling, even if he had an outboard on his canoe and even if he was used to lugging it over a portage."

"That's what I figured," Gallagher agreed. He made a face and rolled his chewing gum between his front teeth and threw it away. "This stuff doesn't keep its flavor like it used to when I was a kid," he complained, and took out a fresh stick. He stuck it in his mouth, then swung his feet up on his desk luxuriously.

"So that's another suggestion that's not going to help us," I said, and he nodded. We looked at one another for a while, realizing the case wasn't going to solve itself just because we'd proved we were right about Prudhomme. Finally I asked him, "Okay, so what did you learn about those other phone numbers?"

"Ver–r–ry interesting," Gallagher allowed. "Three of the others are pay phones. One of them is in Thunder Bay, another is in Timmins, and the third one is in the Soo."

"Anything in common about the locations?" It was the kind of question you ask without having any particular reason, just trying to narrow the focus of your search. But he had an answer for me.

"Yeah. They're all in the bus station lobbies, all three of them."

"Well, maybe he had a schedule, maybe he called people there at certain times. A guy could come into town, walk into the bus terminal all casual and wait around the phone box at set times. Then when the phone went, he stepped in and the contact was made."

"That's the way it looks to me," Gallagher admitted. "Only I was wondering why he'd have three towns so far apart, and why he wouldn't have a more personal number for these guys. I mean, who doesn't have a telephone? Everybody does. And there's no check on incoming calls, we couldn't trace where a call was coming from, not like if a guy dialed out and had the number on the phone company record. Why would he go to this kind of trouble?"

"Beats the hell out of me," I shrugged. "And he's never going to tell us."

"Right." Gallagher put his feet down on the floor and sat hunched over as if the case had a weight of its own that was pressing on his back. "So I've arranged to have the numbers staked out, just today. Once word gets into the paper that Prudhomme's body's been found, whoever's been using those boxes will steer clear of them. I'm calling each one of them on the hour, then the half hour, then both quarters. It's kind of hit-and-miss. We don't know what their schedule was. But if anybody answers, the local cops can pick the guy up and ask him some questions."

"What about the other number—weren't there five on that list?" I asked, and Gallagher grinned.

"Yeah, that one was the strangest of all. You're never gonna believe this one."

"So break it to me gently," I said. "Is it going to help us, that's all I'm asking."

Gallagher dropped the grin and his face settled into an expression I hadn't seen there before. He was sad. "This one was a number you get through the mobile operator."

"Whose car is it?" This was important. It could be the break we were waiting for.

"It's not a car," Gallagher said slowly. "And it's not in use anymore."

"Okay, but you must know who owned the truck, whatever."

"I do," he said. "And this one's a puzzle. It's the number of the phone in the trick truck that Eleanor drove."

"Maybe she handed it out to all her tricks."

"Not likely. It had the area code on it so it would be for calling long distance. You couldn't expect her to drive down from the Soo if you were in Timmins and felt lonely. There had to be more to it than that."

"Maybe he had something going with her."

Gallagher shook his head. "No, I don't think that would be it. He wouldn't have it on this piece of paper if he did. He'd have known her number right off. Hell, you know what it's like when you're involved with a broad."

I said nothing. He had the hangdog wistfulness about him that I'd seen the night before when he spoke about Alice. I would have bet he had her phone number memorized perfectly and I felt a quick pang of sympathy for him. He hankered for her and it was hurting him to know that I was the one she had chosen. I could still remember how it felt from the time after Amy left.

I waited a moment or two and he spoke again. "No, I figure it must be another contact number, something connected with this business. And it made me wonder if he had anything going with Eleanor's pimp."

"The homicide guy at Thunder Bay said she didn't have a pimp," I reminded him, and he waved one hand impatiently. "He just meant she didn't have some big nigger in a red fur coat beatin' up on her," he said. "Hell, I've been a copper for more years than that kid's been living and I want you to know that every hooker I ever met had a pimp. Sometimes it's her old man, sometimes it's her brother, sometimes it's her goddamn mother. They all have pimps." He looked at me as if he was defying me to argue. I didn't.

"Well, did you call the guys in Thunder Bay? Maybe they can dig. Hell, it could be this pimp who killed her."

"I called," Gallagher said. "The homicide guy doesn't know, but I spoke to the Morality office. Their guy's away today and they can't reach him. But they said he'd call."

"I doubt he'll have much for us when he does," I said. "The homicide guy would have chased that one down the day after the murder."

"We'll have to wait and see," Gallagher said.

"And while we wait, what?" I queried. I hadn't got any new suggestions. He was handling his facts the way I would have done it, the way any competent investigator would.

He straightened up slowly and put his cap on, tapping it down over his thick hair. "While we wait we'll go see Sallinon. "Find out why he lied about the bearskin he sold Prudhomme."

"Good. I'll come with you." I stood up with him and Sam hustled to his feet in my shadow.

Sallinon was in his store, handing over a fair-sized lake trout on a wall shield to a guy who looked as if he'd just won the lottery. The customer turned to us as Sallinon wrote out the receipt. "How about that for a fish?" he asked proudly. "On eight-pound test. That's all. Just eight-pound. Sonofabitch weighed seventeen. He could've snapped it like that."

Gallagher was a good copper. He nodded and looked impressed. "Must've taken you all day to land him."

"An hour," the guy said. "That beauty's going on the wall." He got his receipt, thanked Sallinon, and left.

Sallinon looked at us and smiled a buddy-buddy smile. "Fancy getting excited about a seventeen-pounder?"

"Don't knock it, Arnie," Gallagher said. "It's guys like him pay your rent."

"Yeah, I guess," Sallinon said. "So what brings you two fellas down here?"

"Prudhomme," Gallagher said, and let the word sit there, as lifeless as one of the stuffed animals.

After a long pause, Sallinon nodded. "Yeah, I heard about that. Incredible, eh?"

Gallagher leaned on the countertop and nodded agreement. "Fer sure," he said. I watched Sallinon. He licked his lips quickly, the way a man does when he's going to lie. And suddenly Gallagher reached out and held him by the front of his wool jacket. "Listen, Arnie, I wanna know why you've been jerking Mr. Bennett around."

Sallinon tried to be dignified. He drew himself up to his full height, bringing himself eye to eye with Gallagher, and he reached down and removed Gallagher's hand as if it were something that had fallen off one of the dead animals above him. "You'd better explain what you're talking about," he said. It was the right thing to say, but there was so much tension in his voice that the words trembled.

Gallagher looked him straight in the eye and spoke so softly I could hardly hear him from a yard away. "You'd better tell me why you lied about selling him a bearskin."

Sallinon licked his lips again. "I didn't lie. I sold him a mink, just as I told this gen'leman."

Gallagher sniffed. It was as if he had a bad smell under his nose, a contemptuous wrinkling of his nostrils. "Then how come he had a bearskin in his gear, up at the motel? And how come he turns up dead a couple of weeks after he's been buried? Or at least after some poor sucker with bear claw and teeth marks all over him has been buried?"

Sallinon shrugged. "What's that got to do with me?" He was afraid, I could almost feel it. He might or might not be involved in the plot we thought Prudhomme had been running, but he was quilty of something.

Gallagher shook his head, looking down at the counter, then up again into Sallinon's face with a gesture as sharp as a whiplash. "Work it out, Arnie. Soon after you don't sell a skin to a guy, some other guy ends up chewed up by what looks like a bear. Now for that to happen, the killer would either have to be a bear, which is bullshit, or else it has to be a guy with a set of bear claws and bear teeth working to disfigure a stranger so he could head off into the sunset under an assumed name." He waited and Sallinon said nothing, just licked his dry lips once more.

"So," Gallagher went on, "if you earned your living trying to keep this town free from crime instead of stuffing chipmunks full of sawdust, what would you think?"

Sallinon said nothing and Gallagher suddenly reached over and grabbed his jacket again with two hands and drew him close up. I could see Sallinon trembling as he struggled to pull back. "I tell you what you'd think, Arnie," Gallagher roared. "You'd think, Why is Arnie Sallinon lying to me about the bearskin? If he had nothing to do with this, why did he bother to lie to me in the first place? That's what you'd think."

He released Sallinon abruptly, shoving him a little so that he staggered back against the cupboard behind the counter. A gray squirrel on top of the cupboard rocked and I thought it was going to fall on Sallinon's head but it didn't. He did good work, the base was wide enough to stand up to shocks.

So was Sallinon. He staggered to his feet and straightened out his shirtfront. "I don't have to put up with this," he said softly. "And I won't. I'm a member of council in this town and I think they'll take my recommendation that we don't want some slob running the police department."

It didn't fizz on Gallagher. "Dry your eyes, Arnie," he said. "Nobody's gonna take your word for nothing when you're in

Kingston pen." He leaned on the counter again, as relaxed as a customer waiting for his parcel to be wrapped. "And while we're talking about what a good citizen you are, how about getting your sister to give you a reference?"

Sallinon looked at him quickly, then away, a darting little motion like a dog would make if he thought you were going to swat him with a rolled-up newspaper. But again he kept himself in check. "What about my sister?"

"Well, if I was on the town council, hearing how our big rough police chief had come asking questions, I might want to know why the dead man all this is about had the phone number of the honorable council member's sister in his pocket. Now, just to get in practice for when you get me fired, why don't you tell me why that would be? Were they going steady, what?"

"I don't know anything about my sister's private life," Sallinon said. And again he pulled himself together. "And if you're harassing her like you're harassing me, she will say the same as me."

"Harassing?" Gallagher laughed. He turned to me. "Did you see any harassing?"

"I've been here the whole time while you and the accused talked," I said equivocally. I don't like this kind of investigation, but so far Gallagher was keeping his anger under control. I didn't think he would get rougher. If he did I would stop him.

"See," Gallagher said, "Mr. Bennett says we've been talking nice."

Sallinon looked at me, then back at Gallagher, the speed of his head move making his jowls tremble. But he didn't say anything. Gallagher said it for him. "We haven't finished yet, Arnie. Your sister's not home. She's at the drugstore, where she works. I've saved her the embarrassment of having a Thunder Bay cop come calling for her, but he's waiting at her door for when she does show. Then we'll find out what all you're up to."

"I'd be interested to know what your twisted mind will come up with," Sallinon said. "It's going to be amusing."

Gallagher straightened up, tall and amiable, the way he must have looked at the grade school, lecturing the kids on how to cross the street. "Happy to oblige," he said. "You can laugh your way right into the goddamn pen."

He turned away and I followed him, but before reaching the door I stopped and asked the question Gallagher had overlooked. "If you didn't sell him that bearskin, where would he have got it?"

It worked. The relief of an apparently innocent question loosened him up at once. "The only man in town who sells skins, aside from me, is Jack Misquadis."

"Thanks," I told him and followed Gallagher out, past the clank of the cowbell.

15

By now it was three in the afternoon. The sun was still high but the air was colder and the northwest wind had picked up, whipping the dead leaves on the street into tight little spirals. I shuddered. Indian summer was over. It would be cold in the bush the next day. I could dress for it, but I still had to hope we didn't get a sudden cold snap that locked the lake surface tight in inch-thick ice, too thin to walk on, too thick to let us use the canoe. But there's no sense in borrowing trouble so I put the worry out of my mind. I would check the weather forecast before we let the chopper go. If it looked bad we wouldn't start on the island, we'd start on the mainland where we could portage back to the river, which wouldn't freeze up for another month.

There wasn't any more to do right away. All our irons had been put into the fire. Now it was just a question of waiting for something to heat up. When we got back to the station I went in with Gallagher to check if anybody had answered his calls to the pay phones. Nobody had, so I took Sam and left. I was hungry, but figured I'd be eating dinner fairly soon so I made do with a coffee at the bus station, then drove back to the motel.

Alice wasn't painting today. She was on edge and wouldn't talk about it. I've been married and I recognized the signs.

She was upset and I was the cause. It's not smart to labor the point when that happens. Either you ignore it or you suffer. I was fond enough of her that I wished our mood of the last few nights would last, but if it didn't, I wasn't going to play games. So instead I suggested taking her out to dinner for a change.

This time she didn't object and so, quite early, I drove her back up the highway to the place I'd intended visiting that first night and we ate steak and drank the house red wine and acted like a couple who have been married for fifteen years.

While we were eating I noticed a young couple with a boy of about three sitting very quietly, ordering modestly, and eating in silence. The man had a haunted look to him that piqued my policeman's curiosity. He looked ill at ease, as if he'd just done something illegal and wasn't used to the idea yet.

I found out the truth when they brought him his bill. He couldn't pay. It began as a murmur that grew to a rumble as the waitress went for the manager. Then the manager came out of the kitchen, red faced, either from the heat back there or from the problem. I soon heard what it was. The young guy was flat. He had come up to Olympia hoping to get a job only there weren't any. Now he was making his way back to Montreal. He was Quebecois and frightened, explaining that his wife and kid hadn't eaten since the day before.

As the boss began to rant I stood up and went over, greeting the young guy in French. "Hi, long time no see. Remember me? I met you in Trois Rivieres last year."

He looked at me with his mouth gaping. I could see that the woman was crying silently and the kid was sucking his thumb, wondering what was going on. The manager said, "You know this guy?"

"Of course," I told him, in English now. "He is my good friend Henri Barbusse." I took the unpaid bill out of the manager's hand. "He's my guest, I guess he didn't see me at the other table. We were supposed to meet here."

The manager was relieved. "Oh well, in that case," he began, then trailed off. I smiled and made a little ushering motion and he left and the other patrons turned back to their pepper steaks and fries. Reverting to French, I asked the young man how he was traveling. It seemed he was in a Honda. That was good. He would get a few miles out of a cheap tankful of gas. Trying not to be ostentatious, I slipped out a twenty and stuck it in his shirt pocket. "See the welfare people in the Soo, they'll get you home," I told him, winked, patted the little boy on the head, and went back to the table.

Alice said to me, "I speak pretty good French myself, you know. Do you really know him?"

"I do now," I told her, and went back to eating.

She reached across the table and squeezed my hand. "For a hard-hearted policeman you're an absolute pushover, you know that?"

I shrugged. Playing Samaritan is something I'd rather do in private. I've been broke and hungry myself and it wouldn't have made me feel much better to see somebody buying himself limelight on my behalf. But there had been no other way. "I just finished a little moonlighting in Toronto," I told her. "They paid me a fat bonus, and I've been in his place enough times to sympathize."

She grinned at me as the young family got up and left, the woman waving, the man not looking up. "I've done what you did a few times since the gold rush started, although not too many really broke people make it down to my place from the highway. But you're not supposed to. You don't keep a restaurant." Then she laughed. "You're a disgrace to the uniform," she said, and we both laughed. It broke her mood. We chatted easily all evening, but as we were coming back through the darkness to Olympia she opened up, quietly but insistently. She didn't want me heading out to chase down whoever had shot Jim Prudhomme. He was dead, twice over. Her husband was dead. I was alive. She wanted things to stay that way.

I thought for a while that she wasn't going to invite me back to her place and was prepared to say good night and leave her, but at the last minute she said, "You might as well come in," and I did and lit the stove and drank cognac with her for an hour, listening to Mozart and to her as she leveled with me. The gist of her message was simple. She didn't want me mixed up in any rough stuff.

I was flattered, but she didn't change my mind. She wouldn't have, even if we had been a permanent pair instead of a couple of new friends taking the measure of what we felt about one another. I wasn't any closer to her than that—not yet, anyway. And so, in the end, I stayed the night in the kind of sweet sadness I'd known twice before, on R and R from Viet Nam when you know the bubble is going to burst and another day will find you back on the airplane, leaving her to whatever kind of life she leads while you're out in the boonies, trying to extend your own life, one day at a time, in the face of deadly opposition.

Before I left her at seven in the morning, when the daylight grew around us as we lay in the big bed, I made her promise me that she would stay at the motel while I was in the bush. We hadn't been disturbed in the night but that didn't mean that Tettlinger had given up. It meant that she was safe while I was around, but I was heading out, so I dug my heels in and insisted and she agreed, grudgingly.

"You realize you're depriving me of a night's rent on one of the rooms up there," she said, managing a brave smile.

"If that's all that's stopping you, I'll rent the room," I promised. "A few bucks doesn't matter. What matters is your being somewhere safe. I'm going to be on a hike in the bush, nothing more complicated than that, but if I don't know you're among people, I'm going to worry."

And so she kissed me and promised and I left to head up the highway to the motel where Kinsella kept his bird.

I got there at a little after eight. Kinsella was out, doing his walk-around of the aircraft, checking everything, being watched by the same beefy copper Gallagher had brought with him to the hospital. He was in uniform, including a parka that would have been fine if he'd planned on standing around, but looked too warm for canoeing and the other work we might have to do. He also had bush boots, brown instead of black, with inch-and-a-half soles that brought him eye to eye with me.

Gallagher must have given him my pedigree since the day before. He stopped chomping and nodded. "Morning, Chief, coming with us?"

"We both are," I said, and gestured to Sam.

The young cop looked down at him and then up at me, grinning. "Needs a walk, does he?"

"He's trained," I said shortly. "By the way, his name's Sam, mine is Reid Bennett."

We shook hands and he said, "Yeah, Mike Onyschuk."

Kinsella turned and waved. "All set?"

I nodded. "Yeah. I just have to get my stuff out of the trunk." I turned away and opened the trunk of my car. In it I had the Murphy's Harbour Police Department rifle. It was a Remington .308, just iron sights but accurate to a hair at four hundred meters. I also had my survival gear, a backpack with some cans of food, a bag of rice and a billy and a pan. It's not fancy, but I could last a week with it where we were going. And I had a sleeping bag.

I lugged it back alongside the chopper and Onyschuk looked at it and dropped his lower jaw in a one-second gesture of respect. "You were ready for this?"

"Ready enough, I guess. There's nothing fancy in the bag, but we can manage a few days."

He nodded, creasing his heavy jowls. "I got ready m'self," he said. "I got a pack of groceries an' a jug." He thought about that for a moment, remembering I was a visiting chief and added a small joke. "In case of snakebite, eh?"

"Vital," I assured him. "I hope it's Black Velvet, I find that cures me faster than anything else."

We both laughed and Kinsella waved us aboard and shut the door and we were soon up and away. I was in the front seat, Onyschuk and Sam in the back. I asked Kinsella to take us in a sweep of the whole area, to check for campfires.

He did, bringing us in diminishing circles around the lake from a radius of about a mile out. He was a pro and I gave him the thumbs up. "Don't mean a thing if we don't find anybody," he said, and I hooked a thumb back at Sam.

"If there's anybody been close to the lake, Sam'll track them for us."

Kinsella nodded and brought the chopper lower. "How about the same rock as yesterday?" he asked.

"Yeah. We have to start on the island, we can take out over the lake and try the mainland later."

Kinsella found the sloping rock and settled toward it, moving gently. I glanced back and looked at Onyschuk. He was pale and I figured it must be his first flight. "You get used to it," I told him, and he grinned nervously.

We settled on the rock and I got out first, then Onyschuk, and then Sam, who shook himself and went and lapped the lake water, disturbing the first little fingers of ice that were growing out from the rocks. Meanwhile, we unloaded our gear and paddles from the chopper. We would use the canoe I had found the day before. It was still there, tied to the tree.

Kinsella kept his motor running. "I can't take you to the mainland, I've got another call at nine-thirty," he explained, shouting over the steady whup-whup of the blades.

"Not to worry. Mike's got a radio. We'll get in touch tonight and report progress. If we need you back I'll clear a spot to come down. If it's on the island, I'll report it and you can pick us up here again."

He nodded and shook hands with both of us and got back into the seat. I motioned Onyschuk and Sam out of the way into the trees while the bird took off, throwing up a whirlwind of bitter air filled with dead sticks and dust. When he'd gone

I looked at Onyschuk, who was showing signs of sweat already in his thick parka. I had my combat jacket on. It's not warm enough for the dead of winter but you can work in it without overheating. "Okay, I'll get Sam to check if the island is deserted. Then we can head over to the mainland and look for tracks. All right with you?"

He nodded. He had stopped chewing gum now. He had his rifle in his hands and his backpack on. He looked sure of himself for the first time since I'd met him. I guessed that in spite of the wrong choice of coat he knew the bush. Probably he was a hunter. "Whatever you say, Chief."

I nodded and crouched down to Sam, holding his head between my hands, and told him "Seek." It was his general hunting command. He would look for any human on the island and bark when he found anybody, alive or dead.

He put his head to the ground and started circling, wider and wider, leaving us behind in the thick trees. I turned to Onyschuk, who was still holding his rifle. "He'll give tongue if he picks up a scent. Meanwhile, we can dump our stuff here and wait until we hear him. He'll be all over this island in an hour."

Onyschuk was careful. He squirmed out of the straps of his backpack but kept hold of his rifle, a lever-action Winchester, the kind John Wayne made fashionable. "I figure I'll keep the gun," he said.

I nodded. "Me too. That looked like a hunter's shot in Prudhomme's back. If the guy's around we may need firepower." I stopped long enough to load the magazine on the Remington but without putting one up the spout. Then I trailed it in my left hand. It isn't the way I carried my M16 in Viet Nam, but then I didn't have Sam walking point for me.

"I'd like to see the place where you found the body. Can you find it from here?" I asked him, and he nodded.

"It's up the way your dog's heading. Come on with me." He led the way, moving silent as an Indian on his thick boots.

I followed, swinging around constantly as the old patrol reflexes came back. It was odd to be doing this in a cold climate instead of the crushing heat of the hills in Nam. But I was glad of the coolness and glad not to be humping my pack, just following a smart dog and a bush-wise cop.

There was no trail. We picked our way through the trees, clambering over deadfalls, ducking under branches, heading southwest down the long axis of the island. Sam was ahead of us, moving silently through the bush, head down, working.

After a ten-minute hike through bush that would have put most men off guard, concentrating on their comfort and economy of effort rather than security, Onyschuk turned and pointed ahead, not speaking. He was moving well, sweating in his parka but still silent. He paused until I caught up with him, stopping one last time to check behind us.

"This is the place," he said, and pointed again through the trees down onto a moss-covered rock that lay like a beached whale rolling up from the flat ground. I stood next to him and checked it carefully. I could see nobody out there or in the fringe of trees around. Then Sam came into view, loping easily over the rock and down out of sight again on the far side. That meant it was all clear, so I motioned to Onyschuk and we walked out of the trees.

"We found the body down here." He indicated the base of the rock on the north side. A tangle of blueberry bushes hung onto the thin overburden like the sparse hair on an old man's scalp. "He was facedown, about here."

He walked forward again, stopping to check a couple of reference points with his eye. "Yeah, we were just about on a line between those two trees, the dead pine and the poplar." He stamped the back of his heel onto the edge of the rock. "About there."

I'm not sure what I had expected to find, but the ground had been gone over well. All I got was the satisfaction of having been there myself. Onyschuk grinned. "Yeah, the chief made us go over an' over it. The only thing we found was a tin can, rusted to rat shit, coulda been there thirty years." He thought about it a moment and added, "It was like it had been swept."

"Was there any blood on the rock?" I was crouched, checking the gray crust of lichen that had been underneath the body if his reconstruction of the scene was accurate.

"Nah." He shook his head. "But these weren't bleeding kind of injuries. His face was more like somebody had worked it over with a Carborundum wheel. The flesh was worn away. The blood vessels get all sealed up by that kind of wound."

I nodded, not answering. Another theory could be that the wounds had been inflicted after death. There wouldn't have been much bleeding in that case. I wondered how carefully the doctor had examined the body. Not well enough, I guessed, happy to be able to record the death as a bear attack, the hell with any details that messed up his theory: unshed blood or mysterious absence of face or fingerprints. I wondered how he would feel when he got the news of our discovery.

"You figure the damage could've been made by rubbing the face and hands on a rock?" I asked him.

"Sure looked like teeth marks to me. Individual grooves, like a little kid makes if he scrapes his teeth over an ice cream or something like that, only bigger, same size as bear's teeth." He thought about it for a moment and added, "No doubt about it, the head was gnawed, nothing else for it. The doctor was right."

So that was that. I gave up on the headwork and set to exploring the whole area. It was about a quarter acre in extent. Except for a couple of straggly pines with twisted limbs, the rock was bare.

I took one last long look around, stooping to the ground, not sure what I was after. And then I realized. "Did the chopper land here when you came to the island?"

"No." Onyschuk was confident. "No. The chief wouldn't let

it. He kept it the far side of the rock, in case it disturbed anything before we'd finished the examination of the body." He looked at me curiously. "What makes you ask, anyway?"

"I was just checking this section, right here where the body was. It's as if it's been vacuumed. Look at it."

He crouched with me, checking as I had done. I pointed out the evidence. "See, there's nothing here small enough to blow away. Nothing but a few dead leaves, and they could have fallen anytime. All the sticks and bits of brush, they've all been swept away."

Onyschuk whistled. "A chopper'd do that. They must've landed here in a chopper, Prudhomme and the guy whose body we found. Only it's not right. His regular pickup rendezvous was supposed to be three miles away, on the river." He thought about it for a minute. "Of course, they landed here quite a bit last year, when they were drilling the test hole further on, about a hundred meters south of here on the waterline. I doubt any of them ever came up this far, even."

"Yes. They probably did, but a lot of debris would have built up again with a whole fall and winter in between then and now."

We stood up, thinking through the possibilities. There weren't many. Prudhomme had come into the bush with a canoe and a week's supplies. He had been lifted in and the initial search had been all around the rendezvous. Then the canoe had been sighted on this lake and the search switched here.

Which meant, I decided, that he had been airlifted out, from right on top of the dead body of the other man. Which meant he had some chopper pilot in his pocket. Which also meant that Laval could have been connected with the same pilot. And that would give Laval a back door to this lake. It also meant he could have had a man air-lifted in to shoot Prudhomme the day before.

I waved Onyschuk after me and headed slowly after the track Sam had been taking. Now that I had seen the evidence

150

of the chopper I didn't think we were going to come on the rifleman here. The chopper which brought him in could have taken him out again. I pushed on between the punishingly tight trees until I met Sam coming back, relaxed. I bent to fuss him until Onyschuk caught up with us.

"There's nobody on the island," I said.

He nodded. "Good. So let's get across to the mainland and stop to make up a sandwich. I've got some bread and kielbasa in my pack."

"Good idea." I straightened up again and we headed back to the canoe, moving briskly now we didn't have to worry about making noise.

Onyschuk had lashed the bowline to the tree and he untied it and we loaded our packs into the center. He looked at Sam a little nervously. "Has he ever been in a canoe?"

"All the time." I picked up my end and Onyschuk took the other and we walked down the rock and floated the craft in a couple of inches of water. "He's as good as gold, lies as still as one of these backpacks. Only thing is, it's best if I go in the stern. That's what he's used to. He likes to be able to see me."

Onyschuk wasn't convinced but he laughed anyway. "Talk about trained. Hell, my dog's so sloppy you couldn't take him in a john boat, let alone a canoe. But if you say. It's your ass too."

I called Sam into the canoe, telling him "In" and patting the side, then "Down" so he lay flat and "Stay" so he would keep down and not throw our delicate balance off when we were out in midwater.

Onyschuk got in next, at the bow, his rifle propped ahead of him, the butt between his knees. He pushed his end away from the rock with a quick, efficient flick of the paddle, then I placed my own rifle in the space behind the first cross brace of the canoe. Finally I gave a small shove away from the rock and knelt in on the seat, pulled my legs through my arms, and picked up the paddle. The canoe rocked a couple of times but stabilized, and with Onyschuk pulling strongly on the left side and me on the right, keeping us on course with a J-twist to the blade on every stroke, we set off across the quarter mile to the nearest point of the shore opposite.

Sam was lying, open-eyed, head resting on his forepaws. He wasn't exactly working, but after a morning's hunt I knew he was sampling the air that blew over him from the light headwind coming against us off the far shore. And as I watched him I realized how vulnerable we were, all three of us, for the next few minutes. We couldn't protect ourselves against attack. The shock of a rifle firing could capsize the canoe. We were sitting ducks for as long as it took to cross the water.

As I thought about it, my mind jumped automatically to assess our distance from shore. Just fifty yards now thirty seconds' worth of paddling. Then, in the same moment I saw Sam's ears prick alert and his head lift off his feet, I heard the echoing bang of a big rifle and saw Onyschuk flop back into the body of the canoe, his left shoulder pad exploded into a pulpy mass of down and blood.

16

Instinct took over. I roared and grabbed my rifle, working the bolt to load a shell. Firing dead ahead over Onyschuk's twitching, clawing hands, I let off a round at the sloping rock on the water's edge. It ricocheted off, spinning up in an angry whine that scythed it through the trees, chopping down shreds of greenery. The shock brought the canoe almost to a dead halt but I fired again, a yard wide of the first bullet, putting another spinner up there where the sniper was hiding. Then I told Sam "Seek," and he jumped out, rocking the canoe so it almost tipped, but swimming for shore faster than I could make up ground with my flailing paddle.

I kept the rifle between my knees, my eyes sweeping over the trees above the sloping rock, looking for anything, a flash of red from a hunter's hat, a flicker of life, but nothing moved. It was possible I'd scared him off. Maybe he'd never taken fire before and had run, blowing his advantage. I dug for the shore, hurling the canoe through the water. Ahead of me Onyschuk lay and bled and groaned. I had to help him or he would die. But until I had stopped the sniper I would die first.

Sam reached the shore and as he scrambled out I shouted "Fight." He raced ahead up into the bush, barking, snarling. And over the laboring of my own breath I could hear the crashing of his progress, and of the man he was chasing.

I beached the canoe and leaped out, stopping only to grab up Onyschuk's Winchester as well as my own rifle. His had a leather sling and I slipped it over my shoulder as I ran after Sam into the bush.

I reached the edge of it and rolled into cover against a tree trunk, listening to Sam. He sounded to be forty or fifty yards ahead, among the trees. I could tell from the noise he was making that he had cornered somebody. And it sounded as if the somebody had dropped his weapon. I had Sam trained to terrify, then fall silent before he attacks. And he won't attack until he sees a weapon of some kind in the man's hands.

I moved up the way I would have advanced under fire in Nam, moving for three or four paces, rolling sideways, advancing. I didn't know how many attackers there were and I wasn't going to act confident because Sam had one of them up a tree.

It took me thirty seconds. As I rolled up against the trunk of a big hemlock I saw Sam holding his ground against another tree. A man was backed against it. I could see his hands held high and hear his fearful voice calling Sam a good boy, telling him "Easy." Sam ignored him, barking and snarling as if his dearest wish was to tear the man's throat out. I scrambled to my feet, looking all around. With my rifle trained on the man I moved around in front of him. Before I made it that far I found his gun, an old British Army Lee Enfield, the kind Misquadis had carried. It was lying on the ground with the bolt open. I put my foot on it and called out to Sam "Good dog," and he redoubled his barking. Then I took the final couple of steps that brought me in front of the man and I almost shot him. It was Carl Tettlinger.

"You murderous bastard." I raised the rifle and aimed it between his eyes and he whimpered and covered his face, sobbing like a child. For a moment I almost squeezed the trigger. I was a marine again, up against a killing enemy, but my police training took over. I told Sam "Easy," and he stopped barking. I patted his head while Tettlinger uncovered his eyes in the first dawning of hope. Then I told Sam "Seek,"

154

and pushed him off into the bush. He left and Tettlinger began to relax, the fearful stiffness going out of his arms. I looked at him and he dropped his eyes. His nose was still cased in a dirty plaster from the last time we had tangled. I got no pleasure from the sight.

"Take your boots off," I told him. He looked up at me and swallowed nervously, then did as I said. I waited, then told him, "Take the laces out and toss them to me."

He glanced at me again, but did it. I stood looking at him, with the laces at my feet, and whistled Sam. He bounded up and I told him "Easy." Then to Tettlinger I said, "On your face, hands behind you."

He turned nervously and lay flat on his face. He was craning around to see me over his shoulder so I brought Sam close to him on that side and instructed him "Keep." Sam looked into Tettlinger's eyes and snarled. Tettlinger pressed his nose straight down into the moss beneath him, I picked up his bootlaces. They were stout leather, thirty-six inches long. I used one of them to tie his thumbs together behind his back. I didn't overdo the tension. He didn't have to lose his thumbs. I just wanted him out of commission. Then with the other lace I tied his elbows together behind him. He was braced in two places, too stiff to move. But I still didn't trust him so I rolled him onto his back and took his belt away and unzipped his pants. Now he would have to shuffle, holding up the back of his pants with his fingers. I knew that would keep him from causing any more trouble.

"On your feet," I told him, and he looked at me fearfully and struggled to his knees, then upright. His pants slipped and he crouched to hold the back of them between his fingertips, glancing at me nervously, not sure what he expected me to say. "Make your way to the lake. And don't try to run or I'll send Sam after you for real. You haven't seen anything yet."

He licked his lips but didn't say anything and I turned away, scooping up the army rifle and bursting back through the bush to the shoreline where Onyschuk was lying in the canoe.

He was still conscious, trying to stem the bleeding with his right hand. I lifted him out of the canoe and laid him on the rock. "Don't move," I warned him and took out my clasp knife. His eyes widened in alarm but he said nothing and I cut away the shoulder of all the layers of his clothing.

The wound was bad. The round had hit about an inch and a half below the shoulder, smashing the collarbone. Bits of bone protruded on either side of the smashed flesh.

"You'll be fine," I said and tipped my backpack out onto the rock, scrambling through the contents for my field first aid kit. It had Mercurochome in it and a couple of big sterilized pads. I slapped the liquid on the wound and then applied the first pad. It didn't stop the bleeding so I put the other one over it. The blood seeped through again, more slowly now but insistently. I dug out my spare shirt, clean and pressed from the laundry at Murphy's Harbour. I opened it, not touching the inside, and folded it into a bigger pad that I laid over the others. This time the blood didn't penetrate and I quickly tied my triangular bandage over the pad and under his armpit.

Onyschuk looked at me and tried to speak, but the words didn't come. His eyes were blue and unclouded. Both irises were the same size so I guessed the hydrostatic shock hadn't reached his brain.

"I'll give you a shot of that snakebite medicine in a minute," I promised. "First, where's the radio?" He gestured feebly to the canoe and I looked in. His own pack was in the bottom and I pulled it out and tipped it carefully. The radio was a police-style walkie-talkie. I didn't think it would have the power we needed so I asked him, "What's the range?"

He whispered at first, then found a full voice, trembling and shocked, but clear. "Not sure. We just use them in town. Line of sight, I guess."

I checked the controls. "Is everything set for the frequency?"

He nodded, then lay back, putting his right hand over the pad and pressing gently. There were tears of pain in his eyes but he did not make any sound. I put the radio down and found both our sleeping bags and wrapped them around and under him. He made an attempt to speak but I patted his good arm and told him, "Save it, we'll have you out of here double-quick."

I left him, picked up the radio, and ran to the top of the rock. There I switched it on, gave it ten seconds, and started calling for help. "Mayday. Mayday. Mayday. Bennett at the lake. We have a casualty to be air-lifted out. Mayday. Mayday. Mayday."

There was a rustle of static but no answer. I looked around. There was nothing else to stand on. I switched the radio off and clambered up the nearest big tree. It was full of brushy branches at the lower level so I had to force my way up it. It tore at my combat jacket and scratched my hands and face but I didn't stop until I was high up, at the point where the tree could carry me no further without bending.

Below me I could hear Tettlinger blundering through the brush. I switched on the radio and called again, almost shouting into the radio. "Mayday. Mayday. Mayday. Bennett calling from the lake. Come in please?"

There was more crackling, but this time I could hear the calm voice of the operator at Olympia. "Come in, Bennett, we hear your Mayday."

"Constable Onyschuk shot. Need medical aid soonest. Re peat. Constable Onyschuk shot. Need medical aid soonest, over."

The girl was pro. "You're breaking up. Understand you need medical aid." Her voice faded and came back. "Notifying hospital and airfield. Location, please?"

I shouted down to Onyschuk. "What's the name of this lake?" With his voice full of pain, he called, "Tell them Turtle Lake. They'll know."

"Location Turtle Lake. Landed here an hour ago. West shore. Will light a fire, over."

Again the bush-fire crackle of static and then the voice. "No helicopter available, sending plane. Over."

"Message understood. Will light fire. West shore. Hurry. Out." I switched off and slipped the radio back into my pocket. It was on my mind that I had left the rifles loaded at the base of the tree. I didn't think Tettlinger could handle one but I took the precaution anyway. I shouted to Sam "Fight," and heard his instant snarl and Tettlinger's frightened yelp.

Good. He was helpless. I took a moment then to look around and check what I could see of the lake. There were no canoes or boats anywhere and I couldn't see any of my immediate surroundings for the trees, but I had a clear view of the island with its sloping rock surface where we had landed the day before and its one prominent rock standing out like a miniature Gibraltar. Then I started down, slipping and sliding down the trunk.

Tettlinger was on the water's edge, half a step from falling back and drowning, looking fearfully over his shoulder at the water, then back at Sam who was slavering and snarling six inches from his knees. I called Sam off and he came over to me, wagging his tail. I patted him and told him "Good boy," then called to Tettlinger "Sit down"—and he did, almost in the water.

I went back to Onyschuk. His eyes were closed and his teeth clenched against the pain. I knew how he felt. My last wound in Nam had gone through the bone in my forearm. Bone pain hurts worse than any other. "Hey, Mike."

He opened his eyes. "I got through. Help's on the way. Be here in half an hour, tops."

He tried to grin. "Bullshit," he said softly.

"Sooner, likely. They're just picking up the nurse from the hospital. That Gloria."

"My wife'll kill me," he said, and closed his eyes again.

I left him and pulled together some dry wood, then found a birch and ripped off a piece of the white bark. I stuck it under the sticks and lit it with matches from the waterproof tobacco tin I carry everywhere in my combat jacket. It flared and smoked with that rich dark smoke and the intense heat that makes firelighting so easy in the bush. Within thirty seconds I had the twigs going and was feeding in bigger pieces.

I went to my tipped belongings and picked up the pot and filled it from the lake. Then I found a couple of stones and set them among the flames and set the pot on it. "Coffee's on," I told him, and he groaned again.

"You said you'd give me a drink."

"Not yet. It's bad for growing boys," I kidded, and he groaned again. I took no notice. I had aspirin in my first aid kit and I gave him two with a sip of water, knowing they would do him more good than whisky. It's only in old Westerns that they give you raw hooch. It's lousy for you when you're in shock.

While the water boiled I found more sticks, hacking them off deadfalls with my knife and piling them beside the fire. Then I told Sam "Seek," and he whisked away into the brush again, keeping us safe from other intruders.

When the water boiled I made coffee from the tin of mixed coffee, powered milk, and sugar in my pack, then found a mug.

"Where're you hiding the rye?" I asked Onyschuk.

It took him a half minute to reply, then he reached down to his side pocket, under the sleeping bags. I did it for him, pulling out a mickey of cheap rye with one of those deep caps you can use as a shot glass. I measured out one shot and put it in the coffee, then sealed the bottle and set it aside. "See, I do so keep my promises," I told him.

When it had cooled enough to drink I fed the coffee to Onyschuk a sip at a time, supporting him against my knee as I crouched beside him. He didn't want to drink it. He wanted to lie down and think about his pain but I kept him at it

159

until he had taken it all. Then I laid him down again with his pack as a pillow and covered him up warm.

Tettlinger was watching every move and now I went over and stood above him. He didn't look up so I prodded him gently with my toe. "Look at me, I want to talk to you."

He looked up, craning his neck high, staring into the sun that was playing tag among a flock of woolly cumulous clouds. "Okay. Now there's just the two of us here. You're not under arrest. You're still on the run in the bush. Understand?"

He didn't, so I spelled it out for him. "I'm not a policeman in this locality. I'm a citizen who's been shot at. I'm going to ask you some questions." I kept my voice even and reasonable and he relaxed a fraction. I smiled at him, a big friendly smile, and added the fear element. "You have the right to remain silent. But I also have the right to bring my dog back to tear your guts open. I want you to think about that. Your hands are tied behind you so you couldn't do a thing except scream."

"You wouldn' do that?" His voice ran up in a frightened whine. I looked down at him and smiled again.

"With real pleasure. You're already going in for attempted murder of a peace officer. Nobody's going to grieve if you just didn't come back in one piece."

He swallowed. "It was an accident. You never gave me a chance to explain. I was shootin' at a deer f' crissakes an' your buddy was in the way. I'm sorry."

"You will get a lot sorrier," I promised. "Now tell me what I want to know. Who set you up to shoot us?"

He made the obvious noises. "I dunno what you're talkin' about. It was an accident."

I reached down and grabbed him by the hair. "On your feet," I said, and yanked. He groaned and came up, all the way up, two inches anyway taller than I am. He had lost his hold on the back of his pants and he was standing in his long underwear with the green work pants puddled over his high boots. Without turning I whistled for Sam. Tettlinger's eyes widened with horror and he tried to duck for his pants but I held his head and he gave up instantly.

Sam came loping out of the bush and I summoned him over and patted him. "Good boy. Ready for a feed?"

Tettlinger licked his lips and said nothing. I smiled again and said, "Now, I've heard all the crap I'm gonna take from you. Who sent you to shoot us?"

The words poured out of him. "I don't know his name. It was some Frog. I never even saw him. I just got the message."

"By radio?" It was starting to make sense. Tettlinger was already in the bush. Laval hadn't needed to fly in and shoot Prudhomme, he had simply delegated.

"Yeah. By radio."

"And where were you when this happened?" I knew the answer before he told me. He had entered the country the same way the Indians had always traveled it, by canoe, up Trout River.

"I was in camp, up the river, across the other end of the portage."

I switched my line of questioning. I needed to know where the portage was, otherwise I'd spend the whole day covering those four or five klicks to the river. "Where is it?"

He nodded behind him. "Up the shore a piece, maybe a quarter mile."

"Okay. So what was the message?"

Again the words poured out, fearfully. "It was all in a code. The guy told me to net the salmon."

"So he had set this up. You were in the bush waiting for a signal to kill me, right?"

He lowered his head. "Is that right?" I repeated, and he looked up again, his eyes brilliant with hatred. "If that god-damn gun didn't fire low and left you'd be a dead man."

"Where'd you get the gun?" I'd saved this one, because I didn't really want to know the truth. I respected Misquadis too much.

"Bought it offa Jack Misquadis for a jug."

"He doesn't drink," I said. "And if he did he wouldn't sell his gun. He was up here looking for a bear. You can't catch them in a leg-hold trap."

"He sold it to me." Tettlinger repeated it with the despair that told me he was lying. "Lousy piece a' junk. Jammed first round."

"And where is he now?"

"Back up the portage, pissed, I guess. You know what Indians are like, eh?" He flashed me a quick grin but swallowed it when he saw my expression.

"Now, here's the hard part. Why did you murder Jim Prudhomme?" I asked the question quietly and he looked at me in genuine surprise.

"How d'you mean?" I said nothing and he rushed on, anxious to please, aware of his vulnerability. "Ain' he the guy got mauled by a bear here, few weeks back?"

"That was a ringer. I found Prudhomme's body in this lake yesterday," I said, and Tettlinger's mouth gaped.

"He's dead," he protested stupidly. I stared at him and he shifted his eyes and said, "He's dead, eh? They had the inquest in town. His buddy from Montreal was there, identified him."

He stopped speaking and I heard the buzz of a plane approaching, coming up out of the sun from the south. I told Sam "Easy." Then I beckoned to Tettlinger. "Come up on the shore and sit down. And pull your pants up."

He stooped and found the back of his pants, then shuffled onto the shore and sat facing the water. I went to Onyschuk and unwound my sleeping bag from him. It's a bush bag, waterproof green on the outside but bright orange in the lining. I shook it out and stood at the water's edge waving the orange side toward the aircraft.

It waggled its wings and made a straight, sweet descent, kicking up a white plume of spray, then settling onto its floats with a gentle rocking motion. It was a four-seater, a pleasure plane, not the flying ambulance I wanted for Onyschuk. I swore, then shrugged. It would lift him out somehow.

It taxied in and I saw there were three people aboard. In the copilot's seat was Gallagher. I waved to them, indicating a path to the rock where I was standing. The last thing we needed now was a float puncturing on one of the rocks in the shallows. The pilot crept in with his engine barely ticking over, then cut it and bobbed up to the shoreline.

Gallagher jumped down into six inches of water and splashed up the beach. He saw Tettlinger and asked, "He do it?" but rushed by to where Onyschuk lay.

I followed him. He was stooping over the wounded man, talking to him urgently. "Mike. Mike. You okay?"

Onyschuk opened his eyes and nodded "Yeah," then closed them again. Gallagher turned and bellowed over his shoulder at the big nurse from the hospital who was wading through the shallows, carrying a bag. Millie was wearing a parka over her uniform and the crisp white skirt stuck out beneath it incongruously.

She ran up the rock, opening the bag as she came. "Where's he hit?" she asked me angrily, as if it were my fault he was lying there.

"Compound fracture of the shoulder. I put Mercurochrome on it and stopped the bleeding. It's a bullet wound."

She pulled out a syringe and a little bottle. "Okay, Mike. I'm going to give you a needle for the pain. Then we'll get you back home and fix you up properly."

Onyschuk was at the end of his strength. He blinked slowly and said, "Good." She took out a pair of scissors and made a quick cut in the sleeve of his good arm, exposing the shoulder.

"The chief's going to owe you a new parka," she said as she swabbed the flesh and pushed the needle home. He didn't even wince.

Gallagher straightened up. "Let's get him in the plane."

We lifted him gently, and he groaned. "I can walk," he protested.

"Yeah, sure, son. An' I can fly," Gallagher said. "Don't take any weight, we got you." We supported him between us, out through the chilly water, knee-deep into the aircraft. The rock under our feet was slippery and we inched along until Gallagher could reach the float with his right hand and haul the plane around with a slow pull that had the power of an ox in it. I stood until the float reached me, then grabbed it with my left hand and helped Onyschuk up into the hands of the pilot. He pulled him into the seat behind him and strapped him in. Onyschuk groaned once as the pilot fastened the shoulder straps tight over his wound, then bit his lip and sat silent, head lolling forward.

"Pull," Gallagher instructed me, and we heaved the aircraft sideways until the float was resting on the rock. "Good. Let's get that other bastard," he said, and we sloshed up to Tettlinger.

Gallagher unsnapped the handcuffs from their pouch on his Sam Browne and spun Tettlinger around. He saw my lashing job and laughed. "Hell, you don't need cuffs, do you?"

"Cuff him and leave the other ties in place," I said. "He's a murderous swine. I want him nailed down."

"Me too," Gallagher said. He pulled outward on Tettlinger's arms, making him double up and his pants slip down. He didn't comment, just clicked the cuffs over his wrists and pulled him straight again. "If you can't reach your pants to pull 'em up, kick 'em off," he said, and Tettlinger squatted and felt with his fingers for the back of his trousers again. He straightened up and Gallagher steered him to the plane, handling him gently. He shoved him up and the pilot strapped him in. I heard Tettlinger swear.

"Ignore him," Gallagher told the pilot. "My policeman has a gun in his holster, right side. Take it out."

The pilot did and handed it to Gallagher. He turned and

gave it to the nurse. "Here you are, Millie," he said. "If he makes a move, shoot him."

He winked at her, but she didn't acknowledge it. "Right, Chief," she said. "What are you going to do?"

He laughed. "Me? I'm going hunting with young Reid, here," he said.

17

We helped Millie into the plane and handed her the medical bag. She took it, plumped the gun inside it, and set it down between her big, practical shoes. The pilot leaned past her. He was dressed in a business suit with a leather jacket over the top of it. I guessed he was an amateur Gallagher had press-ganged.

"Any instructions, Chief?"

"Yeah. Sergeant Jackaman will be waiting at the dock. Tell him to put Tettlinger in the cells and keep him there. Hold off on a bail hearing until I get back."

The pilot nodded. "What about you guys?"

"Arrange for the chopper to come for us tonight if he can, with a couple of my men to help in the search. We'll see him on the river where the portage comes out—that's due west of here. If nobody can make it tonight, tell 'em first light tomorrow. And one last thing, tell Jackaman to take care of this. Don't touch it except to take prints." He laid the Lee Enfield rifle across the feet of the two men in the backseat, holding it carefully in his handkerchief. I noticed he set the butt end over Onyschuk's feet. That was the part that would be printed, the end Tettlinger might work to wipe with his feet as he flew.

The pilot nodded. "Will do. Now if you'll shove me off and point me offshore, I'll go."

Gallagher nodded and shut the door. Then we both leaned against the fuselage until the float was clear of the rock and the aircraft was pointing toward the island. The pilot started the engine in a crackle of sound and a blast of the slipstream that made us turn away with watering eyes. He moved majestically out into the open channel and turned north, into the light wind. We watched until he lifted off, turning as he climbed to head south again, down to Olympia.

I stooped then and began repacking my backback. Gallagher followed me, shoving Onyschuk's gear back into his bag. As we worked he asked me, "What happened?"

I filled him in and he said, "That'll be his defense for sure, accidental discharge of the weapon."

"It won't stick," I promised. "He's going inside for a long stretch."

"Hopefully until I'm through with this job," Gallagher said. He pulled the drawstring on Onyschuk's bag. "I figure we'll leave this here. You can't carry a thing like this and a gun and a canoe."

"You figure to take the canoe over the portage?"

"We'll be stuck without it if the chopper doesn't get in. Otherwise we could make it back to the highway in two days."

I nodded. "Okay. I guess I put more faith in choppers than most people. I'm just leery about having one of us looking like a turtle if there's anyone else with Tettlinger and he stands off to drill us."

Gallagher took the bag and dropped it in the canoe. "With your dog along he won't get the chance," he promised. "I've covered the portage before. There's nowhere for him to get a clear shot. He'd have to be close up and Sam would flush him out."

"Okay, let's do it." I whistled Sam back from the bush and set him in the canoe. Then we launched it, stern first, and swung it parallel to the shore. "You take the bow," I told Gallagher. "I want to be where I can see Sam."

He clambered in, bearlike in his heavy parka, and took up the paddle at that end. Then I did the same and we pushed off.

"It's up the shore," he said over his shoulder. "Let's stick close in, 'case any other bastard is around."

We stayed in the shallows, only a canoe-length from the shore where Sam could sniff the wind. He sat up, rigid except for the swings of his handsome head as he tasted the air. But he got no scents and in a couple of minutes we beached the canoe on a tiny patch of sand where somebody had tied a piece of geologist's orange marking tape around a tree trunk.

We prepared carefully for the portage. While I kept watch, Gallagher lashed the paddles inside the canoe. Next he hung Onyschuk's backpack from the branch of a tree.

I reloaded my rifle, putting an extra round up the spout this time. Then Gallagher slung Onyschuk's Winchester over his shoulder, muzzle down, and crouched so I could turn the canoe and lift it onto his back.

I slung my own pack on my back and told Sam "Seek," and we advanced up the narrow trail someone had slashed through the brush. I held my rifle at the ready but I knew that Gallagher was right. Sam would flush any ambusher out before he could aim at us. I concentrated on listening and checking the trail itself as well as looking for anybody who might be hiding there.

The woods were quiet, except for the occasional clank of the canoe and Gallagher's snorting breathing. An aluminum canoe weighs around seventy pounds, and it's awkward to carry. It was a solid load for a man in his late fifties, but Gallagher didn't falter.

When we'd walked for fifteen minutes I stopped and spoke to him, softly. "You want to change?"

He canted the canoe prow up so he could look at me. "No,

I'd rather you walked point, I haven't had to for thirty years. But I'd like a breather."

We set the canoe down and he straightened and arched his back gratefully. "You gotta remember, I'm closer to shuffleboard age than humpin' canoes up mountains."

"It's flat here," I reminded him, and he humphed. "That's what you think," he said.

We waited ten minutes, while Sam ranged ahead, then Gallagher said, "When we get another twenty minutes, let's dump our loads and go on to the river and scout around. Any camp'll be this side for sure, on the portage. Okay?"

"Right. I'll call Sam close so he won't warn anybody off."

Gallagher nodded. "If there's anyone still up there they'll have heard the activity in the air, so we won't be much of a surprise. But it wouldn't hurt to sneak a little."

I let Sam run ahead for another ten minutes, then whistled him back and let him lead us, only a few yards ahead. The bush was still dense. Nobody could have taken a long shot at us and I knew that Sam would give me notice of anybody close in.

Gallagher was tiring. Twice in as many minutes he shifted the weight of the canoe on his shoulders, setting up a hollow echoing clank that seemed to ring like a bell through the silent bush.

I felt for him. This was work. But at least we could be glad it was cool and there were no flies. In spring the blackflies would have been so thick we couldn't have breathed without swallowing them. Gallagher would have been in misery by now.

I checked my watch. We had walked twenty minutes so I stopped, and when Gallagher saw my feet under the rim of his burden he said "Good" and crouched so I could lift the canoe off his back. We set it aside, leaving so little room on the trail that we had to push branches out of the way as we moved ahead of it in Indian file.

I heard Gallagher work the action of the Winchester, the classic k-clack that every John Wayne Western fan would recognize in the dark. I kept Sam almost at my feet, sniffing and probing the air as we moved on, silently now. Ahead I could hear the muffled rush of rapids on the river. It's the same sound you get from a highway—even, ceaseless. It grew louder as we approached, and suddenly we were on the edge of a clearing against the river's edge, just downstream of the rapids, the last possible spot to pull out a canoe before you headed into white water.

I kept Sam with me as I scanned the clearing and as much of the far shore as I could see. It took a moment to notice the drab green tarpaulin strung like an open-ended tent between two trees on the edge of the clearing. I turned and beckoned to Gallagher. He came up beside me and I pointed to the tent.

"That'll be Tettlinger's," he whispered. "Misquadis wouldn't bother with a shelter on a short trip."

"Then some other guy could be around," I whispered back, "Stay here, I'll check it out." I urged Sam forward, silently, and moved ahead around the edge of the open space, checking constantly as I walked. There was nothing in the clearing itself to hide a man, but he could be back in the trees a short way, or across the river, where Sam would not be so likely to scent him.

I watched Sam and suddenly his muzzle lifted and his neck began to bristle. He'd picked up a heavy scent. I touched him on the back and he remained silent as we covered the last fifteen paces. Then I dropped to one knee, rifle covering the interior of the shelter while Sam hurled himself into it.

He worked all through the space, head down, sniffing at something I couldn't identify at first. Then I realized it was a sleeping bag, probably Tettlinger's.

I told Sam "Easy," and he backed off while I searched the shelter. There was only one bag and one set of utensils. I turned to Gallagher who was coming out of the bush behind me. "Looks like Tettlinger was on his own."

"Good," he said. "Last thing we need is some other bastard sniping at us from the bush."

18

Finding Tettlinger's camp had taken the pressure off. The terrain became ordinary bush once more, instead of hostile territory. We sat and talked and rested, like soldiers after a dangerous patrol.

"It's beginning to look systematic," I said. "First of all Prudhomme kills some guy. Then we find him killed in turn. Then we find Tettlinger up here, skulking around shooting at policemen. This isn't random killing, there's a pattern to it, if only we could see it."

I waited, but Gallagher said nothing. He held up one hand, then began to dig into the pocket of his parka. He came out with a pack of Export cigarettes and a book of restaurant matches. Almost sensually he pushed his chewing gum out of his mouth with his tongue. He took out a cigarette and lit it, holding up his head as he inhaled, like a priest elevating the Host at mass. "First in two days," he said, as he breathed out a column of smoke.

"When you're through with your orgasm, I was talking about the case," I said.

He took a quicker, more practiced drag, coughing and recovering. "Yeah, I'm still with you. You're wondering why people are getting murdered left and right." He scowled at me and coughed again. "It hadn't slipped my notice, you know."

"So what's your theory? Here we've had a killing and an attempted murder of a pair of coppers in a couple of days. That's premeditated. My question is, What's behind it all?"

Gallagher nodded patiently. "The obvious answer is money. My guess is, it's about those gold claims we talked about. I mean, if Prudhomme was a shareholder and now he's dead, that's a bigger piece of pie for the rest of the guys, right?"

I nodded. "That makes the most sense yet. I think that the lawyer, Laval, has Mob connections. It must have been him who set me up in Montreal—then torched the dentist. That smells like organized crime to me. So they could be involved here. Now if your buddy McKenzie was right, we're talking big money, maybe billions of honest, legal dollars. All they have to do is eliminate anybody who can connect them with the finding of the mine."

Gallagher exhaled smoke, coughed quickly, and recovered. "Those bastards would kill a guy for a thousand dollars. For the kind of money we're thinking about, they'd wipe out the whole of Olympia."

"Right. That's my reading. I guess they used Tettlinger early on to provide some muscle. Now they got him involved, to kill Prudhomme. Next step is to kill the pair of them."

Gallagher nodded. We stared at one another blindly for a moment and I went on, "I'm wondering how much more we can accomplish up here. I think we'd be better off in town, talking to Tettlinger."

"We can't get back before nightfall," Gallagher said. He was still holding his dead match. Now he folded it between finger and thumb to be sure it was completely out, and dropped it. He finished his smoke before continuing. Then he lifted his boot sole and ground out the butt completely dead before tossing it aside. "I figure we should spend our time up here looking for Misquadis. That was his rifle Tettlinger was using and I figure he wouldn't have parted with that without a struggle. Maybe he's in trouble."

"Right. But let's eat first, we may not get another chance all day. I'll go get the canoe. Why don't you get a fire going?"

"Good idea," Gallagher said. "I'm amazed you thought of it yourself." He turned to find some firewood while I took Sam and went back for the canoe and my pack.

I came back and opened a can of corned beef and put some rice on to boil. I fried up the beef, saving a corner for Sam even though I'd fed him before we came into the bush. When the rice and meat were cooked, I mixed them together and divided them, giving Gallagher the plate and taking my own food straight from the pan. We washed it all down with water from the river and a short taste of Onyschuk's rye. I wished he had bought Black Velvet, but the quick snort gave us fresh heart and after I'd scoured out the pan and plate we repacked and made our plans for the rest of the day.

"I'd like to talk to Misquadis," Gallagher said. "Or at least make sure that bastard didn't kill him."

"Me too. 'D'you think he'd have crossed the river and baited for bear somewhere?"

Gallagher nodded. He was sharpening a twig to make a toothpick and he finished and started probing before he answered. "That's what he was up here for. I'd guess he'd want to kill one close to the river, it's less distance to lug the pelt."

"You don't think he'd go into the bush near the lake back there? Then he could drop the meat on the island and everyone would believe he'd caught the one the bounty was on."

"Nah." Gallagher sucked his teeth and threw the toothpick into the fire. "No need to bullshit people. Nobody's coming up here till spring now. The wolves and foxes would eat the carcass, wherever it was left, drag the bones off somewheres, no need for that kind of trick."

"Well, we know he's not this side of the river, not close,

anyway, or Sam would have flushed him out. I figure we should cross and see if San can find him," I said, and Gallagher stood up and stretched.

"May's well. The chopper won't be here for a while yet." He stooped and picked up the pot and went down to the river for water to drown the fire.

While he went back and forth until the fire was dead out, I unlashed the paddles from the canoe and got ready to launch. Then we loaded Sam in and pushed off into the current.

The river was only fifty yards across and we were over in a minute, grounding our canoe at the base of a big spruce on the edge of a flat rock. We lifted the canoe out and tied it to the tree, making sure it was visible from the clearing opposite, in case the chopper came while we were out of sight.

The bush was dense, with no sign that anybody had ever been into it. North of Superior it's all like this, not like the semicivilized bush of the provincial parks farther south, with their wide portages and campsites maintained by park staff.

Gallagher said, "I didn't bring my compass. You got one with you?"

"Yeah. I figured I'd be in the bush," I said, "so I came equipped." I took it out and checked. The river ran southwest, but aside from that I couldn't see deep enough into the bush to pick out a landmark we could march on. "I figure Misquadis wouldn't go far without picking up a deer trail or something. He'd do all his trapping close to the river."

Gallagher fed himself a piece of gum, his last, then crumpled the pack and stuffed it into the pocket of his parka. "I figure that, too. I think we should send Sam in, see what he finds. No sense draggin' our asses through this for no reason."

I nodded and spoke to Sam, holding his big head between my hands and fussing him a moment, then telling him "Seek."

He faded into the bush, nose to the ground, and we sat on the upturned canoe and waited.

"If he was after bear, he'd likely hang up something dead

from a tree on the riverbank, then watch from the other bank until the bear came for it," Gallagher said.

"Right, and he'd wait downwind, which means the bait would most likely be on the other bank and he'd be this side."

We looked at one another and nodded like a couple of guys in a bar agreeing that the Toronto Maple Leafs needed more muscle on defense, and waited for Sam to come up with our answers for us.

It took him twenty minutes. We had both been sniffing the air, trying to pick up any scent of decay from Misquadis's bait, but had smelled nothing. Meanwhile, Sam had gone a quarter-mile circle around us and was sounding off at the end of our hearing range.

"Sounds close to the river, down there," Gallagher said. "Let's take the canoe."

We relaunched and set off with the current. This time Gallagher took the stern while I watched the bank, rifle at the ready. He knew what to do. If I raised the gun he would back the canoe so I could shoot over the bow and not tip us into the cold water. I didn't think it would happen, but so much was going on that I wouldn't have felt safe without the precaution.

We followed Sam's bark for three minutes by water, paddling silently as the sound grew louder and louder. Then, suddenly, as we came almost up to him, I caught the scent of something dead.

When I got the first whiff I turned upwind and saw a porcupine hanging by its tail from a tree on the far bank, its guts hanging down from the slashed abdomen. I pointed and Gallagher nodded and headed closer to the near bank where Sam was waiting for us, barking restlessly, bringing us to the sight I had hoped not to see. It was Jack Misquadis, lying at the water's edge, and he was dead.

We beached the canoe, running it right up the bank. Then I told Sam "Easy," and we crouched over the body. It was still dressed in the same blue jeans and denim jacket he had been wearing when I met him. There was no obvious injury, but an empty rye bottle lay beside the body.

"I thought he didn't drink," I said.

"He didn't." Gallagher was checking the head for marks. "See this, he's been hit." I knelt and checked. There was a bruise over the ear.

"It didn't kill him outright or it wouldn't have swollen," I argued.

Gallagher knelt closer, sniffing around the dead mouth. Then he got to his feet and his dark eyes were blazing with anger. "You're right. What's happened is, somebody cold-cocked him with the bottle, then poured it down his throat. He was out and couldn't do anything so he got drunk and drowned in his own vomit."

"That's a lousy way for a nice guy to die," I said. I was filled with a cold anger for the man who had done this. It figured to have been Carl Tettlinger. I could imagine him laughing as Misquadis thrashed and kicked and gagged, try-to live. "Have we got enough on Tettlinger to charge him with this?"

"I think we do," Gallagher said. "We caught the sonofa-bitch with Jack's rifle. How much more do you need?"

"Yeah, he told me he'd bought it off Jack for a jug of rye. That sounds like a setup for finding Jack like this," I agreed. "And yet, I'm not convinced. Tettlinger's mean enough to do this, but he's not motivated. I figure it must be Mob people, maybe that guy I saw at the motel."

Gallagher nodded. "You're right. People don't just knock one another off like this unless there's big money at stake. What I'll do is get onto the claims office first thing Monday. That's where we're going to find the really important answers." He sniffed. "But for now, let's do a little police work, check this murder scene out like it was the first one we'd come across in a while, instead of the third."

We did the best we could without equipment. Gallagher

checked the dead man's gear, a kit bag tied with a strip of raw-hide. He had no pelts, it was too early in the season. They don't get valuable until the winter fur grows in.

Meanwhile, I searched the surrounding area. It was a mechanical, almost a meaningless thing to do in this case, with a prime suspect already in custody, but it yielded one thing.

I looked up from the ground and called Gallagher. "Hey, I've found a footprint."

He stood up and came over, planting his feet carefully as I indicated the space to avoid. "If it's a size fourteen work boot, it's Tettlinger," he said.

"No, this one is a lot smaller, smaller than mine, maybe a size ten at most." I pointed at the indentation in the scuffed surface soil where the mat of dead vegetation had been taken aside by some animal or by a careless foot. "Look. Give me your notebook a minute."

He passed me his book and a pencil. I measured the length and the width of the heel, using the line spacing on the page as a scale. Then I sketched the heel pattern as well as I could. "Any chance your guys will bring an investigation kit when they turn up this evening?"

"Not sure. Jackaman's a pretty dead-ahead guy. He'll make sure the men are ready for the bush, but I doubt he'll remember to send anything subtle."

I finished my drawing of the heel, then marked it "Sketch of heel print found at site of Jack Misquadis's death," added the date and my signature, and handed the book back to Gallagher.

He looked at the sketch. "It's about the size of Prud-homme's boots. Could it've been him?"

"His heel pattern was different," I reminded him. "He had those thick, thick soles, the kind of boots geologists all wear in the bush. Heavier and fancier than a worker would buy."

We built a little cairn of rocks around the heel print, saving it in case we could get a cast later, then went over the whole area again, twice more, pushing back as far as we could easily get into the bush, but we found nothing. We decided that whoever had killed Misquadis had come by water, not through the bush. And that made us stop and do some reckoning.

"Where's the canoe?" Gallagher wondered. "Tettlinger came into the bush by canoe. Misquadis came in by canoe. Now we think there was another man. He must've come in by canoe. Only there's no canoe here. There's just the one you found with Prudhomme's body."

"That could mean the murderer is heading downriver in one canoe, maybe pulling the other with him," I said. "If we could get in touch with the station we could search the river by air. We could catch the bastard."

"I've got Onyschuk's radio. It worked before," Gallagher said. "You want to try again?"

"Not a lot, but it's the only hope, I guess." I climbed the handiest tall tree and called for ten minutes. Nobody replied so I gave up on talking. Instead I pressed the transmit button three times quickly, then waited, then did it again. I wasn't sure how good their equipment was at Olympia, but if they got the signal they might realize we had a problem and dispatch the chopper that much sooner. I kept it up for half an hour, but nothing happened so I gave up and climbed back down the tree.

In fact, it was four P.M. by the time Kinsella showed in the clearing where we were waiting. He was packed with help, carrying two well-equipped uniformed policemen. I stood back and watched while Gallagher took charge. He dispatched Kinsella to drop the men downstream, checking all the way to the Trans-Canada Highway bridge first, then back to leave the policemen upstream where any escaper would have to pass on his way to the highway and freedom.

That took thirty minutes. In that time, Gallagher and I recovered Misquadis's body from the other bank and wrapped it in a blanket, then waited for Kinsella to return.

He touched down at the edge of the clearing, the slipstream

fanning everything loose across the ground and into the trees behind us. I was glad we hadn't lit a fire. It would have burned the woods down.

Kinsella stopped the rotors and stepped down into the thickening darkness. "A stiff." He whistled. "This is gonna be one hell of a lift. I think I should come back for at least one of you."

"I'll wait. Can you make it tonight?" I asked.

"I don't like night landings. But if you take three lights and set them out in a safe triangle, I'll try it."

"Right. I'd like Sam to go out on the first load, in case you can't land and we have to winch up."

Kinsella nodded. "Good idea. I'll come back in the other machine, with the winch. D'you have three lights?"

"I've got a couple, mine and the chief's. If I can't get another, I'll line them up north and south where it's safe to set down between. That be okay?"

"Three's better," he said, then grinned. "But I've landed with less." He turned away to supervise the stowing of the body in the rear compartment. It was stiffening, and finally we had to stand it in like a board behind the front seat. Gallagher and I worked on it, sweating with the effort. When we had finished it was almost dark, and I saw Gallagher whisk his cap off and sketch a quick cross over his chest. It surprised me. I hadn't figured him for a religious man.

I handed Sam over to Gallagher and he put him behind the body, under strict command, in the backseat. Then Gallagher got in the front and they lifted off, leaving me with my two flashlights and my rifle. I turned the lights off and went to sit quietly against a tree on the edge of the clearing. I figured it would take an hour for the chopper to return, and I wondered whether the man who had killed Misquadis was going to come drifting out of the bush to check whether we had left anything behind. Sam hadn't checked this side of the river for three hours now; someone could have filtered back close to the area without being detected.

I've done a lot of waiting in my time. This was like Nam, only colder. I sat on my pack, the tree sheltering my back, my rifle across my knees, the big flashlight at my feet turned face down into the dirt so the luminous afterglow wouldn't show. Nothing stirred. Far off I heard an owl huffing away, but nothing was moving on the floor of the bush. I began to relax. Whoever had killed Misquadis was gone, down the stream and out to the highway. I was alone and safe.

As my eyes grew accustomed to the darkness I could see the ring of treetops in the gloom, black against the medium gray of the moonless and cloudy sky. After a while I began to hear the small sounds of the bush, the ones you don't hear when you're with other people, listening to words instead of the wild. The steady rush of the rapids faded into the back of my consciousness, like the noise of a car when you're driving a long distance. Over it I began to hear the tiny rustlings of mice and the slow, scuffly dragging of a porcupine somewhere close, probably heading for the spot where the men who had camped here had urinated, craving for the salt. But there were no snapping twigs, no coughs or groans, nothing to indicate that there was another man anywhere in the woods.

From time to time the clouds parted far enough for me to see the stars. I had picked out the Big Dipper and the polestar when I sat down and I judged the passage of time by the slow rotation of the Dipper. It also showed me where north lay and when I heard the whup-whup-whup of the chopper's return I set down the first light, then shut my eyes to protect my night vision, switched the light on, and paced twelve paces north before setting down the second light and switching it on. Then, with my eyes raised away from the light, I stepped out to the river's edge and crouched to wait for the chopper.

I felt the same kind of tingling anticipation I used to know in Nam. I knew this wasn't the same. Tonight it was just transportation, a ride back to the place where a long night of work would start. But there was something about that sound that stirred responses I had thought were buried. Without conscious thought I clicked off the safety catch on my rifle. I was ready for anything.

It seemed to me that the sound hesitated somewhere down-river. The slow, steady Doppler effect of the approach lagged for a moment. I wondered whether Kinsella had seen something on the ground, some natural luminescence that had made him think he was on target. I waited with mounting tension, not knowing why I felt so strained. And then the chopper ambled into my section of sky and hovered, about eighty feet up, well above the treetops.

I went to the flashlights and picked one of them up, using it as a signal, flapping the light down to the ground, then waist high, then down again, calling him down. The down-draft was washing all around me, kicking up all the debris that had been loosened in the earlier arrivals. I clenched my eyes shut and listened until I could hear the changed beat on the blades and feel the slipstream intensifying as he let down, almost on top of me.

I set the light down and moved to one side, kneeling, automatically facing away from the chopper as it descended, my rifle at the ready. I could have laughed out loud at myself except that instincts stronger than laughter had taken hold of me. I was alone on patrol and the night fears that I had kept off while I was alone were rushing in to haunt me.

Behind me something clattered on the ground. I turned and saw it, the rescue collar, lowered from the chopper. Kinsella wasn't coming all the way down. I wondered why he didn't put his lights on and come down, but guessed he was fighting his own personal demons. I hung one strap of my pack over my head so the load hung in front of me, out of the way, then slipped the collar over my head, put my arms through it, and tugged the loose section three times.

At once it started to crank in and I rose from the ground,

swinging like a kid's puppet. And as I climbed, by inches it seemed, a light shone from the edge of the clearing, playing on my swinging body.

My instincts saved me. Without thinking I fired, in front of the light and low, but close enough to scare whoever was holding it so that his answering shot just missed me, thumping harmlessly into the backpack as I swung sideways to his line of fire under the recoil force of my rifle. Then my shoulder bumped the edge of the skid and I hooked one leg over it and banged on the plastic side of the chopper with the muzzle of my rifle.

Kinsella got the message. He stood the machine on its side and howled away, over the trees, out of sight of the man in the clearing. I fired again as he flew, just banging away to make noise and keep the guy's head down, two more shots, then slung the rifle and clambered into the open door, pulling it shut behind me.

Kinsella's face was stretched by the light from his instruments. He looked impossibly Irish. I couldn't tell whether he was horrified or laughing.

"Sonofabitch," he shouted. "I thought we left all that bullshit behind us in Nam."

19

I shrugged off the harness and my pack, dropping them on the coil of rope that lay in the backseat, then strapped myself in and sat very still, staring blankly ahead, clutching my rifle with the same kind of superstitious force I had hugged my M16 in an earlier day. It had saved my life—it, and my own Marine's instincts. I had been as good as dead. If the guy on the ground hadn't flashed his light to be sure of my position, if I hadn't fired so quickly, if Kinsella hadn't acted like a trained combat pilot—if, if, if.

Kinsella called Olympia tower and told them he was taking me direct to the police station, to let Gallagher know. They rogered and he spoke to me for the first time since I'd settled in. "Who the hell was that?"

"Answer that one and we've got this case bagged," I told him. I was still jumpy. I haven't been shot at so many times in a day since I came back to Canada after the war. I was shaken.

Kinsella took his left hand off the controls and patted his side pocket, coming up with a heavy pewter flask. He handed it to me and said, "Take a taste of this."

I did. It was good Irish Whisky and I filled my mouth and swallowed slowly, taking it in like fresh confidence. Then I held it out to him, but he shook his head. "Not yet. When I'm down I'll finish it for you."

He came in high over Olympia and followed the main road down from the Trans-Canada to the police station. Gallagher had closed off a section of the street, setting two flashing police cars at each end of a fifty-yard stretch. It was well lit and clear and Kinsella set me down gently as an egg in the center of it.

I unsnapped my harness and reached over to shake his hand. "Thanks for moving so fast, Paul, it's all that saved me."

He laughed, the high, hectic laughter of a man who has been badly scared. "What's this 'me, paleface'? I figured it was my ass I was saving."

I ducked out, bending back in to pick up my pack, then pushed the door shut. He took off at once and headed back to the motel where he housed his bird.

Gallagher was in one of the police cars and he swung it back beside the station and came over to me as I walked in through the door. "How'd it go?"

"Not good. The guy we want is up there in the bush. He fired at me as we took off."

"He did what?" Gallagher roared in surprise. "Jesus God. I thought we'd checked that area earlier. There was nobody close to that clearing."

I held up my pack. There was a bullet hole in one side. "Believe me now?" I asked him.

Gallagher waved me inside, bursting with anger. "Sonofabitch! We went over that area with a fine-tooth comb. Sam checked it out and everything. It was clean."

"Sam hadn't checked it out for three hours, not that side of the river. Whoever it was snuck back and waited until I was hanging out of that chopper like a yo-yo on a string. He shone a light on me and I fired first, otherwise you'd be checking my butt for bullet holes right now, instead of me checking this pack."

184

I set the pack on the counter top and started going through the contents. My fingers found my billy can. It had an explosive hole punched in the side of it. And inside, where I had packed my spare can of beef, there was a mess of spilled meat. But the bullet had been slowed by the meat and metal and had spent itself in denting the other side of my pot. I took it out and tipped it into Gallagher's hand.

Gallagher took it and whistled. "Okay. I believe you. Now come and sit down a minute and get a coffee while I holler for some help." Sam was lying on the mat behind the front desk of the station and he rose to his feet and wagged his tail when I noticed him. Gallagher went through the routine of handing him back to me, then poured me coffee, adding sugar, which I don't take but needed right now. I thanked him and sat and went over the events again. He heard me through twice, then lifted the phone and called the OPP detachment at Wawa. I listened, still shocked into the near-apathy that settles on survivors when there are other people around to take up the slack for them. I knew that if Gallagher hadn't been in charge, my adrenaline would be running and I would be doing all the things he was doing now, but in the warmth of that station with coffee in the cup, I felt like sleeping.

He hung up after ten minutes. "Good, that's taken care of. They're sending reinforcements at first light. A team of guys with tracking dogs and SWAT gear, the whole manhunt paraphernalia. They'll comb the bush, starting there, circling until they know he's not in the area, then beating the river back down to my men." He stopped talking long enough to light a cigarette, quickly and without ceremony, showing he was back on the weed as badly as ever. "We've got the bastard in a vise. The river's the only road out for him."

I downed the last of my coffee and stiffened my shoulders to come back to the land of the living. "Not necessarily. He could walk out through the bush if he chose. It would take him a week maybe, but he's only thirty miles from the highway. He could come out anywhere."

185

Gallagher shook his head. "No," he said firmly. "You've seen that bush. If he could make a mile a day he'd be doing well. He won't want to put himself at risk that long. It's my bet he'll make it out at night on the river. Only there's gonna be my guys waiting for him a couple of miles from the highway, just when he might try to get cute and cut out through the bush."

I nodded. I didn't share his horror of the bush. It was no worse than the terrain I'd humped through in Nam and we'd covered eight, ten klicks a day, carrying an eighty-pound pack and watching for enemy all the way. But at least he had a plan that made sense, and that was something to be glad about. "So what about Tettlinger? Have you questioned him yet?"

"I've started. But he's playing it cagey. Wants to see a lawyer before he'll say a word. The guy who fronted for him after he took a swing at you is out of town for the weekend, so I'm waiting for a ringer to drive in from Thunder Bay. Along with all the bloody media people in the world. Two murders in a day has got everybody churning. Anyway, the lawyer ought to be here by midnight. We can start then."

"Maybe I can have a word with Tettlinger, off the record," I suggested. Gallagher looked at me, breathed out a stream of cigarette smoke, and shook his head.

"No. For two reasons. First, you're in shock. You need a break from this bullshit. And second, it may queer it for us if he doesn't have a lawyer there at the time, even though you're not a cop in this town." I said nothing, and he said, "Okay?"

I nodded wearily. "If you say so. And what are you going to do with your time?"

He butted his smoke purposefully and stood up. "I'm going back to Sallinon's place to ask him some more questions."

"Need company?" I wasn't sure I wanted to go with him. I'd had enough of direct violence for one day. I didn't feel up to the fencing and evasion that Sallinon was going to stage for us.

Gallagher solved it for me. "No," he said firmly. "But I'll bet Alice Graham could stand a little company. She's heard the news about the shooting of Onyschuk. She may give you hell, but she'll be glad you're back. Meanwhile, I'll have ballistics check out the slug you gave me."

I nodded and stood up. I was drained, ready to call it a day and head home to lie down, too weary to contemplate going to bed with Alice. I needed time to get my head back together. But one last thought nagged me and I gave it to him. "You know, I figure this guy, or guys, whoever they are, have got air support."

He frowned. "What makes you say that?"

I told him about the winnowed ground where the body had been found. "Somebody had let down there with a helicopter. I know the signs. And another thing. He, or they, whoever it is, moves too fast in the bush to be doing it alone."

Gallagher stood up slowly and looked at me as if I were a mirror and he was practicing his thoughtful face. "Did you hear anybody up there, while you were waiting?"

"No." I shook my head. "No, but that doesn't mean it wasn't happening. We know there's other choppers in this area. If Laval and whoever is in the bush has a line to one, that's all they need, we can't police all the comings and goings."

Gallagher took out his notebook and opened it at the back, writing himself a quick unofficial note. "Maybe we can't," he said, "but I can sure as hell check the log books of all the aircraft in the area. I'll get on it first thing in the morning. But for now, go and sleep awhile. I need you bright-eyed and bushy tailed tomorrow."

He offered to drive me to the motel, my own car still being out at the helicopter home base, but he had only one man to spare so I called a cab. The driver looked at Sam warily. "You blind, Mac?"

"No. He's not a Seeing Eye dog, he's a police dog, trained to a hair. Let's go."

He shook his head. "It's in our rules, no dogs." He hesitated. "Wanna see the book?"

I was too tired to play games. I just shook my head. "You wanna see his teeth?"

He flinched. "No. I don't want no trouble."

I sat down wearily and patted the seat beside me for Sam. The interior was old and scuffed and smelled of vomit and pine-scented disinfectant. "Good," I said. "Head up to the motel beside the highway and I won't make any."

He still shook his head officiously so I told Sam "Speak," and he filled the cab with terror.

The driver held both hands up and shouted "Okay," and drove me to the motel without another word as I quieted Sam and sat back, patting him gratefully.

I got out at the motel office, not sure if Alice had kept the room open for me—I had told her I would be away overnight and she probably needed the space. She wasn't in the office. Instead, there was a card propped up against the locked door. "Manager in the dining room." That made my shoulders droop a little. I needed a shower and change of clothes before I was fit for human company, but I walked over to the dining room anyway, still carrying my pack and rifle. I set them down in the shadows beyond the circle of light around the doorway and told Sam "Keep," then went inside.

Alice was standing with a tableful of customers—noisy, cheerful men wearing leather coats with cloth sleeves and sports-club insignias or Legion badges on the pocket and hats with the crests of their companies. Men in the north put their hats on as they shave in the morning and take them off for bed, so I knew these were all locals.

I stood in the doorway for a moment, gathering my energy for polite chitchat. Then one of the men saw me and pointed and spoke to Alice. She turned, mouth open in surprise and delight. She came toward me so quickly that she knocked a chair over. One of the men laughed, but another straightened it and looked around for a second one to put next to it.

She weaved between the tables to reach me as I came in from the door. "Reid" was all she said, but it sounded like a prayer.

She reached out both hands and I held them and looked down into her face and grinned. "Hi." I squeezed her hands gently to let her know how I felt, then put an arm around her shoulder and pulled her toward me.

"I heard you'd been shot at, that they hit Mike Onyschuk. I was so worried," she said.

"No need to be," I grinned. "I've been shot at before, they generally miss." She looked at me and the care glowed in her face.

"Thank God," she said. "Do you have to go out again?"

"Not tonight, anyway. I'm off duty. I was hoping for a shower and a steak and some sleep."

The corners of her mouth turned down in a suppressed smile. "Which will it be first?"

"In the interests of public welfare, it should be the shower. I haven't even washed my hands since morning." I held them up and she pretended to wrinkle her nose.

"Well, I was a good girl and checked in here, like you told me. I'm in unit four, and I've got your bag there with me. Why don't you head over and shower while I dig out the best steak they've got in the icebox and make sure Hector doesn't set fire to it."

"That would be great. Just fifteen minutes and I'll be ready for anything."

She laughed and ducked away from under my arm to take her key out of her pants pocket. "You had better be," she said.

So I collected Sam and my gear and went back and showered and changed and left Sam in the room while I came back for the steak. When I arrived the miners all managed to somehow fill one table and leave another one vacant. Rough they may be, but there are no more courteous people anywhere. I

189

knew they would be all over me with questions about the shooting later, but they left me alone with Alice while I ate.

The steak was perfect and Alice had whipped up a rich sauce to go with it and opened me a Heineken, the only imported beer she carried. She sat opposite me and said, "Forget about conversation, we'll talk when you've finished."

"Very considerate," I told her with my mouth full, and she laughed.

"I remember my mother quoting from *Punch* magazine, something about the old wife's advice to the bride—feed the brute," she said, and we both laughed.

It was perfect. I could wash away the memory of hanging from the rope, a helpless target for the killer in the clearing. I knew the memories would come back later, just as I was falling asleep, the way they always do until your mind has had enough time to digest them all, but for now I was a happy man. And then the dining room door opened and Gallagher came in. He was wearing his parka and he kept his hat on so I knew this wasn't a social call.

He moved between the tables, nodding briefly to everyone who greeted him. When he reached our table he gave an old-fashioned salute to Alice and said, "Hey, Alice, nice to see you. Mind if I join you for a minute?"

"Sure," she said, but I could see her happiness withering. She watched anxiously as he pulled up a chair from the first vacant table and sat down across from me.

"How's the steak?" he asked me, but it was not lighthearted, it was a stroke, getting the courtesies out of the way for the next words he spoke, even before I could answer. "Can Alice spare you for an hour when you're through? We have a problem."

Alice said, "Well, excuse me, I should take care of my customers," and left, smiling politely. We both half stood as she left, then Gallagher slumped down again.

"What's up?" I asked him, pushing the plate away.

190

He sniffed. "The circle is getting smaller, buddy. I was just down to see Sallinon at his house."

"And?" I finished the last of my Heineken.

"And his wife said he was out in the garage, so I went out back and he was." He paused again and coughed. "Poor sonofabitch was hanging there. Been dead an hour by the look of him."

20

"Y ou need me to handle the investigation?" It wasn't really a question, I already knew the answer.

He nodded. "I really do, Reid. I know you've had one hell of a day but I've only got one man available, what with guys in the bush and Onyschuk in the hospital. I need Jackaman with me when I talk to Tettlinger, to play the usual games. My other guy is a rookie, I only hired him last spring. He couldn't handle a homicide."

"Let's go." I stood up. I could see Alice standing beside the cash register at the bar, careful not to look at me. "Give me a minute."

"The car's outside," he said, and left, not stopping to talk to any of the people who spoke to him.

I went over to Alice. She looked up nervously. "What's happened, Reid? It's something bad, I can tell it."

"It's Sallinon, the taxidermist. He's died suddenly. Gallagher wants me to handle the investigation for him while he gets on with the rest of the work that's piling up."

Her hands were resting on top of the cash register and as I watched she clenched them into fists and squeezed until the knuckles whitened. "Where is it going to end?" she asked softly.

"I think this is just a coincidence," I lied. "But it's routine for the police to investigate. Should take a couple of hours, that's all."

She unclasped her hands and laid them flat over all the keys on the register, making it a deliberate calming motion. "Reid, I get scared around you. Since you came we've had more trouble than this town has seen in its whole history."

"It was coming anyway," I said. "It started when that guy was killed up on that island and Prudhomme changed places with him. All I've done is trudge around after him, picking up the pieces." She said nothing, just stood looking down at her fingers. I felt powerless. I knew she was suffering from the shock that women feel more deeply than men in the presence of violence. It's not that they are more afraid. Most times they're not. But they have an inner logic and rationality that men lack. They can't understand violence, it makes no sense. And that disturbs them.

She looked up at last. "Will you be very late?"

Now I reached out and touched her hands, lightly. "I don't think so. It's a suicide. A couple of hours should take care of it and then I'll come back. Do you want to keep Sam with you while I'm away?"

She shook her head. "No. I'll be fine," she said, and as her eyes locked on mine she added, "I'll still be here when you get back. Room four."

I stooped and gave her a quick kiss on the cheek, then turned and left.

The police car was outside the door and I spoke quickly to Gallagher. "I have to bring Sam, he's in Alice's room." Gallagher growled something and I went and got Sam and put him in the back seat, then jumped in and Gallagher pulled away, a seasoned policeman's way. You don't see many veteran coppers laying rubber even for a killing.

"Looks like suicide," he said as we drove. "I've cut him down and left my guy to guard the scene until you get there."

"How high off the ground was he?" It's a good starting

question. Many suicides don't even take their feet off the ground, they tie the rope around their necks and loll against it.

"He had an extension cord tied over one of the rafters and he'd stood on a toolbox and stepped off. He could have stepped back on again if he'd changed his mind."

"No signs of a bang in the head, nothing?"

"Nothing." Gallagher was positive. "I took a careful look, he hasn't got a hair out of place." He turned onto Sallinon's street. There were four or five cars outside, and Gallagher swore. "Dammit. Looks like the whole goddamn ladies' aid is over cheering up the widow."

"Good thing there's somebody with her. It'll keep her off our backs," I said, and Gallagher humphed and said nothing.

He pulled up behind a car as close as he could get to the house and we got out. "I better introduce you," he said. "As far as they're concerned, you're working with me because Prudhomme was involved in your jurisdiction. I phoned the pastor for her and he turned up before I came away. He's a good guy but a bit of a mother hen. He may get sticky about you talking to her, use whatever charm you haven't used up on Alice, otherwise you'll be out of there in two seconds."

I let Sam out of the car and told him to stay, then walked behind Gallagher up to the front door. He tapped and entered and we were greeted at once by a pretty blond woman in her forties. Gallagher took his cap off. "Hi, Mrs. Andersen. I just wanted to introduce my deputy, Police Chief Reid Bennett. Can I have a quick word with Ida?"

"She's through here," the blonde said. She was wearing a sleek blouse that looked a little dressy for this end of the world and her hair was swept back from her face with a carelessness that had taken hours. She looked at me the way my Marine recruiting sergeant weighed me up when I first walked into his office. "How do you do, Chief. My name is Gretchen Andersen." She extended her hand and smiled a formal little smile.

194

I took her hand, which was cool and firm. "Reid Bennett, Mrs. Andersen. I wish we could have met under happier circumstances." Above her head I could see Gallagher doing his best to swallow a grin. I let go of her hand and she led us through to the sitting room out behind the original parlor Sallinon had used as his storefront. This place was no more lively. It was full of dark, heavy furniture with an enormous TV and plastic flowers. At a glance I could count eight stuffed birds and animals scattered around it. A big woman in a flowered dress was sitting on the couch with a gaunt young minister beside her and two other women sitting opposite in big chairs.

The minister looked up. He nodded to Gallagher and then stood up and approached us. "Pastor Aalto," he said, not giving me his hand.

Gallagher spoke to him first. "Good evening, padre. Thank you for coming over. I just stopped in to introduce my deputy." He turned and indicated me as if I didn't speak the language. "This is Police Chief Reid Bennett. He's a very senior investigator who happens to be in town and he volunteered to help me."

Aalto nodded and looked at me out of oyster-colored eyes. "Are you a private detective or something?" He had a cool, resonant voice and he was proud of it. I figured he was something of a showboat and would be trouble if he didn't get stroked.

I used the same formality Gallagher had, the military courtesy. "No, padre. I'm an accredited chief of police. I also happen to be a friend of Chief Gallagher's. I've been visiting with him and he's asked for my assistance. I'm only sorry that it's necessary."

"So am I," Aalto said. "Arnold was a good, kind man. I cannot imagine what pain he must have been suffering." He turned back to the widow, who was looking up blankly. There were no tears. They would come later, perhaps a week later, when the neighbors stopped calling and the world rocked

195

back onto its axis, without the bulk of the man in the garage. "Ida, I believe Mr. Bennett can help."

She tried to smile at me, but it collapsed in a puckering of her cheeks and a nervous dropping of her head. I said, "I'm very sorry for your sadness, Mrs. Sallinon. I'll leave you with your friends for a while," nodded, and turned away with Gallagher close behind me.

The blond bombshell followed us to the door. She touched me lightly on the shoulder as I paused to open it. "Ida is terribly distressed," she said, "but if there's anything at all I can do to help . . ." She opened her eyes very wide. Lord, she was sincere!

"I'll remember that, Gretchen," I said, and did my best to look like John Travolta. Sometimes police work calls for skills they don't ever teach at the Ontario Police Academy in Aylmer.

I went out and Gallagher led me back around to the garage. "Don't feel too flattered," he growled quietly. "She's got the hottest pants in Olympia. Her husband's a salesman for the mill, he's away a lot, and I've seen her in more parked cars than you've had hot dinners."

"Just doing my job," I told him cheerfully. "You want charm, I've got charm."

"I'd call it bullshit," he said, "but it seems to be working."

The door of the garage was closed and he swung it up. Inside, the light was on and a young uniformed constable was standing looking down at Sallinon's body, which lay on its back on the clear space to one side of the parked car, a 1983 Cadillac.

I nodded to the constable and Gallagher said, "Bill, this is Chief Bennett, he's handled a lot of things like this. Help him anyway you can."

The young guy stuck out his hand. "Glad 'a know you, Chief, I'm Bill Pigeon."

"Bill." I shook hands. "Ever had a suicide before?"

"No." He shook his head. "I've seen a few stiffs in traffic accidents, but this is my first suicide."

"Okay. There's no magic, just work, but a good trick is to stick your hands in your pockets, then you won't touch anything and change the scene at all."

He said "Sure," and put both hands in his pants pockets.

I turned to Gallagher. "When did you get here?"

"Right after you took off from the station. Drove up, spent a couple of minutes at the house, then came out. Altogether, that was, say, twenty minutes ago—maybe seven-thirty." He crouched beside the body. "Like I said, it looks like a suicide. See for yourself."

I stopped to check Sallinon's face. It was congested, but he had been flabby so it did not appear deformed. It had the pinpoint red marks that sometimes erupt on the skin during strangulation. There were also scratch marks on his neck, close to the cable, an indication that he had scrabbled to try and unfasten it before he lost consciousness.

The white, plastic-covered extension cord he had used as a ligature was still in place around his neck. I checked the knot. It was a clumsy slipknot. The wire had been twisted twice and then pulled through itself, a casual knot for such a formal purpose.

"If this guy worked sewing up skins, you'd think he'd know some fancier knots than this one," I said.

Gallagher nodded. "I noticed that. It sure looks amateur, doesn't it? But that doesn't mean somebody else did it, maybe he just wasn't figuring he'd be on display anywhere."

I crouched there, staring at the knot and wondering why it seemed familiar to me, and then I understood. "Tell me, was this guy a fisherman?" I wondered.

"Not to my knowledge," Gallagher said. "You can tell he didn't spend much time outdoors and I never heard him talk fishing at all." He turned to his constable. "Did you ever hear anything about him?"

The constable shook his head silently and Gallagher turned back to me. "What makes you ask?"

"Well, that knot is exactly what I make when I'm tying on a new leader to a spinning line. It's the knot a real fisherman would make without thinking." I stood up and walked to the beam from which the end of the wire still hung, clipped with a pair of pliers Gallagher had found and dropped when he cut the body down. The wire went over it and down to a six-inch nail driven into the wall. It was tied around the nail in a clove hitch. I stood up on the hood of the car and examined the beam over which the wire had run. It was made of soft lumber, spruce by the look of it, and there was a groove lying under the wire for the whole width of the rafter.

I jumped down and Gallagher asked, "What's up there?"

"Pressure marks on the beam. But not static, the way they would be if he'd hung himself. There's a groove sliced into the wood, the way it would be if somebody had hoisted him off his feet, pulling the wire back over the beam." I walked over to the nail in the wall. "And another thing, look at this knot. There's three feet of wire below it."

"Okay, Sherlock, so what?" Gallagher wasn't mocking me, he was teasing, the way a father might have been with a bright son, happy to impress his constable with the smartness of the help he'd brought in.

"So there's precisely enough wire on the business side of the nail to make a loop the right height from the floor. I think that means it was tied after the loop had been put over Sallinon's neck and the wire had been pulled tight enough to lift him off the ground."

Gallagher frowned. "He could've planned it himself so it was just the right height," he argued, but I could see he didn't believe it.

"Unlikely. He'd have been more likely to tie the wire to the nail with lots of slack, then take it up by making the noose higher in the wire."

"Sonofabitch!" he said slowly. "I think you're right. I think he was murdered." He bent down and picked up the dead man's hands. "Look. His nails are all broken. He died trying to get that cord off o' his neck."

21

We spent five minutes planning the things we had to do. First, Gallagher would arrange to have the scene photographed and fingerprinted. His own expert was one of the two officers up in the bush, but he had used the town's civilian photographer before so that was no problem, although he would have to do the fingerprinting himself. After that he would start a door-to-door canvass of the area. It's the bread and butter of police work, checking if anybody had seen anything suspicious. You can usually bet that nobody has, but you don't know until you've knocked on enough doors. My job was to question Ida Sallinon and see if her husband had given her any indication that he was in danger.

"Something strikes me as wrong, anyway," I said. "I mean, how much money does he make, stuffing chipmunks?"

"Not a lot," Gallagher agreed. "He does all right during the summer when tourists are up here, wanting their fish mounted, but once the fishing and hunting seasons are over, nothing."

"And yet he can afford last year's Cadillac," I said. "Seems a bit out of whack to me."

"Maybe he has family money," Gallagher said. "He's been a member of council for years and those jobs generally go to the boys with bucks."

"Let's go ask," I said, and Gallagher agreed. He stopped to brief his constable on which photographs he would need when the man arrived, and warned him against touching anything until the whole place had been fingerprinted.

I left Sam out there, with no special commands. He would be a peaceful part of the scenery until I was finished inside, and we went back in. Gretchen poured on the charm like a second helping of syrup, but we smiled by and went into the sitting room. The women were all listening to the pastor, who was reading the Twenty-third Psalm. It was the version from the new Bible, nowhere near as beautiful as the old Authorized Version they sang at my father's funeral, an Anglican ceremony. He saw us come in but continued reading. I waited until he had finished and he stood and came over to me, holding his place in the Bible with his finger. "What is it?" he asked icily. There didn't seem to be much charity in his makeup.

"Could I speak to you in private a moment, padre?"

He inclined his head regally and we went out into the hallway. Gretchen tried to follow us out but he smiled at her and shooed her back into the room with the rest of the women. She went, and he closed the door and asked again, "What is it?"

Gallagher spoke first. "It looks as if this might not be suicide, padre. We've found a few signs that indicate that Arnie was murdered."

His response was classic. "Thank God." He closed his eyes and bowed his head. We waited a moment until he finished his prayer. He opened his eyes and said, "I didn't think Arnold could be guilty of taking his own life."

Gallagher moved in with diplomacy I hadn't expected. "I share your relief, padre. But as a policeman I have to deal with the new problem this raises. Who murdered him?"

The pastor waited and I took over. "It's a shocking idea, but we think it happened. Now I need to talk to Mrs. Sallinon and then look through Arnold's things, to see if there's any clue there. I'm wondering if you will help me by advising her to talk and assist us."

He looked at me solemnly for about half a minute and then said, "Of course. Come with me."

I turned and nodded to Gallagher, who stuck his hat on and left. Then I followed the pastor back into the room.

There was the expected amount of fluttering when he made his announcement that there were some questions I would like to ask and would the other women please leave us alone in the parlor. And then I set to work.

It took only a few minutes to learn the obvious answers. No, Arnold Sallinon had no enemies. He was universally liked. Except by Gallagher and me, and the murderer, I thought, but pumped further. Nobody had called for him this evening. No, there had been no phone calls since he came in from his shop. Yes, he went out every evening to the garage and worked. His radial arm saw was there and he built cabinets and plaques to mount his specimens on. Yes, he did have some other income. He had speculated shrewdly a few years before when nickel became a scarce commodity and had made big money. She didn't know how he handled it. It seemed she was a typical Old Country wife. He earned the money, she kept the house and went to church.

This gave me the lead for the next question. Would she object to my looking through his accounts? I needed the pastor's help here. Small-town people would rather talk about their sex life than about their businesses, but I knew that the answer I needed could be among his papers. And I wondered whether I would find anything to connect him with the rest of the case, the other murders. They were all tied together with the same string, I figured.

She consulted with the pastor over the ethics of letting me see Arnold's papers, but he backed me and within minutes I was in the office beside his showroom with the key for his file cabinets. The pastor was itchy to help. Every man has a weakness somewhere and I thought perhaps his was nosiness, but I managed to talk him out of it. And then Gretchen wanted to come with me but I got rid of her, too. Women like her have never gotten me excited. I'm no saint but I don't want to be a notch on anybody's sexual gun and she was becoming a pain. I sent her for coffee and opened up the cabinets.

Most of the papers were what I would have expected. There were business records, neatly kept, showing he had made a gross income of thirty-two thousand dollars the previous year but that this netted out at less than the price of the Cadillac outside. There were receipts for supplies and copies of his bills to his customers.

Gretchen Andersen came back with coffee and conversation but I got rid of her promptly, and when I failed to turn up anything in the file cabinet, I made a complete search of the room. The desk was locked and there wasn't a key for it among those Ida Sallinon had found for me. I expected it was probably in Sallinon's pocket. I could have gone out for it but I didn't want to leave the room. Getting in there had been a major triumph. If I left even for a moment, the pastor would probably consider I'd had my chance. So, instead of going and searching the body, I harked back to some skills I'd picked up on a slow Sunday in boot camp. A Kentucky kid had shown me how to open a lock as simple as this one with a bent wire. A paper clip did it and within seconds I found out Sallinon's real secrets.

First there was a bottle of Polish vodka, half empty. And then, in the top drawer I found a neat little .22 revolver. I checked the gun. It was loaded in all chambers, but it had never been cleaned. The barrel was dirty but not pitted. That could mean that it had been fired only a very few times. I also noted a rusty-looking incrustation at the muzzle end of the barrel. I'm not a pathologist, but I happen to know that a gun sucks back air into its barrel when it's fired. If it had been used close up to a body it would draw blood into itself. It looked to me as if this gun had been used close up. And that was when the pieces came together in my mind. Eleanor had been shot from close range. I was certain that this was the murder weapon.

There was a box of shells, with eight missing. That added up: two used to kill Eleanor, all chambers filled. I slipped the shells and the gun into my coat pocket and went on looking. There was a flat manila folder and I opened it and knew at once that I was right about the murder. It was full of photographs taken by the hidden camera in Eleanor's mobile home. Some of them were young men in the universal heavy jackets and work hats of the north, but there were about thirty of men in good suits. One was even wearing his Shriner's fez. And at the bottom of the pile, grinning happily, the last recorded likeness of Jim Prudhomme—the picture that had cost Eleanor her life.

I checked the back of it but there was no name or date, although I soon found that there were dates on all the others, in the same round handwriting Sallinon had used in his books. And there were more photographs in another drawer. Some of them had been stroked across with a fine felt pen. These were mostly of working men, people I guessed Sallinon had not thought worth the trouble of blackmailing. The others, any showing men in suits or city topcoats, were clean, and most of these had other photos attached to them, action pictures taken with Eleanor.

I stopped and thought about that for a while. I wondered where that camera had been located in the mobile home, and how she had managed to take pictures without anybody's knowing what was going on. Perhaps Sallinon had been there, hiding in the head or peeking in at the side window, using ultra-fast film. The shots were all grainy enough to have been taken in low light with 1000-speed film. I checked them over. All of them had notes written on the backs. The standard note consisted of name, address, in some cases occupation, license number, and type of vehicle. A lot of them all carried dates and figures, the figure usually being two hundred and fifty dollars. No doubt about it. Blackmail. I made a quick count, rounding out the figures for convenience and found Sallinon had made better than sixty thousand dollars in a little over one year. No wonder somebody had looped a wire round his neck and dragged him into eternity, clawing at his own throat.

There were other papers in the desk, but they were mostly personal—insurance policies, the purchase papers for his Cadillac, for which he had paid cash. Mortgages he held on properties in town and in Thunder Bay, places he had bought with money raised from Eleanor's leads. I sat for a moment and thought about her, trying to remember whether she was a blackmailer by nature. I didn't think so. She had honestly believed that all she was doing by going along with the photography was to provide herself with some insurance. Perhaps she meant it. Maybe the other pictures had been taken from outside the vehicle. In any case her knowledge had killed her. I wondered for a while about the logistics of the blackmail. Sallinon was rooted here. It couldn't have been his finger on the button of the camera. Maybe he had been the guy who thought up the idea and managed the blackmail arrangements. But somebody else was involved as well, someone free to travel with Eleanor. I wondered if it could have been Prudhomme.

And then there was a second puzzle. Why would Sallinon do it? Eleanor was his ticket to easy money. Why would he put an end to it all—unless, I realized quickly, he was scared for his own life. Which meant, my instincts told me, that the order to kill had come from somebody who scared him badly. It added up to Mafia connections, from Laval, through the gunman in the bush, to Eleanor and now to fat, dead Arnie Sallinon.

Gretchen Andersen tapped on the door and pushed in softly as I was looking at the pictures. I shut the file folder, glad I'd had the foresight to close the desk drawers. She tiptoed over to me in that ridiculous look-at-me fashion women use sometimes when they're excluded from some activity and feel they're not getting enough attention. I beamed at her, charm personified. "Hello, Gretchen, could you do something for me, please?"

"Of course." Her eyes widened. If she couldn't score as a sex symbol, she would be the indispensible helpmate. Later we could go our three rounds of wrestling, no holds barred.

"I wonder if you'd go out and find Chief Gallagher and ask him to come in. He's most likely down the block at one of the neighboring houses, that's if he's not still in the garage."

She nodded, a big motion that made us co-conspirators. I figured she had set herself me as a project for the evening. I was the only man within range except for the pastor and Gallagher, who was impervious. "Right away," she said. "Is there anything else you need?"

"Not at the moment, thank you, but I'm sure there will be later on."

It took her about ten minutes to find Gallagher. First she had to put on her mink and high-heeled boots, then she had to let the world know what was happening. But I used the time well. I didn't want to risk losing the material if the widow refused permission for us to take it, so I copied out the names, addresses, dates, and figures from the back of the photographs, concentrating on the more prosperous-looking and younger men, guys who might just have found the personal strength or the money to put an end to Sallinon. Then I went through the rest of the drawers, doing it properly, turning them all out and examining the undersides. There was nothing much else in there except for a little black phone-number book with no names in it, just initials. Then, when I was through with all the routine checking, I found what I had expected. It was on the bottom of the bottom drawer, a pair of flat keys, the kind you get with a safety-deposit box. I laid them on the top of the desk and put the drawer back in place as Gretchen came back with Gallagher.

He thanked her with a crisp nod. I guess if he'd seen her compromised enough times he didn't have to apply as much charm as I did. She smiled at me, affecting a little sadness, and I thanked her and she went out, whisking her bottom like a San Diego bar girl.

"What've you got?" Gallagher asked.

I pushed the file of photographs to him. "A tie between Sallinon and Eleanor. Looks like the pictures she took were being used for blackmail."

He whisked through them, reading the back of the first one, then flicking through the others. "So that's where his bread came from," he said, narrowing his eyes. "No wonder somebody wanted him iced."

"I think it's deeper than that. Look what he had in his desk." I took out the .22, broke it, and handed it to him. He took it and whistled. "You figure he killed her?"

"It was a gun this size that was used. And if we were right to begin with, he was tied in with Prudhomme and the rest of the conspirators in this claims scam." I rocked back on my chair.

"There's another file folder of pictures and at the bottom of the pile is the picture of Prudhomme, just as Eleanor told me on the telephone."

Gallagher swore. "What you don't see when you haven't got a gun," he said disgustedly. "With this information yesterday I could have had the sonofabitch safe inside. We could have tied the whole case up without getting you and Onyschuk shot at."

I waved my hand. "Water under the bridge. The thing is, What do we do next? Ideally we should impound all the evidence and take it away, including this." I handed him the safety-deposit keys. "They were taped under a drawer."

He put the gun down, still broken, and picked up the keys. I swung the cylinder shut and put it back in my coat pocket. "We've got to find out where this fits," he said, shaking the key at me. "There might be something to do with the other killings wrapped up in it. But to do that I'm going to need a court order." He hooked his head back toward the other room. "Otherwise the guardian angel is likely to get awkward and prevent any of it going."

"That's the way I saw it. What I've been doing is copying down names and addresses from the photos. I figure I should keep on until I've got them all, then take the shape of those keys and the numbers off them and tape them back where I found them and leave."

"You're going to keep the heater," Gallagher insisted. "I know for a fact he doesn't have a license for a handgun; there's only two in town, one at the bank, one collector."

"Okay, so you do the arranging for the court order. I'll finish up here and join you. That's what I figured. Tomorrow when the trail's cold we'll start following up on these photos. Oh, and by the way, I found a phone list. No names in it, just numbers."

Gallagher sat on the edge of the desk. He was tired, his shoulders sagged with it. "Let's see it, maybe I'll recognize the numbers if they're local."

I handed it to him and he leafed through. "There's initials but no names," he said. "Cagey little bastard, wasn't he?"

"D'you recognize any of the initials?"

He looked through the book again. "Not offhand. We should try and match them to the blackmail names, maybe that's it." He yawned. "The way I'm feeling, unless somebody comes out soon with his hand up, saying, 'I did it, take me in,' he's safe. I'm still out there knocking on doors. Nobody's seen screw-all. They were all watching television like good little robots."

I felt for him. I've had nights like this myself. If nobody encourages you to stop, you keep on until you fall down and your efficiency dies with every extra move you make. "Why not call it a night? I don't see what else we can do. We've got a mess of work to do tomorrow on what we've found here.

But for now all we should do is call Montreal again, keep the police there looking for Laval. It's my bet that he's the guy behind this killing, as well as the others up in the bush. He's connected to all of them."

"You're right," Gallagher admitted. He ran his hand over his chin with a loud rasp. "I've still gotta question Tettlinger when his shyster gets here. I tell you what. Finish here, like we decided, and go back to the motel. I'm going to make a few more calls about Laval, see if we can turn up anything more on him. Then I'll get a court order for all this stuff and catch a few zzzs until the lawyer gets in." He stood up and tapped his hat more firmly in place. "I'm getting too old for this nonsense."

"All right. You tell the padre about the unregistered gun, make it sound like a precaution we're taking to remove it. I'll finish copying these names and numbers and I'll come out."

"Right." He turned and left, almost colliding with Gretchen, who came bounding in, all anxious smiles, like a little girl out to please her daddy. "G'night," he said to her, and she waved at him with her fingertips and came over to me.

"Would you like a refill on the coffee?" She checked my cup and found it full. "You bad boy, you haven't finished the first one." I thought she was going to slap me on the wrist.

"Sorry, I got busy. But yes, please. If you get me a fresh cup I'll drink it all."

"You'd better." She shook her finger. "Otherwise you don't get any dessert." She left and I rolled my eyes to heaven and went on copying names and addresses.

She came back, set the cup on the desk, and perched on the edge of it, her neatly rounded haunch jutting toward me like a piece of pie. I had shut the folder and she reached for it, but I caught her hand. "Police business, very official," I kidded. "Out you go like a good girl."

She slid off the desk and pouted. "I know you've had a hard

day. The others"—she indicated the other room—"they said you'd been shot at when poor Officer Onyschuk was hit. But you don't have to be nasty to me."

I decided it was time to cut the games out. "Sorry," I said calmly, "getting shot at does that to a man sometimes. Now I'm going to have to ask you to leave, please. I promise to drink the coffee."

She decided to keep her options open. "Bossy," she said with another pout and left, switching her tail like a lioness.

It took me ten more minutes to finish the copying. Then I retrieved Sallinon's vodka and fortified the coffee and sipped it. It was cool but good and the vodka gave it an extra bite. As I sipped I began putting everything back into the desk. First I traced the outline of the two safety-deposit keys, doing it like a brass rubbing. And then, as I finished the coffee, I picked up the phone book and glanced through it.

I was tired to my bones and my head was working at half speed, it seemed, like an engine on a cold morning missing on half the cylinders, but as I flipped toward the middle of the book I came across initials that made me sit up straight. P.K., and a local number. I stood up and looked around for the local phone book. It was on a stand beside the door and I went and picked it up and checked the connection my memory had made. I was right. The number belonged to the helicopter company I had used for the last two days. I looked back in the little book, rechecking the initials. P.K. Paul Kinsella.

22

I picked up the little book and put it into my shirt pocket, then I relocked Sallinon's desk and shut and locked his file cabinets, just like a banker finishing up for the day. I picked up my cup and saucer and put my coat over my arm, the gun heavy in the pocket, and went back into the living room of the house.

Ida Sallinon was kneeling with the pastor, praying silently. The rest of the women had gone, including Gretchen, for which I was glad. I stood and waited for them to finish and when the pastor said "Amen" and opened his eyes, I waited further for some kind of sign I could move.

He gave it at once, getting to his feet and helping the widow to her seat on the couch. Then he came to me. "Have you finished?" He made it sound like I was a storm trooper ravishing a convent.

"Yes, thank you, padre. I guess the chief spoke to you."

He nodded impatiently. "It's all very distressing," he said.

I wasn't about to apologize. It was his job to lay on the relief. My job was to solve crimes. "It's a dreadful thing to happen," I said. "We can't let it go without trying to find the person responsible."

"I suppose not." He stared at me with his colorless eyes.

I went over to the widow. "Thank you for your help, Mrs.

Sallinon." She looked up slowly, as if she were smoked up. I guessed her emotions were all jammed with the horror. She nodded, looking through me, as if I were the glass in an aquarium.

"You're welcome," she said.

I left, nodding to the pastor, and went out to the garage. There was a hearse in the driveway with two men in black topcoats beside it, leaning on a gurney, smoking cigarettes. The media people were all gathered at the mouth of the driveway. Gallagher was inside with his constable and a photographer.

Gallagher looked up when I came in. "Ready to go?"

I beckoned him to one side with a flick of my head and he joined me out in the darkness, out of earshot of the other men.

"I think so. One of the sets of initials in his little black book was Paul Kinsella's."

Gallagher straightened his tired back as if he'd been galvanized. "Sonofabitch! You said these guys had air support."

"May be innocent, but let's check it out." The wind was cold on the back of my neck and I shrugged deeper into my combat jacket.

"Let's go talk to him." Gallagher was excited, all his tiredness gone. "I'll just brief the kid."

He stepped back inside the garage and spoke to the constable, then to the photographer. They nodded. The constable looked less than eager. I guess he was cold. Pity Gretchen had gone home; she would have warmed him, once he was alone. We walked down the drive and out to the patrol car. The constable came after us, walking ahead to the corner. Sam came, too. I walked over to Gallagher's police car and let Sam into the backseat. Then I got in the front, glad to be out of the wind. Gallagher got behind the wheel and whisked away up the street, past the constable who immediately stepped into the roadway and flagged down the procession of cars full of reporters that was trying to follow us. I grinned. What we had to do would be done more easily without cameras sticking over our shoulders while we did it.

Gallagher said nothing until we were out of town, heading up the side road to the highway, gunning the Chevy to 130 klicks an hour over the undulations. "You said you thought you heard him pause on his way back to pick you up," he said at last.

"Not for long. He didn't change note enough to make me think he had set down," I said. I wasn't anxious to paint Kinsella black. He had the same battle scars as me, we were blood brothers.

"Maybe he just let somebody down on the hoist, like he picked you up," Gallagher ventured, braking for the intersection with the Trans-Canada. A truck passed, heading east, and he swore. "Have to pass that bastard now," he complained.

I sat quiet, thinking over the events of those crowded few minutes when the chopper had come for me, and then I had a thought that had eluded me then. I reported it. "One thing I forgot to mention. He had a spare coil of cable in the back of the chopper. I'm wondering if that was part of it."

"How?" Gallagher wondered aloud, flicking on his flashing lights to bring the truck over to the shoulder, then flying past him, speed building to the right-hand limit on his gauge.

"I'm wondering if he was planning to have me killed, then leave me dangling, maybe cut me loose over the middle of the bush somewhere. Nobody would ever have found me in a million years."

Gallagher sniffed, "Could be, I guess, but if he was gonna do that, why didn't he?"

"Training," I said, and Gallagher took his eyes off the road far too long to stare at me.

"Training? What are you smokin'?"

"No, I thought about it at the time. He was in Nam. Chopper pilots were more gun-shy then most grunts. They knew they were the prime target any time they were in range. I think the sound of gunshots, plus the fact that I was close

213

enough to look like I was ready to shoot him myself, had him spooked."

Gallagher wound his window down and spat into the cold slipstream, then wound it up again. "Possible," he allowed. "And another thing. When you see how they've been knocking one another off, maybe he was afraid the guy on the ground would hit him, kill two birds with one stone. After all, if he's part of this he's as vulnerable as any of them. If there's a couple of billion dollars involved and the Mob wants it, they'll make sure they knock off anybody who could get in their way."

I said nothing. It was only guesswork on our part, but the amount of blood that was flowing in this case was phenomenal. It had to be a Mob action, and if it was, Kinsella was just as expendable as Misquadis or Prudhomme had been. He must have known it.

It took us fourteen minutes to cover the twenty-some miles. The needle of the big Chevy had been hanging on the peg most of the way. As we rounded the last curve and saw the motel beside the highway, Gallagher shouted, "He's back. Look ,the chopper's on the pad and there's a light on in the shed."

He swung in, squirting gravel every way, and pulled to a stop in front of the shed. "Let's go," he said, and ran out of the car toward the shed.

I followed him, groping in my pocket to get a grip on Sallinon's peashooter. It wasn't much, but it was the only card I had to play. Gallagher hit the door running, but it was locked and he swore. And then the door at the other end of the hut clattered open. I could hear it as I wrenched the rear car door open to release Sam. Gallagher heard it too. He ran around the hut, drawing his gun, turning the corner at the moment the sound of the shot reached me, then buckling backward, clutching his left leg. I pulled my gun and ran up behind him, crouching, holding Sallinon's pistol as I stepped

214

around the corner and fired twice, not aiming, just returning fire.

I heard a yell and a clatter of something falling. It was dark there except for the lights at the front of the motel, fifty yards back from the road. I dived to the right, away from the hut, rolled, and came up pointing my gun the same way. This time I saw the figure on the ground move, an anguished flopping like a landed pickerel. I ran up to it glancing around me. On the far side of the hut I heard the churning of the starter on the chopper. Kinsella was getting away. I stooped for a second over the fallen man. It was the guy I had seen at the motel when I got back from Montreal. He was dressed in the same kind of combat jacket I was wearing, and a rifle was lying beside him. He was alive, squirming in pain.

I grabbed the rifle, stuffing the pistol back in my pocket, and ran around the hut. The helicopter was lifting away, tilting its blades toward me. I thought Kinsella would be using both hands and prayer to lift so hard but as I stood there he snapped off a shot at me, missing by a foot. I fired back, but he was lifting too fast so I aimed this time at the stopping point, the hub of the tail rotor.

He was thirty feet up now, climbing like an elevator, but I scored. The bullet whang–g–ged away off metal and suddenly the chopper was pirouetting around and around in the air, all directional control gone.

Kinsella was cool. He did the only thing he could, cutting the motor to stop the spinning, letting the bird crunch back to earth. It fell like a brick, still turning, hit the ground, and half rolled. The air was full of the smell of jet fuel and I heard him cursing in a frightened wail over the dying echoes of the spranging metal and plastic.

Keeping the rifle at the ready I ran forward and looked in through the shattered side, covering him. His face was covered with blood but his hands were empty, fiddling with his escape harness. Out of the corner of my eye I saw a lick of flame spring up on the edge of the spreading pool of jet fuel. I reached through the door and grabbed him, unsnapping the harness and hauling him out of the seat, through the door and behind me in a one-handed motion, using strength I wouldn't have had in less dangerous circumstances.

He landed loosely and rolled as I dived after him. Behind me the flames had raced over the surface of the fuel and were eating into the fabric of the chopper. I came up on one knee, still holding the rifle, pointing it at his body, but it didn't matter. He was scrabbling away from the burning craft on knees and elbows the way he had been taught a million years ago by experts. I crouched and ran up to him, grabbing him by the collar and hauling him away behind the shelter of the hut. Beyond us, at the motel, the doors had burst open and crowds of customers were standing on the steps, shouting, screaming.

I roared at them, "Get down," and fell with Kinsella on the other side of the hut as the fuel tank finally cooked off and exploded like a bomb. Chunks of metal thunked into the side of the hut, but it didn't burn. Up at the motel the shouts changed to screams of terror. I ignored it all, running my hands over Kinsella's pockets, seeking his gun. He was clean. "I'm sorry, Reid. I'm sorry. These guys wanted you out of it, you were too close to them," he babbled.

"Where's the gun?" I prodded him with the muzzle of the rifle. "Where is it?"

He put both hands up on top of his head. "Gone. Honesta God. Search me if you want. I dropped it when you hit the rotor."

I ran my hands down his back, sides, and legs. He had nothing hidden so I left him and ran back to Gallagher. He was pulling himself around to the front of the hut, farther away from the heat and light of the fire. I could see his left thigh was a pulpy mass of blood. "You got him?" was all he asked.

"Yeah. Be back in ten seconds." I unsnapped his handcuffs

and ran back to the two fallen men. Kinsella was sitting up and I caught his wrist and handcuffed him to the other man. Then I ran to the motel porch. Men and women were swearing, weeping, shouting, but I couldn't see anybody hurt.

One man looked less dazed than the others. I grabbed him by the lapel. "Listen up. I'm a policeman. We need medical help at the hut. Call the hospital and send two ambulances. The police chief's hurt and there's two other guys in trouble too. Got that?"

He looked at me, slowly getting his mind back in focus. "Okay," he said slowly. Then he asked me, "What's the number?"

"Dial the operator. Two ambulances, police backup. Now." I shoved him by the shoulder and he ran off inside. I turned and grabbed the nearest big man. "Come with me, there's someone hurt out there."

We carried Gallagher in and laid him on a bed in one of the motel rooms. I cut his pants away and was starting to cover the thigh wound with clean towels when the door opened and a middle-aged man came in. He was American, by his clothes, a fisherman passing through like all the dozens of others, only this time we had gotten lucky. "Here, let me do that," he commanded. "I'm a doctor."

Gallagher managed a snort. "Good," he said. "Do your stuff, Doc."

23

I left the doctor in charge and went to check on my two suspects. It was still pandemonium outside. By some miracle nobody had been hit by any of the flying metal, but the shock was enough to have sent ordinary civilians into panic. There was still a lot of screaming and weeping. One man was saying to a woman, "Yes, but you don't know you're all right until you've been to see a doctor. Don't keep saying it. We're gonna sue."

I trotted down the steps and out to the back of the shed. It was lit bright as day by the flames from the chopper. The local fire department hadn't arrived yet, wouldn't get there in time to save anything. Meanwhile a group of the tougher patrons of the motel had gathered around my two prisoners. They were angry, remembering their recent fear, ready to punish. They would have been touble if I hadn't had Sam along.

I'd left him in charge when I went to look after Gallagher, and he was my salvation. He was standing over the two men on the ground, but turning as needed to keep the onlookers back a respectful distance from them.

I walked up to him and fussed him and told him "Good boy," then I unfastened the cuff around the injured man's wrist. Kinsella pulled his hand away eagerly, ready to run now he had his wind and his control back, but I told him, "Forget it. My dog would eat you," and cuffed his hands together behind him.

He swore, but softly, and I examined the other guy. My Marine snap-shooting practice had stood me in good stead. I'd hit him in the arm and the leg. Neither one alone was a stopping shot, especially with Sallinon's popgun, but the pain had frightened him.

"You'll be fine. We'll get you to the hospital right away," I told him. I told Sam "Easy" and called to the crowd, "I need somebody to help get this guy inside."

There was the usual twenty-second silence and then three men came forward at once. I tapped the first one on the shoulder. "You. Get this guy's arm over your shoulder."

We crouched and each took an arm. I took the wounded side and the man groaned when I touched him. "Okay. Up," I said, and we lifted him and walked him to the motel, his feet dragging two scuffs in the gravel. Over my shoulder I told the other two, "Bring the prisoner in, and don't try to hurt him."

Immediately everybody in the crowd volunteered. They all crowded around Kinsella and jostled him after us. One of them said, "Hey, it's the chopper pilot. What'd you do, guy?"

I took them both into the room where I'd left Gallagher. The doctor was still working on him, but looked up when we came in. "Lay the injured one down there," he said, pointing to the rug. "Give him a pillow."

We did, then I sat Kinsella on the floor beside him. He looked at me sadly. "Why'd it have to be this way? We could've been on the same side like we were in Viet Nam."

"That was before you set me up to get greased," I told him.

"I saved your ass, didn't I?" he protested. "I could've left you dangling there, but I didn't. And now I'm in this mess."

"Just cooperate and I'll do what I can for you at the trial," I promised.

The doctor finished with Gallagher, tying the pad over his wound, covered him with a blanket, and knelt beside the casualty. He looked up at me. "Did you do this to him?"

"After he did that." I nodded at Gallagher, who was trying to grin.

The doctor shook his head. "You sure know how to stop people," he said, and suddenly Kinsella brayed with angry laughter.

"There's nobody around like an ex-grunt for stopping people," he said savagely. "I'll bet he was a real cowboy in Nam."

"I made it through," I said. "That's all. Just a whole bunch of days of not getting killed. I was hit, but they didn't kill me." His laugh and comment had angered me. Already I was tasting the cold bile of violence, the sick knowledge that you've hurt somebody, possibly permanently. The older I get, the harder it is to take, but I've never managed to find any other way of earning my keep. I guess I'm one of nature's soldier ants. It's my function to protect society, to fight while others work. I wish I could get used to it.

I turned to Gallagher. His eyes were closed, but he opened them and blinked wearily. "Listen, how good is your sergeant, can he untangle all this crap?" I asked.

He shook his head. "I think he'd be over his head. Better call the OPP investigation unit. Tell them what happened, have them send some guys down the station to take care of things until I get out and about again."

"Will do. You rest." I patted his shoulder and went over to the telephone.

While I was phoning, the ambulance arrived and the other police car with Jackaman and their last remaining constable. Them, plus the wagon train of reporters we had left behind us. Jackaman supervised loading the two casualties into the ambulance and then waited respectfully for me to get off the phone. I did, and told him what the chief's instructions had been. He sighed. This had been his chance for glory and now it was gone.

220

"The chief thinks it's such a mess he needs an outside investigation, so none of the mud sticks to the department. That's why he wants the provincial police," I explained, and he brightened a little.

"Okay, if that's the reason. But I could've handled it."

I soothed him down and he offered me a ride back to Olympia, but I refused. "My own car is here, I'd rather take it back, I'll need it tomorrow."

He stood, lifting his cap off and scratching his scalp with the fingers of the same hand. "Can I ask you for one favor?"

"Of course." There's nothing like winning it all to bring out the generosity in a man.

"Well, we still haven't printed that garage where Sallinon was murdered. I need the scene protected until tomorrow. Can you put your dog in charge? Our guy goes off duty at midnight. He's got to double up anyway." Before I could answer he rushed on. "I'm having to bring him in to take over in the station and we don't have a spare man for the crime scene. I want to get it printed, I think it's not connected with these other killings."

"All right. I'll go by the place and put Sam in charge, and drive your man back to the station," I promised. After which, I thought, I'd make my statement to the OPP and head back to the motel to fall into bed.

I drove back down the highway at normal speed. There is only one radio station within range of Olympia and it plays nothing but rock. At night you can pick up other stations, but they float in and out so I switched off and just followed my headlights down to the turnoff.

The young constable was sitting sullenly on the workbench in Sallinon's garage. He brightened when I gave him the sergeant's instructions. I installed Sam and told him "Keep." Then I drove the kid down to the station.

Jackaman was there, talking to the lawyer who had finally arrived from Thunder Bay to represent Tettlinger. He told him about the upcoming investigation, gave him a few min-

221

utes with Tettlinger, and sat him down to wait for the OPP to start questioning his client. Me he took through to the chief's office and fed coffee.

I should have waited for the OPP to arrive, but I was too tired. Instead I made a statement, using the station tape recorder, setting out all the events as Gallagher and I had deduced them before: the phony killing of Prudhomme, the evidence Eleanor had given me, our suspicions that Prudhomme had staged the whole event to profit from his knowledge of the ore body, our belief that the Mob was involved and had started wiping one another out—everything.

Jackaman listened without comment, and when I'd finished he switched off the recorder and said, "Now I'm glad the chief asked the OPP to take over. This is more than just a shooting."

"A whole lot more," I told him. "And now I'm quitting. Tell the OPP I'll be back at nine tomorrow to answer their questions. Right now I'm going home. Three guys have taken shots at me tonight and I want to rest up."

He thanked me and showed me out past the angry lawyer— a junior partner, I judged, pale faced and restless on the station bench. Outside the reporters crowded around me, shoving tape recorders in my face, but I smiled and waved them all away. It wasn't until I was sitting in my car that I realized I hadn't surrendered Sallinon's pistol. I debated going back inside, but weariness won out and I started the car and drove off.

I still had my motel key to the outer door so I let myself in and went along to unit four. There was a note taped to the door and I stood close and read it. "Heard the news. It's safe. Have gone home." It was signed with four kisses, no name.

I took it down and went back to the car, wearier than ever. Twice in the mile drive to Alice's house I almost went off the road as my eyelids drooped, but I made it and pulled in gratefully beside her house. There were no lights on, which didn't surprise me, it was after one A.M. I closed the door quietly and went to the side entrance. It was unlocked and I let myself in.

The warmth of the stove greeted me like a blessing and I eased my shoulders back and called out softly, "Hello." And then every nerve in my body blazed alive as I heard a soft whimper out of the darkness.

I dropped to one knee and edged away from the door, feeling in my pocket for Sallinon's gun. I called out, "Are you all right?" and rolled silently sideways toward the stove, away from the direction from which the whimper had come. I found the stove by its heat and crouched behind it and suddenly the room was bright with light from the big central chandelier.

A man was standing at the top of the stairs, holding Alice by the hair. He was wearing a ski mask and he had a bowie knife in his right hand. He spoke softly. "Drop the gun or she dies." I did as he said and he added, "Good, kick it away from you." I did that too, and while his eyes followed it I made another move, invisible to him. I pulled out the box of .22 shells I had taken from Sallinon's desk and set it on top of the stove. Then I stood up straight, looking at him.

"Who are you?"

He didn't answer. Still holding Alice, he came down the stairs one at a time, keeping her in front of him, his knife at her throat. "Look, she doesn't have any money," I said. "I'm carrying a real wad, let go of her and you can have it."

"I'll have it anyway," he said. He was tall and by the look of him fair skinned, a blonde. This wasn't Laval, and I had thought he was the only wild card left in the deck.

The man came down further and I closed in, not near enough to scare him but ready to move if he cut her. If he did he would die. I'd made up my mind about that.

"You must be Bennett," he said.

"That's right. What's your name?" I didn't care. All I cared about was his knife, but I wanted him off guard. Talk can do that, if you're careful.

"You don't need to know," he sneered. He reached the bottom of the stairs and edged around to his left, toward the dropped gun. "You won't live long enough to have it matter," he said.

I could smell thick smoke of burning cardboard behind me and knew my moment was almost here. He sniffed the air like a deer in the presence of wolves, but kept edging toward the gun. When it was at his feet he shoved Alice away from him and picked it up. Alice got to her feet and ran toward me but I threw her aside onto the couch. He raised the gun toward me and in the same instant the bullets on the stove began to cook off with the rapid crackle of automatic weapon fire.

He froze. I used the single moment to dive headlong into his diaphragm. He went down like a tree and I knelt up on him and smashed him back and forth across the face with my elbow, back and forth more times than I needed until he lay still, eyes rolled up, broken jaw sagging open against the wool of his bloody ski mask.

I turned to Alice. She was lying on the couch, weeping helplessly. "Did he attack you?" I knew the signs. She was traumatized almost out of her mind. But she shook her head.

"Who is he? Do you know him?" I was intense enough to grab her and shake the information loose.

"Oh Reid," she sobbed. "Oh Reid. I thought he was dead. It's Ivan. My husband."

224

24

He hadn't hurt her. He had been inside the house when she came home, looking for money in the secret cache they had established to hold the Saturday-night take at the motel bar, back before it was enough money to warrant installing a safe. When Alice came in he'd pinned her, covering her mouth, making sure she wasn't with anybody. Then he had heard my car in the driveway, turned the lights out, and waited.

I poured her a drink and called the hospital to come for her husband. I had to explain everything three times over before the dispatcher understood that this was a real emergency. His shock mechanisms were still buzzing from the excitement at the helicopter pad.

Alice was too shaken to leave on her own, so I drove her to the hospital behind the ambulance. She didn't speak, but sat crying quietly all the way there. Millie was on duty and she took over, giving me a stern look before she found out about the reappearance of Ivan Graham. Then she turned all maternal and took Alice away to be tucked in for the night.

I went back to the police station. I'd gone past the point of being tired. Now I was wide awake, the way you get on long patrols in enemy territory. I was fired up on natural speed.

The OPP team was there and they latched onto me at

once. I filled them in first and they thanked me, separated their prisoners, and began to question them. First Tettlinger, then Kinsella, and then, as dawn broke, they went to the hospital and talked to Ivan Graham and the man I'd shot at the helicopter pad. He was the man I'd seen at the motel, only his name wasn't Wallace, it was Huckmeyer, and there were warrants out in New York State for his arrest on a weapons charge. The news heartened everybody except him.

Graham's arrival opened up all of them except Huckmeyer. The others competed with one another to get the story out fastest.

They all blamed Graham for the mess. It had been his idea, his and Prudhomme's. They had met in a bar in the Soo one night when Eleanor was in business. Both were clients of hers, Prudhomme a first-timer, Graham a regular. Graham was half in love with her and had a bantering relationship that amused her and made her do favors for him sometimes, like setting up the camera. The camera had been Sallinon's idea. He was the third member of the plot locally. They let him into it because he was a regular trick of Eleanor's, visiting her on his "Lodge Nights." The other two men had needed someone as a go-between to link up with Misquadis, who would go out and stake the claims Prudhomme identified and register them.

Later, Sallinon had helped again, in Prudhomme's disappearance, finding him the bearskin he wanted. But a lifetime of slavish attention to his books had tripped them up. He'd given Prudhomme the receipt that led me to his store in the first place. And now he was dead, killed by Graham when the net started to tighten around them all. Graham had been the real force. That night in the Soo, when he recognized Prudhomme, a man he knew from his stay at the motel in Olympia, Graham had started talking and Prudhomme had brought forward his idea.

They set it up, carefully. First Graham arranged for his own disappearance. This left him a free agent. He moved in with Eleanor, pimping for her except in places around Olympia

226

where he was known, living off her earnings, and helping Prudhomme to stake out claims on the island in the lake.

"The main ore body is there," Graham explained to his investigator painfully, with his broken jaw. "There reckons to be ten million ounces of gold. And if Jim had reported his findings to his company, they would have said thank you very much and given him his month's pay and forgotten about him."

They asked Graham about the unproductive hole that had been drilled there, putting the Darvon people off the place. He explained that one very simply. Prudhomme's boss had a share of the action. He had substituted useless rock cores for the ore they had found. Kinsella had made the switch when he flew the samples out. It was all so clean then. And then Prudhomme was too clever.

He knew that the startup costs for a gold mine could range anywhere from ten to a hundred million dollars. The size of this ore body made it likely that the figure would be high, not low, because they would go after it full tilt. He was afraid that if anyone started looking for that kind of money in the legitimate mining community there would be an enquiry and the plot would be uncovered. So he went to Laval, knowing that Laval had Mob connections.

The Mob had done what it always does. It had moved in, politely, and then taken over. They had sent Huckmeyer north to cut down the number of their shareholders. Prudhomme had to go. So did Misquadis, whom Huckmeyer killed. So did Sallinon, killed by Graham under Huckmeyer's instructions, for leading the police into the case. Next on the list were Tettlinger, as expendable muscle, and Graham himself. Only he got lucky—I put him in the hospital and later in jail, before the Mob had chance to finish him.

But in the beginning, Prudhomme had been smart. He had registered the claims he wanted by using a dummy company with Misquadis working as the errand boy. Misquadis hadn't known anything illegal was involved; Prudhomme

227

and Graham had stayed away from him, working through Arnie Sallinon. All of them grooving on the money they thought would be coming in. They expected to make a royalty of ten percent of the gold extracted, millions of dollars between them.

And so they had worked out how to make Prudhomme disappear. At first they were going to pull the same stunt Graham had pulled. He would go overboard from his canoe and vanish. But they worried about the coincidence. And on top of that, he needed another identity, something that would put an end to any chance of blackmail when he tried to get phony identification. So he had pulled in a transient the same size and age and general coloration as he was and had taken him out to the island in Kinsella's helicopter.

"That was why Prudhomme didn't have the samples bag with him," Gallagher said when I gave him the news next morning. "I'll bet he took the guy out with that first bang, the one that broke his skull. He probably swung at him with a rock in the bag, then had to get rid of it because of bloodstains."

I agreed, stirring my coffee which had come with an unexpected shot of rye in it, courtesy of Millie. "And then he used the teeth and the claws from the bearskin he'd bought off Sallinon to muddy up the face and hands. His lawyer identifies the body, they cremate it, and they're home free."

"Well, they would've been for a year or two, anyway, if it hadn't been for that long nose of yours," Gallagher said.

"Well, Prudhomme screwed himself with that receipt from Arnie Sallinon for the bearskin," I argued. "And then, the bloody arrogance of keeping the skin and passing it on to Laval. They must have thought they were so smart and the rest of us were too dumb to think."

"They figured me for a lame duck," Gallagher agreed. "They'd never seen me do anything more clever than write a parking ticket. They thought that was all I was good for." He was pale and unshaven and there was an intravenous drip in his left arm, but he was as sharp and gruff as ever. I could sense his pride.

"Dammit, I've done more detective work from this bed than I had chance to do the whole year I've been here. I've already had Jackaman check Huckmeyer's boots. They're the right size and sound like the right shape for that print you found near Misquadis. So he's getting charged with that killing too."

"What about this guy Laval?" I had a personal grudge with him and I wondered just how much of a figure he'd cut in the exercise yard of the big old St. Vincent de Paul penitentiary in Montreal.

"The Montreal police are looking for him already. They went around to Prudhomme's house and had a word with his widow. According to the detective who talked to Jackaman, she didn't have anything to do with the case. She and Laval were an item and she just accepted her husband's reported death as an act of God, kind of gratefully."

"Well, the whole thing's in pieces now," I said and he nodded.

"You bet," he said happily. "The Thunder Bay guys talked to Sallinon's sister. She's a female him, blonde and soft, the officer called her. Anyway, she was just collecting money for dear Arnie. He told her he was gambling and didn't want his wife to know. We'll look in his safety-deposit box when the banks open, see how much he was socking away."

"Must have upset him, having to kill Eleanor. She was, if you'll overlook the pun, the goose that laid the golden eggs."

"Hurt her worse," Gallagher said. "And it was all out of greed and I just know they'd have been caught anyway. Once they'd started collecting their royalties in all those millions, somebody would've done some digging. I'd have got them someway."

"I wonder who's going to get the money now," I said, sipping the wonderful coffee and yawning.

Gallagher laughed. "It's just my legs hurt, not my phone

finger," he said. "I called the claims office and got them to check it out at nine. The company that owns that island is called Turtle Holdings. Jack Misquadis is listed as the president. That means the profits will go to his family. And that means his whole band."

We both laughed at that one. Native rights are very touchy news in Canada today. If any sharp mining lawyer tried to skate around the ownership he would have to come up against the Indian Affairs Department. They would see an easy way to win some popularity for themselves by taking the side of the Olympia band against the big bad multinational mining company. That would mean success for the locals. They would have good modern homes to live in, instead of the shacks they lived in now. Their kids would grow up with investments to worry about instead of traplines. Misquadis would have liked that, even though he might have thought it softened them too much, made them poor trappers.

I left Gallagher after a while, when Millie came back in and shooed me out maternally. Gallagher sighed, but I had a feeling he was enjoying himself. And it looked to me as if she wanted to make looking after him a life's work. But then, coppers and nurses have always been close. We both do society's dirty work for them.

Me, I went back to Alice's house. I didn't count on being welcome, but I didn't have a room anywhere else. On the way I reclaimed Sam and fed him, then went in, restarted the stove that had saved my life the night before, and fell asleep on the couch. As I dozed off I noticed it was marked with tiny cuts from the bullet casings that had exploded, but I've seen damage a lot worse so I just grinned and slept.

I woke in mid-afternoon and found Alice sitting across from me. She smiled and I sat up and tried to look alert. "You looked so peaceful I left you to it," she said.

"Hell, I shouldn't have slept like that. I would never have done it when I was younger, not with somebody moving around me." I still felt sluggish, but she only smiled a sad smile.

"How are you feeling now it's settled down?" I asked, running my hands through my hair and trying to look less ragged.

"Lousy, if you want the truth," she said. "Ivan is my husband. I loved him but he would have killed me for enough money to run away with. That's a tough one to swallow."

"But it's all over now. The worst is behind you. The trial will come and go. He'll go inside for years. You can start your life from today as if he never existed. I'm not sure what your legal status is, but I'd imagine the marriage is ended." She said nothing, so after a pause I asked her, "What will you do, carry on running the motel?"

She shrugged. "I guess so." Then she shook her head. "That sonofabitch. If he'd robbed a bank or murdered somebody without disappearing first, I'd have stood by him to the end. But instead he just treated me like I didn't exist, let alone matter to him."

"Maybe you could hand over the motel to somebody for a while, come on down and spend some time at my place, do some painting and cussing, if it makes you feel better."

She rewarded me with the ghost of a smile. "The cussing sounds about my speed right now. But I can't go. This place would fall apart without me and it's the only asset I've got."

There was nothing else to say to her. I wasn't going to add to her problems by coming on dependent. If she wanted to leave this place she would but she might be better off staying here, putting up with the local gossip and the pointing fingers, making good money against the time she decided to branch out somewhere else.

After a moment or two I stood up and walked away to the wall, to the painting of her husband that dominated the collection. Looking at it, I recognized the rock on which he was sitting. It was on the island where the gold lay, the island at the center of her misery. All this time it had hung there, mocking her with its secret.

She looked up at me and smiled blankly, a stranger's smile. "Thanks anyway, Reid. It's been good, but things have changed now. I'm going to have to work it all out on my own."

I didn't argue. I figured she was probably right. I was only glad that the magic hadn't happened, that we hadn't developed anything it would hurt to break. We were two friends, parting on good terms. For now, the best thing I could do for her was to get in my car and head back to Murphy's Harbour.

"I have to be on my way," I told her. "You know where I live." I found my combat jacket and slipped it on. "I've been away too long. That's where I earn my pay." She smiled again but didn't speak and I stopped and kissed her cheek gently. "Take care of yourself," I said.

She smiled a braver smile. "I will," she promised. Then she stood up and kissed me with more warmth. "Thanks," she said, and patted my arm as if I were a kid.

I walked toward the door and she followed me. When I reached it and put my hand on the doorknob she stopped and picked up a picture from the floor. It was wrapped in brown paper. She offered it to me without speaking.

"For me?" I was surprised. She had been so secretive about her painting.

"Yes," she said. "Think of me when you look at it."

"Can I look at it now?"

She shook her head. "Please don't. Unwrap it when you get home." Then she craned up and I kissed her very softly on the lips and left. She watched from the door and waved as I drove off down the drive with Sam tall beside me in the front seat.

I waved back and kept driving until I was almost out of gas and daylight, a hundred miles east of her. Then, as the attendant filled the tank I opened the brown paper around

232

her present and looked. It was a picture of me, with Sam, standing on that same bloody rock. I showed it to him, but he just looked over it at me until I let him out for a run. He'd seen rocks before. And so have I, and this one was behind us now, like a lot of other painful landmarks in my mind.